HARDCASTLE'S FRUSTRATION

Recent Titles by Graham Ison from Severn House

The Hardcastle Series

HARDCASTLE'S SPY
HARDCASTLE'S ARMISTICE
HARDCASTLE'S CONSPIRACY
HARDCASTLE'S AIRMEN
HARDCASTLE'S ACTRESS
HARDCASTLE'S BURGLAR
HARDCASTLE'S MANDARIN
HARDCASTLE'S SOLDIERS
HARDCASTLE'S OBSESSION
HARDCASTLE'S FRUSTRATION

Contemporary Police Procedurals

ALL QUIET ON ARRIVAL
BREACH OF PRIVILEGE
DIVISION
DRUMFIRE
JACK IN THE BOX
KICKING THE AIR
LIGHT FANTASTIC
LOST OR FOUND
WHIPLASH
WHISPERING GRASS
WORKING GIRL

HARDCASTLE'S FRUSTRATION

Graham Ison

This first world edition published 2012
in Great Britain and in the USA by
SEVERN HOUSE PUBLISHERS LTD of
9–15 High Street, Sutton, Surrey, England, SM1 1DF.
Trade paperback edition first published
in Great Britain and the USA 2012 by
SEVERN HOUSE PUBLISHERS LTD.

British Library Cataloguing in Publication Data

Ison, Graham.
  Hardcastle's frustration.
  1. Hardcastle, Ernest (Fictitious character)–Fiction.
  2. Police–England–London–Fiction. 3. Great Britain–
  History–George V, 1910-1936–Fiction. 4. Detective and
  mystery stories.
  I. Title
  823.9'14-dc23

ISBN-13: 978-0-7278-8171-7 (cased)
ISBN-13: 978-1-84751-431-8 (trade paper)

All Severn House titles are printed on acid-free paper.

Severn House Publishers support The Forest Stewardship Council [FSC],
the leading international forest certification organisation. All our titles that
are printed on Greenpeace-approved FSC-certified paper carry the FSC logo.

Typeset by Palimpsest Book Production Ltd.,
Falkirk, Stirlingshire, Scotland.
Printed and bound in Great Britain by
MPG Books Ltd., Bodmin, Cornwall.

GLOSSARY

A FROM A BULL'S FOOT, to know: to know nothing.
ACT UP: temporarily to assume the role of a higher rank while the substantive holder is on leave or sick.
ALBERT: a watch chain of the type worn by Albert, Prince Consort (1819–61).
ALL MY EYE AND BETTY MARTIN: nonsense.
ANDREW: Slang term for the Royal Navy.
APM: assistant provost marshal (a lieutenant colonel of the military police).

BAILEY, the: Central Criminal Court, Old Bailey, London.
BEF: British Expeditionary Force in France and Flanders.
BLIGHTY: the United Kingdom.
BLIGHTY ONE: a wound suffered in battle that necessitated repatriation to the United Kingdom.
BUCK HOUSE: Buckingham Palace.

COUGH to: to confess.

DABS: fingerprints.
DARTMOOR: a remote prison on Dartmoor in Devon.
DDI: Divisional Detective Inspector.
DIP a: a pickpocket.
DOGBERRY: a watchman (*ex* Shakespeare).
DRUM: a dwelling house, or room therein. Any place of abode.

FEEL THE COLLAR, to: to make an arrest.
FOURPENNY CANNON, a: a steak and kidney pie.
FRONT, The: theatre of WW1 operations in France and Flanders.

GLIM: a look (a foreshortening of 'glimpse').
GUV *or* GUV'NOR: informal alternative to 'sir'.

JIG-A-JIG: sexual intercourse.

KC: King's Counsel: a senior barrister.
KATE CARNEY: army (rhyming slang: from Kate Carney, a music hall comedienne of the late 19th early 20th century).
KNOCKING SHOP: a brothel.

LONG BOW, to draw the: to exaggerate _or_ to tell unbelievable stories.

MI5: internal counter-espionage organization.
MONS, to make a: to make a mess of things, as in the disastrous Battle of Mons in 1914.

NICK: a police station _or_ prison _or_ to arrest _or_ to steal.
NICKED: arrested _or_ stolen.
NOT PYGMALION LIKELY: a euphemism for 'not bloody likely', from George Bernard Shaw's play _Pygmalion._

OLD BAILEY: Central Criminal Court, in Old Bailey, London.
ON THE GAME: leading a life of prostitution.

POLICE GAZETTE: official nationwide publication listing wanted persons, etc.
PROVOST, the: military police.

QUID: £1 sterling.

RAGTIME GIRL: a sweetheart; a girl with whom one has a joyous time; a harlot.
RECEIVER, The: senior Scotland Yard official responsible for the finances of the Metropolitan Police.
ROZZER: a policeman.

SAM BROWNE: a military officer's belt with shoulder strap.
SKIP _or_ **SKIPPER:** an informal police alternative to station-sergeant, clerk-sergeant and sergeant.
SLÀINTE: (_slän'cha_) Gaelic salutation for 'Good health'.
SLING ONE'S HOOK, to: to run away, hastily or secretly.
STAGE-DOOR JOHNNY: young man frequenting theatres in an attempt to make the acquaintance of actresses.

SUB: Police shorthand for sub-divisional inspector, the officer in charge of a subdivision.

TOPPED: murdered or hanged.
TOPPING: a murder or hanging.

WAR HOUSE: army officers' slang for the War Office.
WAR OFFICE: Department of State overseeing the army. (Now a part of the Ministry of Defence.)
WIPERS: Army slang for Ypres in Belgium, scene of several fierce Great War battles.

ONE

The detectives' office in Cannon Row police station, in a turning off Whitehall in London, was thick with tobacco smoke on that Monday morning at the beginning of March 1918. The police station and New Scotland Yard opposite had been erected 28 years previously to the plans of Norman Shaw and constructed, fittingly, from Dartmoor granite hewn by convicts from the nearby prison.

All the windows in the office were firmly closed and the only heating came from a solitary and inadequate smoky fire. However, the Receiver for the Metropolitan Police District was obliged to be parsimonious in his capacity as controller of the Force's finances, and spent no more on the comfort of junior police officers than met the minimum requirements. The thinking of the hierarchy was that such officers should be out on the street, not languishing in their offices.

In this stark and essentially functional room, four or five detectives were seated around a long wooden table, each working on reports, applications for warrants and all the other paperwork that was a necessary part of a CID officer's lot. There was, however, only one typewriter in the office, and fewer chairs than there were detectives, a state of affairs that was regarded by the senior officers as an incentive for their juniors to arrive early.

Close to the door of the office, Detective Sergeant (First Class) Charles Marriott, being the senior officer in the room, was privileged to have his own desk. This morning he was drafting a complicated report that would eventually find its way to the office of the Solicitor to the Metropolitan Police and thence to the Director of Public Prosecutions. But it was not proving easy, and several times, he had begun it again. In common with other detectives, Marriott had often thought that it was easier to solve a crime than to commit the details to paper afterwards.

'Excuse me, Sergeant.' The young uniformed constable on station duty hovered in the doorway.

'Yes, what is it now?' asked Marriott, throwing down his pen in exasperation and heaving a sigh. 'And don't tell me you're applying to become a detective. Take it from me, it's not worth the trouble.'

'No, Sergeant, it's this message that's just come in from Thames Division.' The PC crossed to Marriott's desk and handed over a form.

Marriott quickly scanned the brief missive. 'All right, leave it with me,' he said, standing up and dismissing the constable with a wave of his hand. He buttoned his waistcoat and donned his jacket. Crossing the narrow corridor, he tapped on the divisional detective inspector's door and entered.

'What is it, Marriott?' DDI Ernest Hardcastle, head of the CID for the A or Whitehall Division, looked up with an expression of annoyance at having been interrupted. He too was engaged in writing a difficult report about ex-Inspector John Syme that would eventually find its way to the Commissioner. Since 1910, Syme had held a continuing, and often violent, grudge against the Metropolitan Police for his reduction in rank and subsequent dismissal for a variety of disciplinary offences. At nine o'clock last Saturday evening, he had been arrested, yet again, outside Buckingham Palace with a brick in his hand. Syme, who would throw a brick through any government window he could find, including 10 Downing Street, had been charged with intent to commit malicious damage and would appear later that morning at Bow Street police court. It was unfortunate for Hardcastle that most of Syme's protests were conducted on A Division, and that it fell to him to be the one writing the reports.

'A Thames Division crew from Waterloo Pier has reported dredging up a male body, sir.'

'Waterloo Pier's on E Division, Bow Street's patch. What the hell's that got to do with us?' demanded Hardcastle, placing his pipe in the ashtray.

'It was found floating near one of the uprights of Westminster Bridge on our side of the river, sir.'

'Well, if he committed suicide it's not a crime, Marriott,' said Hardcastle. 'You should know that you can't prosecute a dead man. Only *attempted* suicide's a crime,' he added archly. 'A successful suicide's not a matter for the CID.'

'I don't think it's a suicide, sir, unless his name's Harry Houdini,' said Marriott, again referring to the message form and permitting himself a brief grin. 'The body was tied up in a sack.'

'You could've said that to start with, Marriott,' growled Hardcastle irritably. 'We'd better go and take a look, I suppose.' Relieved that he had an excuse for not completing his report about Syme, he stood up, put on his Chesterfield overcoat and seized his bowler hat and umbrella. 'Starting the week with a dead body that'll probably turn out to be a murder is something I could well do without.'

'Indeed, sir.' Marriott knew that such an investigation was likely to put the DDI in a bad mood for the next few days, and possibly longer if the enquiry dragged on.

Before descending the stairs Hardcastle paused to put his head around the office door of his deputy, Detective Inspector Edgar Rhodes.

'If anyone wants me, Mr Rhodes, I'm going to have a look at a body at Waterloo Pier that the river police have obligingly found for me floating by Westminster Bridge.'

'Very good, sir,' said Rhodes.

'I really don't know why they withdrew the CID from Thames Division last year, Mr Rhodes,' muttered Hardcastle, 'and that's a fact. I sometimes wonder what they're thinking about over there.' He cocked a thumb in the general direction of Scotland Yard. 'And now I'm stuck with a suspicious death.' He was still complaining when he and Marriott left the police station.

There was a slight breeze on Victoria Embankment as Hardcastle and Marriott turned out of Scotland Yard's east gate. A dense fog clung to the river and drifted on to the pavements where it was knee-high. But there was a hint of rain in the air and that and the breeze were slowly dispelling the mist. And the temperature had yet to reach forty degrees Fahrenheit.

'Well, I'm not walking all the way to Waterloo Pier in this weather,' complained Hardcastle, and promptly hailed a taxi. 'Waterloo Pier nick, cabbie, and be quick about it.'

It was Monday the fourth of March 1918. The Great War had now been in progress for three years and seven months. In Flanders the British and French armies were bogged down in opposing trenches that stretched for over three hundred miles from the North Sea to the Swiss border. Between the allied forces and the Imperial German Army there existed a killing ground called no-man's-land where countless soldiers of the warring factions had lost their lives in this interminable war. Some remained buried there, to be recovered if ever the conflict came to an end. Some would be recovered years later, and some would never be found.

But now that the American Expeditionary Force, under the command of General John 'Black Jack' Pershing, had entered the war, things were, at last, beginning to look hopeful for a swift and decisive victory.

'I'm DDI Hardcastle of A,' announced Hardcastle as he and Marriott descended the steps from the Embankment and entered the front office of London's only floating police station.

'All correct, sir.' The station officer, a sergeant, had a moustache and spoke with a Scots accent. He was a short man and, Hardcastle surmised, barely met the minimum height requirement. But he was well built and looked as though he might have been a useful wrestler. That he was a good swimmer went with the job.

'Matter of opinion,' muttered Hardcastle, who was always irritated by the formal report junior officers were obliged by the regulations to make, whether all was correct or not. 'I understand you've found a body for me.'

'Yes, sir,' said the sergeant. 'He was spotted drifting downriver near Westminster Bridge. The crew was lucky to come across him in this weather.' As if to emphasize the sergeant's comment, a foghorn sounded loudly close by; and the police station rocked in the swell of the passing vessel.

'You might've done me a favour and let him drift on to E Division's manor,' muttered Hardcastle.

The sergeant grinned and lifted the flap in the counter. 'If you'd care to come through, sir, we've got him laid out in the side office.' He nodded to Marriott. 'How are you keeping, Charlie?'

'Fair to middling, Jock.' It was not the first time that Marriott and the river policeman had met to discuss a dead body. It was one of the penalties of Cannon Row police station being responsible for that half of the river closest to it.

Hardcastle spent a few moments surveying the corpse that the river police had placed on a bare wooden table. The victim, clothed in a suit with a celluloid collar and a tie, appeared at first sight to have been affected only by immersion in the dirty water of the Thames. Neatly folded at one end of the table was the sack in which the victim had been found.

'Looks like some sort of clerk to me, Marriott,' said Hardcastle as he studied the apparel in which the body was attired. He turned to the river policeman. 'Any personal belongings on him, Skipper?' he asked.

'Yes, sir. These were found in his pockets.' The sergeant handed over a few pieces of sodden paper and a wallet. He pointed to a couple of banknotes and some small change. 'The money was still there, too, sir,' he added, implying that robbery did not appear to be the motive for the man's death.

'Ah, I was right, Marriott.' Hardcastle spread the papers out on the table. 'According to this pay packet, his name appears to be Ronald Parker and he works at the Kingston upon Thames Gas Company.' He put the pay packet back on the table, took a letter from its envelope and spread it out. 'It's a bit smudged by the water, but I can just make out what it says. It's from a woman called Daisy Benson with an address in Gordon Road, Kingston. She wants to know when he's coming to see her again and suggests that next Saturday afternoon would be a good time. It looks like she might've been his fancy piece on the side.'

'Might be his mother-in-law, sir,' suggested Marriott, half in jest.

Hardcastle scoffed. 'Has your mother-in-law ever written to you, Marriott, expressing a desire to see you again?'

'No, sir.'

'No, I thought not. Nor has mine.' Hardcastle turned back to the body. 'Well, so far so good. I'll be interested to see what Dr Spilsbury makes of it.'

'D'you want me to send for him, sir?'

Hardcastle pondered Marriott's question. 'I doubt he'll see much point in coming down here,' he said. 'After all, our Thames Division colleagues have already unwrapped the body, so to speak, and I don't suppose much will be lost if we get it straight up to St Mary's. Arrange it, Marriott, there's a good chap.'

Dr Bernard Spilsbury, the pre-eminent forensic pathologist of his generation, always conducted his post-mortem examinations at St Mary's Hospital at Paddington. Renowned for his painstaking investigation into the cause of death, his appearance in the witness box was guaranteed to send a frisson of concern down the spines of defending counsel. Many were the cases in which Spilsbury's detailed analysis had resulted in a conviction for murder that, without his testimony, might well have been dismissed as accidental death. And on other occasions his interpretation of the victim's fatal injuries had been instrumental in negating a killer's plea of self-defence.

'I'll give him a ring, sir,' said Marriott.

'You'll do *what*?' demanded Hardcastle, with a frown on his face. He broke off from his study of the body to stare at his luckless sergeant. 'What on earth are you talking about, Marriott?'

'I'll, er, telephone him, sir,' said Marriott, hastily translating his comment into proper English.

'Oh, that thing,' said Hardcastle dismissively. He always pretended ignorance of the workings of what he called 'that newfangled instrument'. It was a piece of equipment he abhorred, even though he was competent in its use. But in common with many of his contemporaries, he regarded it as an infernal invention that would not last. 'Better use the thing to get a couple of our people down here to shift the body to St Mary's, then, and while you're at it, alert Dr Spilsbury as to when they're likely to arrive. And bring that sack with you, Marriott. It might tell us something.'

'The telephone's in the front office, Charlie,' said the Thames Division sergeant.

'Thanks, Jock,' said Marriott, and left the room to make his calls.

Hardcastle spent the next few minutes closely inspecting the body. With the assistance of the river policeman, he turned it on to its face.

'Aha! What have we here?' he said, moving closer to examine an injury on the back of the dead man's head. 'Looks like a bullet wound.' He stepped back and tucked his thumbs into his waistcoat pockets. 'That settles it; it's a murder without a doubt.'

'Looks that way, sir,' said the river policeman cautiously. He was convinced, from his long experience in such matters, that a body tied up in a sack had been the victim of a murder, and wondered why the DDI had at first appeared to be in some doubt.

'With your knowledge of the river, Skipper, have you any idea where the body might've been put in?'

'Difficult to say, sir. It depends on the date and on the flow of the tide when he was dumped, and he might've been caught up on some obstruction before floating free again. But I'm surprised it wasn't weighted down.'

'So am I, Skipper,' said Hardcastle. 'Bit of an amateur killer by the looks of it. I suppose you've not been advised about a missing person,' he asked hopefully.

'No, sir. Reports of that sort are usually made to a land station.'

'Everything's been arranged, sir,' said Marriott, returning from making his telephone calls.

'Good. In that case, we'll get back to the nick and put our thinking caps on, Marriott,' said Hardcastle. 'And we'll get Mr Collins to go to St Mary's and take fingerprints from the victim. You never know, he might find that there's a record of him.'

Detective Inspector Charles Stockley Collins was an expert in the comparatively new science of fingerprint identification. It was only thirteen years previously that such evidence had been accepted by the courts, and had been a factor in securing the conviction of the notorious Stratton brothers for the murders of a Deptford oil shop owner and his wife.

'We could always chop off the fingers and send them straight to the Yard, if it'll help, sir,' volunteered the river sergeant.

'I think we'll let Dr Spilsbury have the whole body, Skipper,' said Hardcastle with a wry grin, 'otherwise he might come to the wrong conclusion. Sorry to deprive you of your fee.' It was well known that Thames Division officers coveted the small remuneration they received for such primitive surgery.

Mounting the steps to Victoria Embankment, Hardcastle hailed a taxi. 'New Scotland Yard, cabbie,' he said, and turning to Marriott, added, 'Tell 'em Cannon Row, Marriott, and half the time you'll end up at Cannon Street in the City.'

'Yes, sir,' said Marriott wearily. He had been the recipient of this advice on almost every occasion that he and the DDI had returned to the police station by cab.

'Learn anything from the sack our body was tied up in, Marriott?' asked Hardcastle, when his sergeant joined him.

'It's a sugar sack, sir, stamped Henry Tate and Sons. They've got a refinery at Silvertown.'

'Well, that doesn't help much,' grunted Hardcastle. 'There

must be hundreds of sacks like that knocking about, although it could mean that this here murder's down to a grocer.' He placed his pipe in the ashtray and stood up. 'We'll have a trip to Kingston while we're waiting for Dr Spilsbury to come up with some answers. See what Parker's employers have got to say. Then we'll have a chat with this here Daisy Benson and find out if she's got anything useful to tell us.' He paused in the act of donning his overcoat. 'How do we get there?'

'Train from Waterloo station, sir.' Marriott sighed inwardly. Hardcastle was playing his usual trick of pretending not to know. But Marriott was fairly certain that the DDI could not have forgotten that they had frequently travelled to Kingston two years ago when investigating the murder of Colonel Sir Adrian Rivers.

'Ah yes, I suppose so,' said Hardcastle.

'D'you know where the Kingston upon Thames Gas Company's got its offices, cabbie?' asked Hardcastle, addressing the driver of the first cab on the rank outside Kingston railway station.

'Of course I do, guv'nor,' said the cabbie, yanking down the flag of his taximeter. 'It's in Horse Fair.'

'Damn funny name for a street,' muttered Hardcastle, as he and Marriott clambered into the taxi.

It was only a short journey and the cab stopped outside offices that were close to Kingston Bridge.

A young woman seated at a desk looked up as Hardcastle and Marriott approached her. 'If you've come to pay a bill, it's over there,' she said curtly, pointing her pencil at a grilled counter where a short queue of people was waiting.

'I've not come to pay a bill,' snapped Hardcastle. 'We're police officers and I'm here to see the manager. Be so good as to direct me to his office, young woman.'

'One moment.' With a toss of her head, the woman rose from her desk and walked the short distance to an oaken door. Knocking, she went in, returning moments later. 'Come this way.'

The manager, who appeared to be in his sixties, rose from his desk. One hand brushed at his heavy moustache, the other played with the albert stretched between his waistcoat pockets. 'Good morning, gentlemen. I'm Frank Harvey, the manager.' He indicated two upright chairs. 'Please sit down.'

'I'm Divisional Detective Inspector Hardcastle of the Whitehall

Division, Mr Harvey, and this is Detective Sergeant Marriott. I understand that Ronald Parker is a member of your staff.'

'Ah!' The manager leaned back in his chair and steepled his fingers. 'It's interesting that the police are taking an interest. What can you tell me about him?'

'It's more a case of what you can tell me, Mr Harvey.'

'He didn't report for work on Friday or Saturday. There was no explanation, no sick note, nothing. It's most irregular and extremely unusual in Parker's case. I did wonder whether he'd been caught up in an air raid somewhere and is in hospital. One can never tell these days. I sent one of my clerks to his home, but he received no answer. Parker's neighbour said that Mrs Parker is working for the war effort somewhere, but she declined to reveal where. She said it had something to do with national security.'

'Sounds like a shrewd woman,' commented Hardcastle. 'In what capacity is this here Parker employed, Mr Harvey?'

'He is the chief clerk,' said Harvey, 'but might I enquire why you're interested in Mr Parker, Inspector? Are you searching for him, perhaps?'

'We've found him,' said Hardcastle bluntly. 'He's dead.'

'Good heavens!' Harvey stared at the inspector open-mouthed and fiddled with his watch chain again. 'When did this happen?'

'We're not sure, although the pathologist might be able to tell us, once he's completed the post-mortem examination. However, I can tell you that his body was found in the river near Westminster Bridge this morning.'

'What happened? Did he commit suicide?'

'That's something I'm trying to find out, Mr Harvey.'

'You say that you sent one of your staff to his home,' said Marriott. 'Perhaps you'd tell us his address.' Although the letter from Daisy Benson that had been found on the body was just legible, the water had washed away the address on the envelope.

'Certainly.' Harvey took a book from the top drawer of his desk, and thumbed through the pages. 'Yes, here we are. He lived with his wife Mavis in Canbury Park Road, Kingston. I'll write it down for you.' He scribbled the details on a piece of paper and handed it to Marriott.

'What age was Mr Parker?' asked Marriott.

Harvey referred to his book again. 'He was thirty-eight. Born on the twenty-third of July 1879.'

'What sort of man was Ronald Parker?' asked Hardcastle.

Harvey considered the question and then replied as though he were furnishing a reference for a trusted employee. 'He was a sober man, very punctual, and fastidious in his work. In fact, I could find no fault with him whatsoever. I understand he was a regular churchgoer too. We'll miss him, and a replacement will be hard to find. I suppose it'll mean employing another woman.' Harvey sighed. 'Most men are in the army or the navy now.'

'Talking of which, have you any idea why Parker wasn't called up?' Hardcastle knew that Lord Derby's 1916 Military Service Act had been widened to include all men under the age of forty-one, whether married or single. 'Being a gas company clerk is hardly what you'd call a reserved occupation.'

'He was not a well man,' said Harvey. 'He suffered from breathlessness quite badly. I told him it was because he smoked too many cigarettes, but he wouldn't give them up.'

'Was his marriage a happy one?'

Harvey appeared to bridle at that question. 'I don't enquire into the private lives of my employees, Inspector,' he said loftily. 'All I ask is that they do a decent day's work, and Parker was one of the best people I had here. Which was why the board promoted him to chief clerk a year ago.'

'Thank you for your assistance, Mr Harvey,' said Hardcastle. 'I'll not bother you further today, but we may need to speak to you again. Perhaps you can direct me to this here Canbury Park Road.'

'It's no more than half a mile from here.' Harvey stood up and indicated a large-scale street map pinned to his notice board. 'We're here,' he said, pointing with a pencil, 'and Canbury Park Road is there.' He moved the pencil to indicate the road where the Parkers lived.

'I'm much obliged,' said Hardcastle, turning to leave.

'Perhaps you'd let me know when the funeral is to take place, Inspector,' said Harvey. 'I should like to attend, to represent the company, you understand.'

'Very well, Mr Harvey, and good day to you.'

TWO

T he Parkers' house was a narrow, detached Victorian villa with a bay and, above it, a single sash window. Hardcastle and Marriott walked past a well-kept garden and up the side of the house to the front door. Marriott hammered on the knocker, but there was no reply.

'I've got a feeling that this murder of ours ain't going to go the way we want it to, Marriott,' muttered Hardcastle. 'Better try next door, I suppose.'

The middle-aged woman who answered the door of the adjacent house was neatly dressed and her hair was swept up and secured with an inordinate number of hairpins. She studied the two men with an enquiring gaze, as if they were itinerant salesmen.

'We don't buy at the door,' she said curtly.

'Very wise, madam,' said Hardcastle, as he raised his hat. 'We're police officers.'

'Oh God!' The woman put a hand to her mouth. 'It's not Jimmy, surely?'

'Jimmy, madam?' queried Hardcastle.

'Our son Jimmy is in the navy. Has he been killed?'

'Not to my knowledge, madam. We're enquiring into the death of Mr Ronald Parker. I believe he lives next door.'

'Ron is dead?' The woman's face displayed predictable shock at the news. 'My God, how awful. What happened, was it an accident?'

'I'm afraid our enquiries are at an early stage. May we come in, Mrs er—?'

'I'm Martha Middleton. Yes, of course. I'm working in the kitchen at the moment. I hope you don't mind, but I'm just finishing the washing up.'

'Not at all,' said Hardcastle, as the woman led the way into the small kitchen at the rear of the house. 'We knocked at Mr and Mrs Parker's house next door, but there was no one at home.'

'No, there wouldn't be. Mavis works at the Sopwith Aviation Company,' said Mrs Middleton. 'It's just down the road, at the corner of Elm Road. It used to be a skating rink until 1912,' she added unnecessarily.

'Very interesting,' murmured Hardcastle. 'When did you last see Mr Parker, Mrs Middleton?'

'It must've been about a week ago, I suppose, but I'm not altogether sure,' said Martha Middleton thoughtfully. 'But I saw Mavis yesterday evening, just after she got in from work. I was taking in my washing, and she was taking in hers.'

'Did she mention anything about her husband?'

'No, and I never thought to ask.' Mrs Middleton finished putting away the last of the crockery in a large dresser. 'Well, you don't, do you, not every time you meet, not living next door, if you know what I mean. I'm sorry, do sit down. I've just made a pot of tea. Would you like a cup?'

'Very kind, madam,' murmured Hardcastle, as he and Marriott sat down at the kitchen table.

'Presumably Mrs Parker is at work now,' said Marriott.

'I should think so,' said Martha Middleton, pouring tea. 'She's there every day except Sundays, of course, helping to make Sopwith Camels for the Royal Flying Corps, but I suppose I shouldn't mention that, it being sort of secret. Sugar and milk?'

'Your secret's safe with me, Mrs Middleton. D'you happen to know what hours she works?'

'She usually goes out at about twenty-five to eight, and gets back at just after six. Mind you, I s'pose she's better off than the poor souls who work the night shift.'

'Tell me, did the Parkers enjoy a social life?' Hardcastle asked, taking a sip of tea.

'I doubt they had much time, Mr Hardcastle. They both work six days a week and they always go to church of a Sunday morning. Mind you, Mavis sometimes worked on a Sunday too, when they had what she called a rush on.'

'The manager at the gas company said that he'd sent a clerk to enquire why Mr Parker hadn't shown up for work, but as he got no answer, he spoke to a neighbour.'

'No one called here, Inspector. He must have gone to the neighbour on the other side of the Parkers' house.'

A bearded policeman stood in the centre of the main entrance to the Sopwith Aviation Company. Being March, his greatcoat was buttoned on the left. It was another bizarre idea to emanate from the Receiver's Office and was intended to reduce wear by alternating the side upon which the coat was buttoned month by month.

'Can I help you?' he asked, fiddling with his whistle chain.

'I'm DDI Hardcastle of A.'

'Ah! All correct, sir.' Having given Hardcastle's warrant card a cursory glance, the PC came to attention and saluted. Although curious, he knew better than to enquire why a Whitehall Division detective should be in Kingston.

'Where can I find the management offices, lad?' Hardcastle always addressed constables as 'lad', regardless of how old they were, and this PC was probably about the DDI's age.

'I'll get someone to take you, sir, if you'll follow me.' The PC pushed open one of the heavy gates and led Hardcastle and Marriott to a small hut just inside. 'Two police officers to see the management, Fred,' he said, speaking to the gatekeeper through a small window.

'Righto, mate.' Fred put down his mug of tea and his newspaper, wiped his moustache and emerged from his hut. 'This way, guv'nor,' he said to Hardcastle.

Ascending a wooden staircase on the outside of the main building and through a maze of corridors, the two detectives were eventually shown into the works manager's office.

The manager was in his forties, immaculately dressed and prematurely bald. He had the studious air of a scientist and, Hardcastle thought, was probably an engineer, given the post he held. Taking off his horn-rimmed spectacles, he introduced himself as George Quilter.

Hardcastle effected introductions and came immediately to the purpose of his visit.

'I'm given to understand that you have a Mrs Mavis Parker working here, Mr Quilter.'

'Quite possibly, Inspector, but I don't happen to know the names of all the workers here.' Quilter was somewhat disconcerted by mention of the woman's name, but covered his apprehension by smiling apologetically. It was not the first time that the police had called on him with regard to Mavis Parker. In fact, he knew of the woman only too well, but deemed it impolitic to mention that fact, even to a DDI from the Metropolitan

Police. 'We have hundreds of personnel here. However, if you'll
bear with me, I'll find out.' He crossed the office and opened a
door. 'Miss Douglas, would you find out if there's a Mrs Mavis
Parker on the payroll and where she works. As quickly as you
can, if you please.'

'Yes, Mr Quilter,' came a voice from the outer office.

'Won't keep you a moment, Inspector,' said the manager.
'Please sit down.' He moved a couple of chairs closer to his desk
and resumed his seat. The humming and clatter of heavy
machinery could be heard, even in the manager's office.
Somewhere an aeroplane engine was being run up on a test bed.

The efficient Miss Douglas appeared a minute later. 'Mavis
Parker is a day worker employed in the paint shop, Mr Quilter,
and I'm told that she's here today.'

'Thank you, Miss Douglas. Just wait a moment, if you please.'
Quilter turned to Hardcastle. 'Do you wish to speak to Mrs
Parker, Inspector?'

'Yes, I do. I have the unhappy duty of telling her that her
husband has been found dead.'

'Good grief,' said Quilter, but asked no further questions.
Nevertheless, he could not help wondering whether this tragedy
had anything to do with his previous conversations with the
authorities about the woman. 'Miss Douglas,' he said, glancing
at his secretary, 'perhaps you'd be so good as to go down to the
paint shop and bring Mrs Parker up here immediately.'

'Yes, Mr Quilter.'

'But don't tell her why, or that the police wish to see her.'

'No, Mr Quilter.'

'What happened?' Quilter asked, once Miss Douglas had
departed on her errand.

'Beyond saying that Ronald Parker's body was found in the
river at Westminster this morning, I can't really say,' said
Hardcastle.

'Did he commit suicide?'

'We don't think so, Mr Quilter,' said Marriott, not wishing to
divulge too much information about Parker's suspicious death.

The woman who entered the office looked to be about thirty
and was quite possibly attractive, but it was difficult to tell; she
was clothed in rough trousers, a paint spattered smock overall
and a mob cap beneath which her hair was completely hidden.

Hardcastle never ceased to find the sight of a woman wearing trousers distasteful, even though it was all too common among female workers these days. He reflected, yet again, that this damnable war was producing the most extraordinary changes in the life of the country. And not always for the better.

'You wanted me, sir?' Mavis Parker said to Quilter and then glanced apprehensively at the two policemen.

'Yes, Mrs Parker. These two gentlemen are from the police and they wish to speak to you. You'd better sit down.' Quilter glanced at his secretary. 'Miss Douglas, if you'd be so good as to fetch that chair for Mrs Parker.'

Miss Douglas moved a chair closer to Hardcastle and Marriott, and Mrs Parker sat down.

'Whatever is it?' Mavis Parker had a worried look on her face, possibly thinking that she was in some kind of trouble, but it was an expression that the DDI subsequently discovered he had misinterpreted.

'I'm sorry to have to tell you that I have bad news, Mrs Parker,' Hardcastle began. It was the one task that policemen disliked the most. 'Your husband was found dead this morning.'

'Glory be!' Mavis Parker put a hand to her mouth and blanched, and for a moment Hardcastle thought that she might fall from the chair in a faint.

The efficient Miss Douglas poured a glass of water from the carafe on Quilter's desk and handed it to the woman.

Mavis Parker took a sip of water and returned the glass to Miss Douglas. 'Did this happen in Holland?' she asked, when she had partially recovered.

'*In Holland?*' It was the strangest reaction that Hardcastle had ever heard in response to the news of the death of a loved one. 'Whatever makes you think that he died in Holland?'

'It was where he was going, sir.'

'But why? Why should he have gone to Holland?'

Mrs Parker stared guiltily at Hardcastle. 'To avoid being called up for military service,' she said, but she sounded unconvincing.

'But how was your husband proposing to get to Holland, Mrs Parker?' Hardcastle became immediately suspicious. He knew that the ferry service between Harwich and the Hook of Holland had been suspended as long ago as 1915, and he was now wondering whether this woman had had any involvement in her husband's death. Set against that was her reaction; if it was not genuine, then Mrs Parker was a clever and convincing actress. But possibly a guilty one.

'I don't really know.' Mrs Parker extracted a handkerchief from somewhere within her clothing and dabbed at her eyes. 'He said something about going to one of the south coast ports in the hope that he could get a passage in one of the cargo vessels. I think he mentioned Harwich. Would that be right?'

'When did he decide to do this?' asked Marriott, without answering the woman's question.

Mavis Parker switched her gaze to Hardcastle's sergeant. 'Last Thursday,' she said, dabbing at her eyes again. 'What happened to him?'

'His body was found in the River Thames early this morning,' said Hardcastle.

'Did he fall from a ship, then?'

'We are still trying to find out what happened.' Hardcastle was not about to tell Ronald Parker's widow that her late husband's body had been shot in the head and was found tied up in a sugar sack. 'You said just now that your husband was trying to avoid military service, Mrs Parker. But I've been given to understand from his employers that he suffered from severe breathlessness, possibly consumption or some chest complaint, I suppose. Surely that would have exempted him from military service.'

'Yes, sir, that's true. He wasn't a well man and he'd been before a tribunal once before, but a couple of weeks ago he'd been called back for another examination. He was worried that this time they'd pass him fit. It wasn't that he didn't want to go; he just thought that his health wouldn't stand up to being in the trenches. One hears such terrible stories about what it's like out there.'

'So I believe.' Hardcastle had witnessed some of the results of total war during his visit to the Belgian town of Poperinge eighteen months previously. He would never forget seeing badly wounded soldiers at the railway station, lying on stretchers in the open air, awaiting evacuation. 'Well, I think that's all, Mrs Parker. You have my sympathy,' he muttered as a gruff after-thought; he was not good at expressing words of condolence.

'You'd better take the rest of the day off, Mrs Parker,' said

Quilter. 'In fact, take as much time as you need. I'll get one of the other women to see you home.' He glanced at his secretary. 'Perhaps you'd arrange that, Miss Douglas.'

'Yes, Mr Quilter,' said his secretary.

'Thank you, sir.' Mavis Parker glanced at the works manager, but said nothing to Hardcastle.

'I may need to see you again, Mrs Parker,' said the DDI. 'What time d'you normally finish work?' He had been told by Martha Middleton, Mrs Parker's neighbour, but as usual was confirming the information he had received.

'Six o'clock, sir,' said Mavis Parker.

'A bad business, Inspector,' said Quilter, once Mrs Parker had been escorted from the office by Miss Douglas. 'D'you think he committed suicide?'

'I have no idea at this stage, Mr Quilter,' said Hardcastle, well knowing that it was murder.

'What time is it, Marriott?' asked Hardcastle, when the two officers were back at the main gate of the factory.

'A quarter past four, sir,' said Marriott, wondering why the DDI had not looked at his own watch, but dismissed it as another of Hardcastle's little perversities.

'I see you've still got that wristwatch, Marriott. I'm surprised you haven't knocked it off on something.' Hardcastle, attached as he was to his half-hunter, could not understand the modern trend of wearing a watch attached to the wrist by a strap.

'Yes, sir, and it keeps good time.'

'So does mine,' muttered Hardcastle, declining to become embroiled in a debate about the relative merits of watches. 'What was the address on that letter that was found on Parker's body?'

Marriott took out his pocket book and glanced at it. He had made notes of the letter, knowing that Hardcastle would, sooner or later, want to know the details.

'Gordon Road, sir, and it was a woman called Daisy Benson who wrote the letter.'

'So she did,' said Hardcastle. 'I wonder how far that is.' He turned to the policeman standing guard. 'Where's Gordon Road, lad?'

'Turn right into Queen Elizabeth Road, sir,' said the PC, pointing off to his left, 'then go under the railway bridge and it's the first turning on the left. It's not much of a stride, sir. Less than half a mile, I should think.'

It took the two detectives just under ten minutes to find the address. The detached house was similar to the one in which the Parkers lived, except that Daisy Benson's house had two windows on the upper floor and the door was on the front rather than at the side.

The woman who answered Hardcastle's knock looked to be in her late twenties or early thirties. Attired in a dress that revealed a good twelve inches of well-turned ankles, she had dispensed with a chemisette thus displaying a rather daring décolletage.

'Good afternoon, gentlemen,' said the woman, carefully appraising the two officers. 'I'm afraid I don't have any rooms vacant at present.'

'We're not here looking for accommodation, madam,' said Hardcastle, 'we're police officers. Is your name Daisy Benson?'

'Yes, it is.' A look of concern crossed the woman's face. 'Oh my Lord, it's not about my husband, is it?'

'Your husband?' queried Hardcastle.'

'Yes, my Sidney's a staff sergeant in the Army Ordnance Corps somewhere at the Front.'

'No, it's not about your husband, Mrs Benson.' Hardcastle wondered why the woman had volunteered so much information so quickly. 'We want to talk to you about Ronald Parker.'

'I'm afraid I don't know anyone of that name.'

'But you wrote him a letter,' said Hardcastle tersely.

'Oh, heavens!' Daisy Benson glanced up and down the street.

'You do know him, then,' said Hardcastle.

'Yes,' said Daisy Benson, almost whispering her reply. 'You'd better come in.' Her mind was in turmoil as she wondered how the police could possibly know that she had written to Ronald Parker.

The parlour was a comfortable room furnished with easy chairs, a sofa and a diamond-patterned Axminster carpet that must have cost at least five pounds. Net curtains excluded the prying eyes of the outside world, and a fire burned cheerfully in the grate.

'What's all this about Ronnie?' asked Mrs Benson, having invited the two detectives to take a seat. She sat down opposite them and carefully arranged her skirt.

'His body was found in the River Thames this morning, near to Westminster Bridge,' said Hardcastle bluntly.

'Dead? Good grief, how awful.' Mrs Benson's hand went to her mouth as she absorbed the shock of the news. 'But that's terrible.'

'Among his belongings was a letter from you in which, among other things, you expressed a desire to see him again soon. You suggested next Saturday afternoon would be a convenient time. From the date on your letter, I presume that referred to the Saturday just gone.' Hardcastle sat back and waited to hear what Daisy Benson had to say about that.

'Oh, how silly of him to have kept that letter.' Daisy waved a hand in front of her face, clearly flustered. 'I realized afterwards how silly of me it was to have written it.'

'Yes,' said Hardcastle. 'His wife might've read it.' He was already convinced that Daisy Benson and Ronald Parker had been having an affair.

'What exactly was your relationship with Mr Parker?' asked Marriott. 'Are you a relative, his sister perhaps?'

Daisy Benson coloured slightly. 'We were lovers,' she said, once again lowering her voice to a conspiratorial whisper, and confirming Hardcastle's view. 'His wife didn't understand him, you see, poor Ronnie.'

Hardcastle had heard that well-worn excuse for an affair many times before, but he declined to say as much. It was a familiar reason put forward by philandering husbands and adulterous wives as a fallacious excuse for their behaviour; nor was it the first time that a woman had so openly discussed her love life with him. 'How long had this affair been going on, Mrs Benson?'

'About a year, ever since my Sid got posted abroad. He was in Aldershot before that, but then they sent him to France,' said Mrs Benson. 'Well, it gets lonely for a girl when her husband's away and . . .' She allowed the sentence to lapse, but there was no need for her to elaborate; Hardcastle understood only too well what she meant.

'Did Mr Parker say anything to you about going to Holland, Mrs Benson?' Marriott asked.

'To Holland?' Daisy Benson emitted a girlish giggle. 'Why on earth would he have wanted to go to Holland? It sounds a very dangerous thing to do, what with the war and everything. But no, he never said anything about going to Holland.'

'We spoke to Mrs Parker less than an hour ago, and that's

what she told us,' said Hardcastle. 'She said something about Mr Parker having been interviewed by a medical tribunal recently and that he apparently feared being called up for the army.'

'That's nonsense. He's not fit. He told me that he felt quite confident that they would reject him. He wasn't in the least worried about it. In fact, they said they would write to him with the results, but he was fairly certain that it would be all right.'

'You knew where he worked, I suppose.'

'Of course. He was with the gas company in Horse Fair. That's how I'm able to have a decent fire. Ronnie was able to wangle me some extra coal from time to time.' Mrs Benson smiled guiltily.

'How did you manage to arrange your meetings?' asked Marriott. 'Mr Parker was working six days a week, and Mrs Parker is a day worker at Sopwiths.'

'Once a fortnight Ronnie would have a Saturday afternoon off, but Mavis would be working, of course. So we'd meet then. Mavis would even work on a Sunday occasionally, especially if they were particularly busy at the factory, and Ronnie would skip church and come to see me.' Parker's paramour was quite blatant about their arrangements.

'Weren't you afraid that the neighbours might talk?' Hardcastle did not really care what they thought, but had posed the question out of idle curiosity.

'I let rooms to commercial gentlemen,' said Daisy. 'The neighbours are quite used to seeing different men coming and going all the time.'

'I see.' Hardcastle had already formed an opinion about Mrs Benson's commercial enterprise, but it differed from that which the woman was attempting to convey.

'D'you think that Mrs Parker knew about your affair, Mrs Benson?' asked Marriott.

'Crikey, I should hope not.' Daisy emitted another giggle. 'I don't think she'd've been too happy about it.'

'I don't suppose she would,' commented Hardcastle drily. 'But wasn't there a danger that Mrs Parker might've seen the letter you wrote?'

'I doubt it,' said Daisy. 'Ronnie told me that he always picked up the letters from the doormat.'

'When did you last see Mr Parker?' enquired Marriott.

'A week ago last Saturday,' said Daisy promptly. 'It was one of those Saturdays when Ronnie had the afternoon off. And Mavis, of course, was at work painting her aeroplanes.'

'Did Mr Parker seem to be in good spirits?'

'Very much so.' Daisy gave a coy smile. 'You wouldn't've thought that he was unfit for active service,' she added, and giggled again.

'But you had made an arrangement to meet again?'

'He sort of suggested he might have an extra Saturday afternoon off which is why I wrote what I did in the letter. That was the day before yesterday, but he didn't arrive and I assumed he'd had to work.'

'Thank you, Mrs Benson,' said Hardcastle, as he and Marriott stood up. 'We may have to see you again. I presume you're here most of the time.'

'Yes, I am.' Daisy Benson briefly touched the back of her hair. 'How did Ronnie die? Was he drowned?'

'No, Mrs Benson,' said Hardcastle. 'We believe him to have been murdered.'

Daisy Benson's mouth opened in shock. 'Murdered? But why should anyone want to kill poor Ronnie?'

'That is something I'm trying to find out, Mrs Benson.'

THREE

'It seems that our Mr Parker was a bit of a Lothario, Marriott,' said Hardcastle once the two detectives were back at Cannon Row police station. 'What you might call a gas board Romeo.' He chuckled at his feeble joke.

'I don't really blame him, sir,' said Marriott. 'That Daisy Benson is a good-looking woman. Enough to turn any man's head, I should think.'

'Yes, and I wonder how many of her paying guests have benefited from her favours.' Hardcastle scraped out his pipe and put it in his pocket before glancing at his watch. 'I doubt that we can do much more tonight, Marriott. Take yourself off home; it might be the last early night we have before this case is closed. I've a feeling that it's going to get complicated.'

'Especially if Parker had more than one lady friend, sir,' suggested Marriott.

'Thank you for that helpful comment, Marriott. Go home before you depress me further. And my regards to Mrs Marriott.'

'Thank you, sir, and mine to Mrs H.'

Once Marriott had left the station, Hardcastle settled down to deal with his accumulated paperwork. But first he read *Police Orders*, the daily publication that reported all that was happening, and going to happen, in the Metropolitan Police. He noted with a wry smile that a constable in one of the outer divisions had been dismissed after being found drunk and asleep in a wheelbarrow. Such a punishment carried with it the very real possibility that the man concerned would be called up for the army and finish up in the trenches.

At half past seven, he decided that he had done enough for one day, and donned his overcoat and bowler hat and seized his umbrella.

But before leaving the station, he looked into the front office. The station sergeant reported that all was correct.

'Anything happened that's likely to interest me, Skipper?' asked Hardcastle.

'A couple of your lads nicked a pickpocket at the guard change at Buck House this morning, sir, but apart from that, nothing.'

'Who were they?'

The station sergeant referred to the charge book. 'DCs Catto and Lipton, sir.'

'They're not trying hard enough.' Hardcastle had an unfair view of Henry Catto's abilities as a detective, but he was good at his job, and seemed only to appear uncertain of himself in the DDI's presence. 'They could do better than a couple of dips if they tried.'

Hardcastle had waited nearly half an hour in the fog for a tram to arrive at the stop on Victoria Embankment, and when it did arrive it was crowded. Once he had taken the fares, the conductor alighted and returned to the front of the tram. For the rest of the journey, he walked slowly ahead of it with an acetylene gas lamp. Trams had been known to run down lost pedestrians in such weather, despite the constant ringing of the vehicle's bell.

As a result of the delay, it was nearly nine o'clock before

Hardcastle let himself into his house, remembering to shake his umbrella and leave it on the doorstep before he entered. It was the house in Kennington Road, Lambeth, in which he and his wife Alice had lived since their marriage some 25 years ago, and was a few doors down from where the famous Charlie Chaplin had once resided.

'Is that you, Ernie?' called Alice from the kitchen.

'Yes, it's me, love.' Hardcastle hung up his hat and coat and, as was his invariable practice, checked the hall clock against his hunter before entering the kitchen. 'Sorry, I'm late, love,' he said, and kissed his wife. 'What's for dinner? It smells wonderful.'

Alice turned from the range and flicked a lock of hair from her forehead. 'I spent fifteen of our meat coupons on a sirloin of beef, Ernie,' she said, 'which only leaves us three points for the rest of the week. But we've got to have a decent bit of beef once in a while.'

Hardcastle nodded. 'At least we're better off than the Germans,' he said. 'I've heard that they're eating cats and dogs over there, and they're making their bread from potato peelings and sawdust.'

Alice stopped what she was doing. 'Is that true, Ernie?' she asked. 'Oh, those poor people.'

'Poor people be damned,' said Hardcastle vehemently. 'They shouldn't have started it by marching into Belgium.'

'Yes, I know all about that,' said Alice, who was an avid reader of the *Daily Mail*, 'but just think of the poor children. They didn't have anything to with the war.'

Hardcastle knew better than to argue with his wife, and changed the subject. 'Talking of which, where are our children this evening?' He always referred to their offspring as children, even though Kitty was twenty-two, Maud twenty and young Walter had just turned eighteen.

'Kitty's got the back shift on the buses, Maud's gone out with her young man, and Wally's gone to the Bioscope in Vauxhall Bridge Road with a pal of his to see some film about cowboys and Indians.'

'It's time Kitty gave up that job on the buses. It's too dangerous.' It was something that Hardcastle frequently said.

'Well, you try to talk her out of it, Ernie, but I doubt you'll have any better luck than me.'

Hardcastle knew that to be true. Kitty Hardcastle was a

headstrong young woman and had taken a job as a conductorette with the London General Omnibus Company to relieve a man to fight. But despite his own attempts to dissuade her, nothing would convince her to change her mind.

'And what's this about Maud having a young man?' demanded Hardcastle. 'I didn't know anything about that.'

'Well, you're never here to find out, Ernie, are you?' said Alice accusingly. 'She met a young army lieutenant who she was nursing, and they've got quite keen on each other.' Maud had been nursing at one of the large houses in Mayfair that had been given over to the care of wounded officers. 'When he'd recovered, he was posted to Armoury Barracks in Hoxton training young soldiers, and he invited her out to the theatre tonight. They've been walking out for quite some time now.'

'An officer, eh?' Hardcastle was impressed. 'It's a shame Kitty can't find someone like that. The last I heard she was going out with a City copper, of all people.' He was unreasonably critical of the City of London Police, and regarded it as little less than impertinence that they should have responsibility for a solitary square mile in the centre of the Metropolitan Police District.

It was not until Tuesday morning that Hardcastle received a message from Dr Spilsbury requesting his attendance at St Mary's Hospital.

'I've just completed my examination of this fellow's cadaver, Hardcastle,' said Spilsbury. 'It was a single gunshot to the back of the head that did for him.'

'I take it you've recovered the round, Doctor Spilsbury.'

'There it is.' The pathologist pointed his forceps at a bullet resting in an enamel kidney-shaped bowl on a side bench. 'I'd estimate the age of this man to have been in the late thirties.'

'You're absolutely right, Doctor. He was born on the twenty-third of July 1879, and I was told that he was unlikely to be fit for the army,' said Hardcastle, repeating the information he had received from Frank Harvey, Ronald Parker's manager at the gas company.

'I can certainly confirm that for you, Inspector. He most certainly was not fit. He suffered from pulmonary emphysema and that would have precluded him from service in the army or navy.'

'He wouldn't have passed a tribunal to assess his physical fitness for active service, then, Doctor?'

'Not if I'd had anything to do with it, Hardcastle,' said Spilsbury.

The cab delivered the two detectives to the main door of New Scotland Yard. Followed by a hastening Marriott, Hardcastle, his agility belying his bulk, bounded up the steps that led to the front entrance of the central building. A uniformed constable pulled open the heavy door for him and saluted.

Once inside, Hardcastle immediately turned left and hurriedly descended the staircase. At the end of a long corridor he and Marriott entered the tiny workshop of Detective Inspector Percy Franklin, the Yard's acknowledged ballistics expert. So enthusiastic was Franklin that the authorities at Scotland Yard had eventually yielded to his demand for somewhere to carry out his tests and experiments. On the wall of his tiny workshop there were cutaway diagrams of rifles, pistols and revolvers, and the bench at which the shirt-sleeved Franklin was working was littered with parts of firearms. To the unskilled eye, it seemed that there was no order to them, but Franklin knew every piece and where it belonged and how it fitted.

In furtherance of his passion, Franklin had struck up a friendship with Robert Churchill, the gunsmith, whose premises were in the Strand. The two of them were frequently to be seen sitting by the fire in the nearby Cheshire Cheese public house, enthusiastically exchanging information about firearms. From time to time, Franklin would call in at Churchill's small establishment to watch the gunmaker firing bullets into the heads of sheep, a ready supply of which came from the butcher next door. From these experiments, Franklin had learned, among other things, about how powder burns could determine the distance at which a firearm had been discharged. On one particular occasion, back in 1913, it had helped Franklin to prove that what at first was believed to be a suicide was actually a murder.

'Good morning, Ernie. Don't tell me, your visit has something to do with a body found floating in the Thames yesterday.' Franklin swung round on his stool, and put down the magnifying glass he had been using to examine a pistol. 'I've been expecting you.'

'You're very well informed, Percy.' Hardcastle placed a round on the bench. 'Dr Spilsbury recovered this bullet from the skull of Ronald Parker, our victim. What can you tell me about it?'

Franklin placed the bullet on a piece of green baize cloth, and with the aid of a jeweller's eyeglass, examined it closely, occasionally turning it this way and that with a pair of forceps. 'A seven-groove, point four-five-five ball round, Ernie,' he said, at last looking up. 'It's almost certainly from a military weapon, probably a Webley and Scott, and anything between a Mark One and a Mark Six.'

Hardcastle was impressed by Franklin's apparent expertise, but at once slightly sceptical that the firearms specialist could deduce so much just by looking at a bullet. 'Can you tell me which particular revolver it came from, Percy?'

Franklin emitted a short, contemptuous laugh. 'Not unless you can show me the weapon, Ernie.'

'I will, Percy, you may rest assured.

'Well, I hope you do, Ernie,' said Franklin, 'because I can't tell you anything more until you do. I'm not a bloody magician, you know.'

'Really?' said Hardcastle. 'And there's me thinking that you were.'

'Come into the office, Marriott,' said Hardcastle when the two detectives were back at Cannon Row police station. He settled himself behind his desk and filled his pipe. Once he had lit it to his satisfaction, he leaned back in his chair, a reflective expression on his face. 'We'll have to give some serious consideration to this here murder of ours, m'boy.'

'D'you think Parker's wife had anything to do with it, guv'nor?' said Marriott, lapsing into the informality of address that his chief had used.

'Not unless she owns an army revolver, m'boy.'

'Daisy Benson's husband might have one, guv'nor. She told us he was a staff sergeant in the Army Ordnance Corps.'

'But would he have had a revolver? The Ordnance Corps isn't an active service regiment, is it?' Unusually for Hardcastle, he was admitting that Marriott's knowledge of military matters was superior to his own.

'Not in the same way as the artillery, the infantry, the cavalry or the Tank Corps, but the Ordnance Corps is responsible for supplying weaponry to the army. If Staff Sergeant Benson works in an ordnance depot, he'd be able to lay hands on a revolver without any difficulty, and cover up the loss by showing that it had been condemned as unserviceable.'

'That's all very interesting, Marriott,' said Hardcastle, reverting to the formal mode of address, 'but there's only one flaw in your theory: Daisy Benson said that her husband is in France. So how does he shoot Parker, wrap him up in a sugar sack and drop him in the river, even if he'd known that Parker was enjoying Mrs Benson's favours?'

'He might've come home on leave and caught them at it, sir. And if he had, I don't suppose it's the sort of thing Daisy would've told us about.'

'He needn't necessarily have caught them in the act,' said Hardcastle, unwilling to let Marriott tailor the enquiry to fit in with his own theory. 'He might've been tipped off, despite what Daisy Benson said about her neighbours not suspecting anything. I can't even scratch myself without my neighbours appearing to know about it. Anyway, he wouldn't be the first soldier to get that sort of letter while he was at the Front.' He put his pipe in the ashtray. 'But that's all pie in the sky. We need solid evidence.'

'We've only Daisy's word for it that her old man's in France, sir,' said Marriott, unwilling to give up on his notion. 'For all we know, he could still be in Aldershot. If he was ever there in the first place. What's more, he could've been on leave at the time Parker was topped.'

'Well, that's easily resolved, Marriott. Have a word with Colonel Frobisher's people.' Lieutenant Colonel Ralph Frobisher of the Sherwood Foresters was the assistant provost marshal of London District, and as such was Hardcastle's point of contact for all matters military. 'But you needn't bother the colonel. Drop in on his clerk, Marriott, and see what he can tell us. What's his name?'

'Sergeant Glover, sir,' said Marriott.

'Ah yes, that's the fellow.'

Charles Marriott crossed Whitehall and strolled the short distance to Horse Guards Arch where the APM had his office. Buses ground their noisy way up and down the broad thoroughfare, and the pavements were thronged with pedestrians, many of whom these days, wore either army or navy uniform.

The outgoing King's Life Guard had just been relieved of its twenty-four-hour stint of duty and Marriott, never tiring of a sight he had seen on many occasions, paused to watch the khaki-clad troopers ride through the archway on their return to Hyde Park Barracks.

Sergeant Cyril Glover of the Military Foot Police looked up in surprise as Marriott entered the office.

'Blimey, your guv'nor not with you this morning, Charlie?' Glover was accustomed to seeing Marriott in the company of his DDI.

'Not today, Cyril. He does occasionally let me out on my own.'

'The colonel's not here at the moment, Charlie, if it was him you wanted to see,' said Glover. 'He's gone to Duke of York's HQ to give evidence at some court martial they've got going on there. Apparently some idiot of a second-lieutenant got involved in a fist fight over a woman outside the Army and Navy Club, of all places,' he added, shrugging as though such events were an everyday occurrence.

'It doesn't matter, Cyril. It's you I wanted a word with. We've got a murder running and one of the names to come up is that of a Daisy Benson who lives in Kingston. She's a bit of a flighty madam, probably on the game, and she told us that her husband's a staff sergeant in the Army Ordnance Corps somewhere in France. But we've got our doubts that he's actually there.'

'D'you think he's up for this topping, then, Charlie?'

'It's a possibility,' said Marriott cautiously.

'And I suppose you want me to find out where he is, Charlie.'

'That's the general idea, Cyril, and possibly if he's had any Blighty leave recently. What are the chances?'

Glover shook his head at the sheer enormity of the task that Marriott had set him. 'Charlie, there are millions of men under arms across the water. It could take a few days at best, but I'll see what I can do.'

'Well?' Hardcastle looked up as Marriott entered his office.

'I spoke to Sergeant Glover, sir, but he said it could take a few days to find out about Staff Sergeant Benson.'

'A few days? You wouldn't think there was a war on, would you?' Hardcastle put down his pipe. 'If someone wanted to know where one of our policemen was stationed, I could find out in minutes, Marriott, not a few days.'

'Yes, sir.' Marriott was ill-disposed to encourage one of the DDI's acerbic diatribes about the army's efficiency or lack of it. But he felt that he had to defend the military, particularly as his brother-in-law was a sergeant-major in the Middlesex Regiment serving in France. 'There are nineteen thousand men in the Metropolitan Police, sir, all in London apart from those at Windsor Castle and the Dockyard Divisions. The army's got millions all over the place.'

'They're not trying, Marriott,' said Hardcastle, loath to admit that his sergeant had a point. 'I suppose we'll just have to wait and see.'

'Excuse me, sir.' The station duty constable appeared in Hardcastle's doorway.

'What is it, lad?'

'There's a Mr Harold Parker downstairs, sir. He wants to report a missing person.'

'Did he say who was missing?' asked Hardcastle, although he had guessed that it concerned his murder victim.

'He said it was his brother, a Ronald Parker, sir.' The PC paused. 'I thought you'd wish to know, because he was the bloke you pulled out of the river yesterday morning, wasn't he, sir?'

'I don't go about pulling people out of the river, as you put it, lad,' snapped Hardcastle. 'Not unless they're still alive. You know I don't stand for that sort of sloppy statement. You wouldn't give evidence in court like that, I hope. The body was found and recovered by Thames Division officers.'

'Yes, sir. Sorry, sir.'

'Where is this here Harold Parker?'

'In the interview room, sir.'

'Come, Marriott. We'll see what this fellow has to say for himself.'

Dismissing the constable, Hardcastle and Marriott descended to the small interview room on the front of the police station.

'Mr Harold Parker?'

'That is I, sir.' Parker stood up and tucked a clay pipe into a pocket. He was a big, ruddy-faced man, dressed in a heavy Guernsey sweater, moleskin trousers, a reefer jacket, and a red kerchief. He had stout boots on his feet, and held a soft peaked-cap in his hand.

'I'm Divisional Detective Inspector Hardcastle, Mr Parker. One of my constables told me that you wish to report a Ronald Parker missing.' He waved a hand to indicate that Harold Parker should sit down.

'I hope I'm not wasting your time, sir, but the missus and me called on his wife Mavis down at Kingston last Sunday afternoon,' Parker began, 'expecting to see Ron as well. But he wasn't there and Mavis said she hadn't seen him since Thursday. She did seem a bit worried though, but I somehow got the impression that it wasn't that that was vexing her. Then she said that Ron had talked about going to Holland.' He shook his head as though unable to comprehend the reason for such a venture. 'Why on earth he should want to go to Holland is a mystery. Apart from which, I've no idea how he'd get there? There aren't any passenger services to the Hook. Anyway, I thought that I ought to have a word with you. I moored nearby half an hour ago and as you're the nearest police station, I came in here.'

'It so happened that you came to the right police station, Mr Parker, but I'm afraid we have bad news for you, sir,' said Marriott. 'Your brother's body was recovered from the Thames yesterday morning.'

'Oh no! Was he drowned?'

'We have yet to establish the exact cause of death,' lied Hardcastle. He did not intend to tell Harold Parker that his brother had been murdered, at least not yet.

'Are you sure it was Ronald?'

'As sure as we can be, Mr Parker,' said Marriott. 'We recovered correspondence and a pay packet that leave us in little doubt.'

'My God! What a tragedy.' Parker shook his head in disbelief. 'He was the mildest man you could hope to meet. Poor Mavis. Ronald was a God-fearing good husband, you know.'

Hardcastle knew that to be untrue. 'We're endeavouring to find out how he died, Mr Parker,' he said, even though he was well aware that his brother had been murdered. 'Would you tell me again when you visited Mavis Parker? Just to make sure.'

Parker took a small diary from his trouser pocket and thumbed through the pages. 'Last Sunday, the third of March, Inspector. It's not often that I get a Sunday off these days.'

'Why is that? Are you engaged in some sort of war work?'

'I suppose I am, in a way. I'm a bargemaster on the Thames, working out of the Pool of London.'

'How far upriver d'you ply, Mr Parker?' asked Marriott, just as Hardcastle was about to pose the same question. Each of them was thinking the same thing: could Harold Parker have had anything to do with his brother's death?

'I have been known to go as far up as Brentford, but not very often. Usually Chelsea Reach is my limit.'

'Were you at Chelsea yesterday by any chance?' asked Hardcastle.

'Yes, as a matter of fact, I was, sir. I took a load of timber up from Dagenham.'

'What time would you have arrived at Chelsea Reach?'

'At about three yesterday afternoon, or thereabouts.' Parker seemed puzzled by the DDI's question, but did not query why it had been asked.

'I see.' Hardcastle stood up. 'There is one thing I'm going to ask you to do, Mr Parker . . .'

'What might that be, sir?'

'I need you to identify your brother's body. I thought it unwise to ask Mrs Parker; the body is not in the best of condition.'

'Certainly. I quite understand. When would you like me to do this?'

'Now would be ideal. Your brother's body has been moved to the Horseferry Road mortuary pending the inquest. Sergeant Marriott here will take you in just a moment.' Hardcastle glanced at his sergeant. 'Take a cab, Marriott.'

'Yes, sir.'

'Thank you for calling in, Mr Parker,' continued Hardcastle. 'We'll keep you informed of any developments.'

'Are you able to tell me when the funeral is likely to be, sir?'

'That's a matter for the coroner, but as soon as he's released your brother's body for burial, I'll be sure to let you know. Perhaps you'd let my sergeant here have a note of your address.'

Parker took Marriott's proffered pocket book and scribbled the details. 'Thank you, Inspector,' he said, and crossed the room, but paused with his hand on the doorknob. 'I presume that Mavis has been told about Ronald.'

'I spoke to her yesterday, Mr Parker.'

'She must be beside herself with grief,' said Parker with a shake of his head. 'The missus and me'll call and see her this evening.'

FOUR

Marriott escorted Harold Parker into the mortuary at Horseferry Road. The attendant showed them into the small room where Ronald Parker's body, covered with a rough sheet, was lying on a table.

With a skill borne of years of practice, the attendant flicked back the sheet sufficient to allow a view of the victim's face. He moved away, allowing Harold Parker to approach.

'Is that your brother Ronald, Mr Parker?' asked Marriott.

Although he was in no doubt, Harold Parker spent several seconds gazing down at his dead brother before eventually turning away.

'Yes, that's Ronald, Sergeant.'

'If you'd be so good as to come into the office, Mr Parker,' said Marriott, 'I'll ask you to make a brief formal statement confirming that you have identified your brother.'

'Of course.' Harold Parker shook his head and followed Marriott out of the room. 'Why on earth did it have to happen?' he said.

Marriott reported to Hardcastle the moment he returned to the police station.

'Harold Parker identified the body as that of his brother straightaway, sir.'

'Of course he did, Marriott. There was no doubt.'

'D'you think he was involved, sir?' asked Marriott.

'He could've had something to do with it, I suppose,' said Hardcastle, slowly filling his pipe. 'He admitted to taking his barge under Westminster Bridge yesterday.'

'But would he have told us that if he'd murdered his brother, sir? I'd've thought that he would've made up some story about being miles away if he was guilty. Anyway, according to him it would've been well after the time the body was found that he went under Westminster Bridge. He said he arrived at Chelsea Reach at three o'clock yesterday afternoon. And it's likely that the body had been in the river for quite some time before it was recovered.'

'Quite possibly, Marriott, quite possibly. But Harold Parker might just be drawing us the long bow. Anyhow, we'll check. Send Wilmot up there to ask a few questions.'

'Yes, sir,' said Marriott, and made a mental note to speak to DC Wilmot the moment the DDI had finished.

'He didn't seem too cut up about his brother's death, neither, Marriott,' commented Hardcastle. 'Where was it he said he lived?'

Marriott opened his pocket book. 'Seven Jacob Street, sir. It's off Mill Street in Bermondsey.'

'Yes, I know where Jacob Street is, Marriott. Handy for the Pool of London, that is.' Hardcastle sat down behind his desk. 'This business of Ronald Parker going to Holland because he was afraid to be called up . . .'

'D'you mean the tribunal might've passed him fit after all, sir?'

'Yes, that's what I was thinking, even though Spilsbury ruled it out. But they're so short of men these days that they're likely to send anyone who's capable of standing up straight for five minutes. Who deals with this business of medical tribunals?'

'The Ministry of National Service, sir,' said Marriott promptly.

'Yes, I suppose they would,' said Hardcastle thoughtfully. 'Where are their offices?'

'In St James's Square, sir.' Marriott knew that the question would be asked at some stage, and had made a point of finding out.

'Not in Whitehall?' Hardcastle took his pipe out of his mouth and stared at his sergeant.

'No, sir.'

'That's a damned funny place for a government office to be, Marriott. I thought they were all in Whitehall, but it seems that this war has turned the world upside down. I suppose we'd better have a walk round there and see what they've got to say about our Mr Parker. But first, I fancy a glass of ale.'

The two detectives walked out of the police station into Derby Gate and descended to the downstairs bar of the Red Lion public house.

'If you're buying, Marriott, mine's a pint of best bitter.'

'Yes, sir.' Marriott grinned; he knew that neither he nor the DDI ever paid for their beer in the Red Lion. It was one of the perks they enjoyed as members of the local CID.

The Ministry of National Service occupied a white three-storied building that had undoubtedly been a fashionable town house before being requisitioned by the government, and had probably been the residence of a well-to-do family. It was evident that some families still lived in the square: straw covered much of the road to deaden the sound of traffic. The Spanish influenza pandemic was taking its toll, but only the more affluent families with sick relatives could afford the luxury of purchasing straw.

A constable from C Division's Vine Street police station, posted there to guard the building, stood on the steps, surveying the passing scene with a bored expression on his face.

'And what would you two gents be wanting with the Ministry of National Service?' asked the PC as Hardcastle and Marriott mounted the steps. 'Look a bit too old to join up, I'd've thought.' He laughed at what he thought was a rather clever quip. 'Anyway this ain't the place for enlisting.'

'What I'm doing here is none of your damned business, lad,' snapped Hardcastle, thrusting his warrant card under the policeman's nose. 'DDI Hardcastle of A.'

'Oh, I do beg your pardon, sir.' The PC hurriedly assumed a position of attention and saluted. 'All correct, sir.'

'Is it indeed?' demanded Hardcastle. 'Well, I'll be having a word with your sub at Vine Street, lad. We'll see if he thinks it's all correct. The charge will be either incivility to a member of the public or insubordination to a senior officer. You can take your pick. Make a note of his divisional number, Sergeant.' And leaving that threat hanging in the air, he pushed open the door. 'Bloody slackness, that's what it is, Marriott.'

'Yes?' A sickly youth of about twenty, seated at a desk inside the door, looked up as the two detectives entered. He had the surly attitude of someone clothed with a modicum of authority.

'I'm a police officer and I want to see whoever's in charge, lad,' said Hardcastle. 'And, as a matter of interest, why aren't you in the army?'

'I'm in a reserved occupation,' said the youth sullenly. 'Anyway, I've got adenoids.'

'Haven't we all,' muttered Hardcastle, as the clerk disappeared through a door behind his desk.

'Come this way,' said the clerk churlishly, as he reappeared moments later. He gave the impression of being annoyed that someone had got past him.

An elderly civil servant rose from behind his desk as Hardcastle and Marriott were shown into his stark office. It seemed that His Majesty's Government was not greatly interested in providing comfortable accommodation for its servants.

'My name's Makepeace.' It seemed an inappropriate name for a man in his employment. 'My clerk tells me that you're police officers,' he said, peering at the two detectives over his half-moon spectacles.

'Divisional Detective Inspector Hardcastle of the Whitehall Division and this here is Detective Sergeant Marriott.'

'Please sit down and tell me how I can help you, gentlemen.' Makepeace indicated a couple of uncomfortable chairs as he resumed his own seat.

'I'm investigating the murder of a man named Ronald Parker, Mr Makepeace,' began Hardcastle, 'and I understand that he recently appeared before a tribunal to assess his fitness for conscription.'

Makepeace gave a short, cynical laugh. 'There are hundreds of them going through the system on an almost daily basis, Inspector. Do you happen to have an address for Parker?'

Hardcastle glanced at his sergeant. 'Marriott?'

'Canbury Park Road, Kingston upon Thames,' said Marriott, and furnished the full details of Parker's employment. 'And he was born on the twenty-third of July 1879.'

'One moment while I look him up.' Makepeace crossed to one of several wooden filing cabinets and after a short search took out a Manila folder. 'Here we are,' he said, sitting down again. He adjusted his spectacles and studied the docket for a few moments before looking up. 'What exactly did you want to know, Inspector?'

'Whether the tribunal found that he was eligible for military service, Mr Makepeace.'

'Definitely not. He was examined by a medical board for the second time on the fifteenth of February this year and declared to be unfit. He was sent a letter notifying him of that result on

Monday the eighteenth.' Makepeace closed the docket. 'But you say he's been murdered.'

'Yes, his body was recovered from the river on Monday last.'

'I'm afraid we'll need to have a death certificate to keep our records straight, Inspector.' Makepeace picked up a pen, dipped it in the inkwell and looked expectantly at Hardcastle.

'I dare say,' said Hardcastle, not wishing to become involved in the administrative niceties of the civil service. 'I suggest you communicate with the coroner at Horseferry Road coroner's court. He'll doubtless be able to assist you, once he's reached a verdict, that is.'

'It's all very irregular,' muttered Makepeace, as he put down his pen and closed the file.

'Yes, it must be,' said Hardcastle, rising from his seat. 'Thank you for your assistance, Mr Makepeace.'

The policeman saluted again as Hardcastle and Marriott left the building, but the DDI ignored him.

'There's definitely something funny going on here, Marriott,' said Hardcastle, once they were back at the police station.

'It looks as though he never got the letter, sir, otherwise he wouldn't have set off for Holland.'

'If he ever did, Marriott,' said Hardcastle. 'Frankly, I don't think he travelled any further than the distance between Kingston and where he was chucked in the river. And remind me to speak to the sub at Vine Street about that PC on the fixed point in St James's Square. The man should be put on the report.'

Detective Constable Fred Wilmot took the Underground train for the tortuous journey from Westminster to Dagenham Heathway. He was tempted to take a cab to Dagenham Dock, but feared that Hardcastle would disallow the cost as an unnecessary expense. Consequently, he walked the two miles to the dock gates.

'Where can I find the dock-master, mate?' he asked a passing stevedore.

'Should be in his office over there, guv'nor.' The docker pointed to a low grey building.

'What's his name?'

'Lynch, Pat Lynch, but everyone calls him Paddy. He's not

Irish though, he comes from Canning Town,' responded the docker, and carried on walking.

The dock-master looked up as Wilmot entered.

'Mr Lynch?'

'That's me, but we ain't hiring today,' said Lynch, 'and you'd be too late even if we was. You know the rules: you have to be here at six o'clock in the morning and take your chances with the rest and hope that the calling-foreman would take you on.'

'I'm a police officer, Mr Lynch,' said Wilmot, cutting off Lynch's short lecture on the hiring of dock hands.

'Oh, sorry, guv,' said the dock-master. 'What can I do for you? Got a warrant for someone here, have you? That's the usual reason the law comes down here.'

'Nothing like that,' said Wilmot. 'D'you know a bargemaster called Parker?'

'What Harry Parker? What's he been up to?'

'Nothing that we know of, but can you tell me if he took a load of timber from here to Chelsea Reach yesterday?'

'Seems to ring a bell,' said Lynch. 'Half a tick, guv'nor.' He thumbed through a pile of manifests that threatened to overwhelm his desk. 'Yeah, he did, on his barge the *Tempest*.'

'He told us that he arrived at Chelsea Reach at about three o'clock yesterday afternoon. Would that be correct?'

Lynch glanced briefly at the large clock on the wall, as though that would give him the answer. 'Yeah, that'd be about right,' he said, looking back at Wilmot.

'So he couldn't have gone under Westminster Bridge at about eight in the morning.'

'Not a chance, guv,' said Lynch. 'Anyway, what's this all about?'

'A body was found in the water there at about eight, and we wondered whether he'd seen anything.'

'Oh, I see. If he had, he'd've reported it to you lot. Very law-abiding is Harry Parker.'

'Thanks for your help, Mr Lynch,' said Wilmot, turning to leave. 'Who in Chelsea Reach would want a load of timber? There's no building going there, as far as I know.'

'Don't ask me, guv'nor,' said Lynch. 'I'm only the dock-master and that keeps me busy enough without enquiring into things like that.'

'Yes, I suppose so,' said Wilmot. 'Thanks.' And with that confirmation of what he had guessed would be the case, he made his weary way back to Westminster.

On the Wednesday morning, Hardcastle made a decision. 'We'll go to Kingston, Marriott,' he said.

'What for, sir?'

'To call on Mavis Parker.'

'But she'll be at work, sir.' Once again, Marriott wondered whether his chief was playing some arcane game.

'I should hope so, Marriott. And then we'll call on her neighbour. What was her name?'

'Martha Middleton, sir,' said Marriott promptly.

'So it is, so it is,' said Hardcastle. 'You see, Marriott, if Mavis Parker is at home, we can't very well then go next door to her neighbour without Mavis knowing and wondering why. But if the worst comes to the worst, I'm sure we can think of a few questions for Mavis Parker if she does happen to be at home.'

'I'm not walking this morning, Marriott,' said the DDI, when the two detectives arrived at Kingston railway station. 'We'll take a cab.'

It was ten o'clock when they arrived at the Parkers' house in Canbury Park Road. As Hardcastle had hoped, there was no answer, but a moment later, the head of Martha Middleton appeared over the neighbouring fence.

'She's at work.' There was a second's pause, and then she said, 'Oh, you're the policemen who called on Monday.'

'That's correct, Mrs Middleton. But perhaps you might be able to help us.'

'Of course, Inspector, do come in.'

'Thank you.' Hardcastle and Marriott made their way round to Martha's front door.

'I've just put the kettle on. I dare say you could do with a cup of tea seeing as how you've come all the way from London.'

'That's very kind of you, Mrs Middleton,' said Hardcastle. It seemed that Mrs Middleton had always just made a cup of tea. He and Marriott stepped over the threshold, removing their hats as they did so.

'Do sit yourselves down in here, gentlemen. We normally only use it of a Sunday.' Martha unlocked the parlour door, showed the two detectives in, and lit the gas fire. 'I won't be a mo,' she said, and disappeared into the kitchen.

'She don't miss much, Marriott,' whispered Hardcastle, as the pair settled themselves on a sofa. 'Thank God!' he added, as he glanced around the room. It was comfortably but drably furnished. There were brown velour curtains and nets at the windows. Above the fireplace there was a large mirror, beneath which was a mantel clock. Bric-a-brac adorned every available shelf and table. In the bay window there was a baby grand piano, the keyboard lid of which was raised and the sheet music of *Titwillow* open on the rest. A photograph of a young man in naval uniform occupied a prominent place on top of the piano.

'Here we are, then.' Mrs Middleton entered the room bearing a tray on which were an electroplate teapot, sugar bowl and milk jug. The teacups and saucers were of good quality bone china, the sort that was only brought out for visitors. There were also some side plates and cake and biscuits. 'Sugar and milk?' she asked. 'Oh yes, of course you do. I remember from the last time you were here,' she said, seating herself opposite Hardcastle and Marriott. 'I can't get lemons for love or money,' she added apologetically.

'Thank you,' murmured Hardcastle. 'Ah, Madeira cake *and* ginger snaps, I see. My favourites.'

'I was lucky to get them, what with the shortages an' all.' Martha Middleton busied herself pouring tea, holding the tea strainer in a genteel fashion between thumb and forefinger with her other fingers spread out. 'A dreadful thing, Mrs Parker's husband being killed like that,' she said, as she handed round the tea and plates and tiny tea napkins.

'I'm surprised she's at work,' said Hardcastle. 'She was told to take as much time off as she needed.'

'Mavis was always one to put a brave face on whatever life threw up, you know, Inspector.' Martha sat back on the sofa and took a sip of tea, her little finger extended. 'I remember when she lost her only child to the diphtheria a few years back.' She paused. 'In fact it was just a year or so after the war started, I think,' she said, 'but she just got on with life. I suppose getting a job at Sopwiths helped to take her mind off the tragedy. D'you know, she said to me only yesterday, that there's no point in grieving and that she just had to get on with things.'

'Very commendable,' said Hardcastle, dunking a ginger snap into his tea.

'Well, what with the war an' all,' continued Martha. 'She said as how the aeroplanes had still got to be made. And, strictly entre nous, Inspector, she said they were developing a new aeroplane that was so revolutionary it could end the war.'

'She shouldn't go around saying things like that,' muttered Hardcastle. 'Walls have ears.'

'You're quite right, of course, Inspector, but I suppose because my husband Gerald is a senior draughtsman at Sopwiths, she thought it would be all right to mention it to me. And what with you being a policeman, I s'pose it's all right to tell you.'

'Having an important job like that's prevented your husband from being conscripted, I suppose, Mrs Middleton,' suggested Marriott.

'Yes, thank the Lord.' Martha gave a little laugh. 'Most people in this road seem to work at Sopwiths. Unfortunately, our son Jimmy had to go. Well, he didn't have to, he volunteered.' She nodded towards the photograph on the piano. 'He's an observer in the Royal Naval Air Service. A lieutenant, he is.'

'Very patriotic of him,' murmured Hardcastle.

'Were they very close, Mrs Parker and her husband?' enquired Marriott.

'Ah, now you're asking, Sergeant.' Martha Middleton leaned forward, intent upon sharing a confidence. 'Strictly between the three of us, I think a bit of a rift had come between them. I oughtn't to be saying this really, but she could be a saucy little baggage at times, could Mavis. I s'pose it was something to do with her working at the factory and him being at the gas board, and not having much time for what you might call a social life. I mean to say, until this lot with the Kaiser started, women never went out to work, did they? But sometimes she'd go out of an evening on her own, even when Ron was at home.'

'Could she have been doing another shift at the factory, perhaps?' asked Hardcastle, fairly sure that she had not.

'Not the way she was dressed, Inspector, if you take my meaning. All dolled up like a barber's cat. She certainly knew how to dress herself up when she was out on the town.'

'I suppose she never mentioned where she'd been?' asked Marriott hopefully.

'Well, she did say once that she'd taken up roller skating. Apparently a lot of the girls from the factory went to the rink. I suppose it was a way of breaking the monotony of spending all day painting those aeroplanes.'

'Thank you, Mrs Middleton,' said Hardcastle, as he and Marriott stood up. 'And thank you for the tea.'

'Any time you're passing, Inspector,' said Martha, primping her hair. 'Always glad of a bit of company.'

'Are you the pianist?' asked Marriott, nodding towards the piano. 'I see you like Gilbert and Sullivan.'

'We love it. We used to go to the Savoy Theatre quite regularly before the war, but we're a bit worried about the bombs in London now. But to answer your question, Mr Marriott, I only play a little. My Gerald's much better. I always said that he could've been a professional.'

FIVE

'The cracks are starting to appear, Marriott,' said Hardcastle mysteriously, as the two of them walked down Canbury Park Road towards the railway station.

'I suppose it would be helpful if we knew whether she'd met anyone at this roller skating rink, sir.'

'There's one way to find out, Marriott. We go to the rink and we ask questions.'

'All correct, sir.' As the two detectives reached the main gate of the aircraft factory, the policeman who had been there on Monday, saluted.

'Ah, the very man,' said Hardcastle. 'A test of your local knowledge, lad. D'you know of a roller skating rink in the town? I'm told that some of the factory girls go there.'

'I think there's only the one now, sir,' said the PC, rubbing a ruminative hand round his chin. 'They built these works on the site of the old one.' He nodded his head in the direction of the factory. 'But I'm fairly certain that the only one left now is in Ceres Road, near the public baths. That's where a lot of the girls go, so I've heard.'

'And where's Ceres Road, lad?'

'Go straight down here to Richmond Road, sir,' said the policeman, extending his right arm, 'left under the railway bridge, right into Wood Street and it's down there at the far end.'

It took the two detectives about fifteen minutes of brisk walking to find the roller skating rink.

A woman seated behind a counter looked up as Hardcastle and Marriott entered, and regarded them with a bored expression. 'What size d'you want?' she asked, removing the pencil that was lodged in her hair.

'Size?' queried Hardcastle.

'Yes, what size skates d'you want?'

'We haven't come here to skate, miss, we're police officers,' said Hardcastle. 'Is the manager here?'

'There isn't one; he went off to the army and got hisself killed by them Turks at Gallipoli. I'm the manageress.'

'I see.' Even after nearly four years of war, Hardcastle still had difficulty coming to terms with women doing men's jobs, even though his daughter Kitty worked on the buses. 'Can you tell me if a Mrs Mavis Parker ever comes here?'

'Half a tick.' The woman pushed the pencil back into her hair and referred to a large book that was open on the counter. 'Yes,' she said eventually. 'She comes in a couple of times a week, usually with some of the girls from Sopwiths. Hires size five skates,' she added, as though furnishing a helpful description of the woman.

'Is there anyone in particular who comes with her?' asked Marriott.

The manageress ran a finger down the entries in her book. 'Yes, a Gertrude Hobbs,' she said, looking up again. 'Why, what's Mrs Parker been up to?'

'Did she ever come with a man?' asked Marriott, declining to discuss his and the DDI's interest in Mavis Parker.

The woman referred to the book again. 'No, but she did leave with a man one night, the week before last that was. Is that helpful?' she asked, looking up.

'What was his name?' asked Hardcastle.

'Gilbert Stroud. He comes quite often. What's this all about, anyway?'

'It's secret business, miss,' snapped Hardcastle, 'and you're not to mention my interest either to Mr Stroud or Mrs Parker. Otherwise you could be in serious trouble under the Defence of the Realm Act. Is that understood?' He found it useful to threaten the draconian measures of DORA even when they were clearly inapposite.

'Yes, of course.' The woman looked slightly taken aback by Hardcastle's warning. 'I won't tell no one, mister.'

'Do you have an address for this Gilbert Stroud?'

'No, we don't take addresses.'

'Do they come here regularly, miss, this Mr Stroud and Mrs Parker?' asked Marriott

'They come here quite often on their own, but I've only ever seen them together the once, and as I said that was Wednesday of last week.'

'What time do they normally get here?'

'Mrs Parker usually comes in about seven o'clock of an evening, but Mr Stroud is usually here about six. When he comes, of course.'

'What does he look like, this Gilbert Stroud?' asked Hardcastle.

The manageress gave the question some thought before answering. 'About his age, I s'pose,' she said, nodding in Marriott's direction, 'and about his build an' all. Oh, and he had a moustache, a bit like that picture of Lord Kitchener. You know, the one on the recruiting poster what they put up before he was drowned. Lord Kitchener, I mean, not Mr Stroud.'

'Thank you, miss, that'll be all,' said Hardcastle, but as he turned to leave, the manageress spoke again.

'I've just remembered. There was another man she came with once or twice.' The manageress ran a finger down her book. 'A Mr Mortimer, Mr L. Mortimer.'

'What did he look like?' asked Marriott.

'I can't remember, I'm afraid. It's only the name I remember. And the size of their skates, of course, but only if they need to hire 'em.'

'It's going to be a bit of a job finding these two men, sir,' said Marriott, once he and Hardcastle were in the street again.

'No it won't, Marriott. I'll put a couple of men on it. They'll find them.'

*   *   *

Hardcastle wasted no time in assigning two detectives to the task of identifying Gilbert Stroud and Mr L. Mortimer.

Once back in his office at Cannon Row police station, he sent for Marriott.

'Who've we got available for this following job at the skating rink, Marriott?'

'Depends on when you want them to start, sir.'

'Tomorrow evening,' said Hardcastle.

'There's only Lipton and Catto, sir,' said Marriott, whose job, as the first-class sergeant, was to know where each of the detectives was at any given time, and to what duty they were assigned. 'Carter and Keeler are both up at the Bailey with that robbery job, the Martin's Bank one.'

'Is that trial still rumbling on?'

'Yes, sir. Mr Rhodes has given his evidence, and the summing-up should start the day after tomorrow.'

'Oh well, Lipton and Catto it'll have to be, I suppose. Fetch 'em in here.'

'You wanted us, sir?' asked Lipton, the senior of the two.

'I've got a following job for the pair of you,' Hardcastle began, 'and I don't want you making a Mons of it, Catto,' he said, glaring at the other detective. 'Is that understood?'

'Yes, sir,' said Catto, as ever, apprehensive in Hardcastle's presence for no better reason than he always seemed to be the butt of the DDI's criticism.

'There are two men who've been seen in the company of Mavis Parker at the skating rink,' said Hardcastle. 'One's called Gilbert Stroud and the other one is a man who goes by the name of L. Mortimer. I want you to follow whichever of 'em comes out first. And if neither of 'em turns up, start again tomorrow. It might be helpful to have a discreet word with the young woman who seems to run the skating rink. But don't let on what you're up to, or you'll have me to answer to. Got that, have you, Lipton?'

'Yes, sir.'

'And you, Catto. Got that, have you?'

'Yes, sir,' said Catto.

'And I don't want to find that either of these men have cottoned-on that he's being followed.'

'No, sir, of course not, sir,' said Lipton.

'Right, start tomorrow. I'm told that they usually turn up at the rink round about six o'clock. I want to know where they live.'

'D'you want them nicked, sir?' asked Catto. It was an unfortunate question, but he tended to ask stupid questions in the DDI's presence.

'No, I do *not* want them nicked, Catto. It seems to me that you're all too fond of feeling collars, except when you should.' And with that reproof, Hardcastle dismissed the two DCs.

On Thursday morning, Marriott received a telephone call from Sergeant Glover in the APM's office.

'I've got some information for you, Charlie, if you'd care to drop in.'

'I'll be down straight away, Cyril,' said Marriott, and made his way the short distance along Whitehall to Horse Guards Arch.

Glover was in the act of making a pot of tea when Marriott entered his office.

'Well, Cyril, have you solved my problem for me?'

'In a manner of speaking, Charlie.' Glover gave a wry smile and, unbidden, poured Marriott a cup of tea. 'This Staff Sergeant Benson of the Army Ordnance Corps you're interested in,' he began, as the two of them sat down.

'You've found him, then. Is he in France?'

'Oh, he's in France all right, Charlie.' Glover laughed and referred to his file. 'He's buried in Boulogne, at the *cimetière de l'est.*' Having served in France at the beginning of the war, he spoke the words confidently enough, but without any attempt at a French accent. 'That's what the French call the East Cemetery.'

'When was he killed?' Marriott had his pocket book open, and had begun to make notes.

'The seventh of May last year.' Glover took a sip of his tea. 'It's always a good idea to check the casualty lists first when we're looking for a name. Apparently he got run down by a gun carriage team in the base ordnance area at the Port of Boulogne. He was killed instantly.' He glanced up with a wry smile on his face. 'They're bloody careless at times, these artillery drivers.'

'Presumably his wife was informed at the time of his death.'

'Bound to have been.' Glover looked back at his file. 'Yes, the War House was signalled by the port commander at Boulogne on the eighth of May 1917, and they in turn advised his wife, a

Mrs Daisy Benson, by telegram on the eleventh. At the time she lived at Gordon Road, Kingston upon Thames.'

'Yes, I know, and she's still there, but she told us that he was still alive.'

'When was this?'

'Last Monday, Cyril.'

Glover laughed. 'Got a fancy man, has she?'

Marriott laughed too. 'I think she's got more than one, Cyril, but you army coppers are terrible cynics.'

'That's rich, coming from a civvy copper,' said Glover. 'Anything else I can do for you, Charlie?'

'No, not at the moment, Cyril, and thanks for the tea.'

'I can tell you how to get to that cemetery if you want to pop over and make sure, Charlie.'

'Thanks very much, but I think I'll give that a miss. My Lorna wouldn't care for that idea at all,' said Marriott, and returned to Cannon Row keen to report this latest twist to the DDI.

Hardcastle applied a match to his pipe and blew smoke at the ceiling. 'There's obviously more to our Daisy Benson than meets the eye,' he said, once Marriott had finished telling him of Staff Sergeant Benson's death. 'I think we'll have to have another chat with her.'

'But how will that help us, sir?'

'We won't know until we ask, Marriott.'

It took a few moments for Daisy Benson to recognize the two men on her doorstep.

'Oh, it's you, Inspector,' she said eventually, and glanced nervously over her shoulder.

'Yes, it's me, Mrs Benson.'

'Good Lord, it's about Sid this time, isn't it? That's what you've come about. I can feel it in my bones. Is he dead?'

'I'm afraid so, Mrs Benson.'

'Oh dear God!' Daisy took hold of the doorpost and contrived to appear shocked by the news. As charades went, it was not very convincing. 'When did it happen?'

'Ten months ago, on the seventh of May last year, to be exact. As you well know, Mrs Benson,' said Hardcastle coldly. 'You had a telegram from the War Office on the eleventh of May, four days after he was killed.'

'You'd better come in, Inspector.' With unseemly haste, Daisy Benson ushered the two detectives towards the parlour, but it was too late. A man descended the staircase, putting on his jacket.

'I'll be off, then, Daisy.' The man glanced apprehensively at Hardcastle and Marriott. He had encountered the police before, and was fairly certain that he had just done so again.

'Oh, this is, um, Mr Smith, one of my lodgers, Inspector,' said Daisy.

'I've left the, er, rent on the dressing table, as usual, Daisy,' said 'Smith', with a broad wink, and hastened towards the front door.

'Such a nice man,' said Daisy, but she could not control the flush of embarrassment that was rising slowly from her neck.

Waiting until Daisy Benson had taken a seat and composed herself, Hardcastle and Marriott sat down opposite her. Hardcastle remained silent, waiting to see what the woman had to say.

'I don't know what you must think of me, Inspector,' she began. Hardcastle still said nothing. 'Of course I knew about Sid getting killed, but I didn't tell anyone. You see, I was worried what the neighbours might think, with me having gentlemen lodgers, so to speak,' she added, rushing into an unlikely explanation.

'Yes, of course,' murmured Hardcastle. 'Do you have a revolver, by any chance?' he asked suddenly.

'A revolver?' Daisy seemed unnerved by the question. 'What on earth would I be doing with a revolver, Inspector?'

'Some people do keep them for protection, Mrs Benson,' suggested Marriott. 'Particularly widowed ladies living alone who have male house guests.'

'Oh, no, I'm not worried by having business gentlemen taking a room here. They're all very respectable and trustworthy.'

'And Mr Smith is a respectable business gentleman, is he?' asked Marriott.

'Oh yes. He's . . . now what was it he told me he did?' Daisy lapsed into thought while trying to think up a spurious profession for her paying guest. 'Yes, of course, he works for the income tax people, I believe.'

'Strange, him starting this late on a Thursday,' said Hardcastle.

'Yes, he does work odd hours,' said Daisy lamely. 'I s'pose it's something to do with the war.'

'However, I've not come here to talk about your lodgers, Mrs Benson,' said Hardcastle, to Daisy's obvious relief. 'I was wondering if you could tell me anything more about the Parkers.'

'Oh, poor, dear Ronnie, such a tragedy. Have you any idea who might have killed him, Inspector?'

'I'm pretty certain that I know his murderer,' said Hardcastle, much to Marriott's surprise. He knew that the DDI had no idea who had killed Parker, but presumed he was playing another of his little games. Although to what end remained a mystery. 'However, I was wondering if you could tell me a little more about Mavis Parker.'

'I don't know what there is to tell.' Daisy Benson seemed more relaxed now that the DDI had moved away from his interest in her lodgers.

'I have reason to believe that she and her husband didn't get on too well,' suggested Hardcastle.

'I never met her, of course, but from what Ronnie told me, they didn't enjoy the best of relationships. Like I said the last time you were here, she just didn't understand him, poor soul. And her working at the aeroplane factory didn't help matters, either.'

'Strictly between ourselves, Mrs Benson,' said Hardcastle, leaning forward, 'd'you know if she was seeing someone else?'

Marriott listened to this exchange with increasing amazement. He knew that Hardcastle often pursued a line of questioning that seemed to have no point, but he could not really follow what the DDI was hoping to achieve. From their enquiries of Mrs Middleton, and the manageress at the roller skating rink, it seemed quite apparent that Mavis Parker was not an innocent party in the marriage. Perhaps he thought that she had murdered her husband or, more likely, that some male acquaintance of hers had done so.

'I wouldn't know anything about that,' said Daisy with a toss of her head.

'Well, thank you, Mrs Benson,' said Hardcastle, rising from his seat. 'If you do happen to think of anything that might assist me, perhaps you'd telephone me. You do have a telephone, do you?'

'Oh yes,' said Daisy, 'it helps with the bookings.'

'Yes, I imagine it makes life much easier for you,' said Hardcastle drily. 'Marriott, be so good as to give Mrs Benson the telephone number of the police station.'

*   *   *

'Have Lipton and Catto left to find out where this here Gilbert Stroud lives, Marriott?' Although Marriott was entirely trust-worthy in his supervision of the detectives in his charge, it was in Hardcastle's nature always to check that his orders had been carried out to his satisfaction.

'Yes, sir, they left in time to take up the observation by half past five. I thought it best if they got there early just in case Stroud and Mrs Parker turned up together. Or, for that matter, Mortimer, although without a description they'll be hard pressed to identify him.'

'Quite right, Marriott,' said Hardcastle. 'I was going to suggest an early start myself.' He took out his hunter and checked the time, wound it briefly and dropped it back into his waistcoat pocket. 'Half past seven. I think we'll take the opportunity of having an early night, Marriott.' He put on his bowler hat and overcoat, and picked up his umbrella, checking that it was tightly furled. 'My regards to Mrs Marriott.'

'Thank you, sir, and mine to Mrs H.'

SIX

I t was twenty past eight when Hardcastle arrived at his house in Kennington Road. The moment he closed his front door he heard the sounds of laughter, including that of a man, coming from the parlour. Although curious to discover the reason for the hilarity, he still made time to check the accuracy of the hall clock against his hunter.

That done, he pushed open the parlour door to be confronted by his wife Alice, his twenty-year-old daughter Maud, and a young man in army lieutenant's uniform. At the sight of Hardcastle, the soldier immediately leaped to his feet.

'I'm glad you're home, Ernie,' said Alice. 'You're just in time to meet Maud's young man before he takes her out to supper.'

'Charles Spencer, sir.' The young man took a pace towards Hardcastle and held out his hand.

'How d'you do?' said Hardcastle, carefully appraising the young man and pleased to note that he had a firm grip. 'What

regiment are you in?' His eyes dropped to the ribbon of a Military
Cross adorning the officer's tunic. On the ribbon was a bronze
oak leaf spray which, Hardcastle had learned, indicated a mention
in dispatches. Clearly Spencer was a courageous soldier.

'The Loyal Regiment, sir,' said Spencer.

'But aren't all the regiments in the army loyal, Mr Spencer?'
Once again, Hardcastle found himself baffled by the complexities
of the military.

'Yes, sir, of course they are, but it's the name especially given
to the Eighty-First of Foot. That's what the regiment was called
in 1793, and it was taken from the motto of its first colonel.
Although officially we're the Loyal North Lancashire Regiment
now. Loyal for short.'

'I see,' said Hardcastle, 'and are you from Lancashire?'

Spencer grinned boyishly. 'No, sir, I'm from Windsor as a
matter of fact, but we don't have any say in where we're sent. I
was in the Essex Regiment before I was commissioned.'

'Do sit down, Mr Spencer. I have to say that I find the army
a very confusing organization.'

'So do I, sir, and I'm in it,' said Spencer, with a self-deprecating
laugh.

'Has Maud given you a drink, Mr Spencer?'

'No, I haven't,' said Maud, 'and why don't you call him
Charles, Pa? I'm sure you don't mind, Charles, do you?'

'Not at all,' said Spencer.

'Well, I'm going to have a whisky,' said Hardcastle. 'What
about you, Charles?'

'A whisky would be fine, sir. Neat, if you please.'

Hardcastle poured two measures of Scotch, and looked enquiringly at the womenfolk.

'I'll have a sherry, Ernie, and so will Maud, won't you, dear?'
asked Alice, glancing at her daughter.

'Yes, please, Pa,' said Maud, who was still growing accustomed
to being treated as an adult by her father.

'I understand that you met Maud while you were in hospital,
Charles.' Having poured the women's drinks, Hardcastle settled
in his armchair.

'Yes, sir. I copped a Blighty one in the leg at Cambrai at the
end of last year. D'you know, sir, that the Canadians actually did
a cavalry charge north of Masnières during that battle,' continued

Spencer, his face lighting up with enthusiasm. 'The Fort Garry Horse rode down a German artillery battery with their sabres out. Put the fear of God into Fritz.'

'Yes, I read that in the paper,' said Hardcastle, 'but I take it you're quite recovered from your wounds now.'

'Fit as a fiddle, sir.'

'Is it bad over there? I mean worse than we read about.'

'It's bad enough, sir, but things are starting to move into the open now. I'd like to think we've seen the last of trench warfare, and I've got a feeling that the end will be in sight before much longer.'

'I hope so,' said Hardcastle. 'This damnable war has gone on far too long.'

'Charles,' said Maud, making a point of gesturing at the clock on the mantel, 'it's time we were going.'

'Yes, of course.' Spencer drained his whisky glass and stood up. 'Jolly good to have you met you, sir,' he said, proffering a hand once more.

Hardcastle stood up and shook hands. 'You take good care of my girl, Charles.'

'Don't worry, sir, Maud's very precious to me. She nursed me back to health.' Spencer dashed into the hall and returned with Maud's hat and coat. 'Well, goodbye, sir, and thanks for the whisky,' he said, buckling on his Sam Browne belt. He glanced in Alice's direction. 'Goodbye, Mrs Hardcastle.'

'He seems a nice young chap, Alice,' said Hardcastle, once the door had closed behind Maud and Charles Spencer.

'If things go on as they seem to be going, Ernie, I might just have to buy a new hat,' said Alice Hardcastle.

'Good grief!' exclaimed Hardcastle, taking his pipe from his mouth. 'You don't mean that—'

'They're very keen on each other, Ernie. A woman can always tell, you know.'

'Good grief!' said Hardcastle again, and immediately tried to calculate how he would be able to afford a decent wedding for his daughter on a DDI's pay of less than two hundred and thirty pounds a year.

A policeman was standing in the entrance to Kingston railway station when Lipton and Catto emerged into Wood Street.

'Any idea where Ceres Road is, mate?' asked Catto.

'I'm not your mate,' said the PC tetchily, as he fingered his beard and glanced disparagingly at the two 'civilians' in front of him. 'And I should've thought that two well set up young gents like you would be looking for the recruiting office in Kingston Hall Road.'

'Well, we're not. We're in the Job,' said Lipton. 'But as we're CID officers we don't have time to stand about all day doing bugger all.'

'Down there.' The PC pointed down Wood Street and ambled away, mumbling to himself about what he perceived to be the comfortable life of a detective.

'Bloody uniform carrier,' muttered Lipton.

The two detectives eventually found the roller skating rink, but undecided what to do next, stood on the opposite side of the road.

'We can't go in there and start asking questions,' said Catto, 'even though the guv'nor said we should. It'd mean showing out.'

'Well, I don't see how else we can find out which of the men going in there is . . . what's his name, Henry?'

'Stroud. Gilbert Stroud.'

'What time is it?' asked Lipton.

'Time you bought a watch,' said Catto, pulling out the Enigma watch he had bought from Selfridges last week for an outrageous four shillings and sixpence. 'Ten minutes to six.'

'And what time did the guv'nor say Stroud arrived?'

'Usually about six, when he does come.'

'Be just our luck for him not to turn up today, then we'll be back here again tomorrow.' Lipton thrust his hands into the pockets of his overcoat and stared moodily at the skating rink, visualizing an unending period of time spent in Kingston.

'Well, I s'pose we'd better just hang about,' said Catto.

'This looks promising, Henry,' said Lipton, a quarter an hour later, as he sighted a man striding towards the rink.

Making his way purposefully along the opposite side of the road was a tall man in a raincoat and a brown trilby hat. He had a large moustache, similar to that of the late Lord Kitchener, and was swinging a pair of roller skates in his right hand.

'Could be him, I suppose,' said Catto doubtfully, 'but on the other hand he looks like a dozen other men. After all, Gordon, most men have got moustaches, you and me included.'

'Don't let him see you're looking at him, Henry,' cautioned Lipton, as he put his hand on Catto's shoulder and turned him, so that both of them appeared to be taking an interest in a shop window display. But Lipton was watching the man in the reflection afforded by the glass. 'He's gone in, Henry.'

'Well, he would've done seeing as how he's carrying skates.'

'So what do we do now?'

'Wait, I suppose,' said Catto.

For just over an hour, the two detectives wandered up and down the deserted street, trying to appear inconspicuous. During that time, several groups of girls entered the rink, usually laughing among themselves. Two or three couples also went in, each girl holding the arm of her male companion, some of whom were in uniform.

'We're going to be here half the night at this rate,' complained Lipton.

At a quarter past seven, the man in the raincoat and the brown trilby emerged, carrying his skates.

'D'you reckon that's him, Gordon?' asked Catto.

'There's one bloody way to find out,' said Lipton, who disliked prolonged observation duty. Before Catto could stop him, he streaked across the road. 'Blimey, if it's not old Tom Pickford,' he said, borrowing a surname he had seen on the side of a removal van. He seized the man's right hand, and shook it vigorously. 'God, I haven't seen you in years, Tom, mate. What've you been doing with yourself? Taken up skating, I see.' He nodded at the man's skates. 'Lord Derby not grabbed you for the Kate Carney?'

'I think you must've made a mistake.' The man was clearly thrown off guard by this sudden confrontation and made an admission he would not otherwise have done. 'My name's Gilbert Stroud.'

Lipton relinquished the man's hand, and took a pace back. 'Crikey, mate, I'm terribly sorry,' he said, 'but you're just like him. They say that everyone's got a double somewhere in the world. Still, no harm done. Sorry an' all that.' He crossed back over the road and hurried to catch up with Catto who had wisely moved away so that the man would not see him.

'It's him, Henry,' said Lipton breathlessly.

'You were taking a hell of a chance, Gordon,' complained Catto. 'The guv'nor said that he mustn't twig that he was being tailed. You might've blown it.'

'Don't worry, mate, he never saw you. He was too busy telling me that he was Gilbert Stroud. Now, as he knows me, the best thing is for you to follow him and I'll bring up the rear.'

Gilbert Stroud set off at a brisk pace along Wood Street. Turning into Clarence Street, he continued into London Road, past the police station, and eventually turned into Caversham Road. Catto maintained his watch on the man from a discreet distance until eventually his quarry let himself into a house. Waiting until the door had closed Catto walked swiftly past the house and noted the number. At the top of the street, he turned into Fairfield Road and waited until Lipton had caught up with him.

'I don't think the guv'nor will find too much to complain about with that, Henry.'

'I wouldn't be too sure, Gordon,' said Catto pessimistically.

'It's Friday morning already, Marriott, and we're no further forward with this damned murder.'

'No, sir.' In fact, Marriott thought that they had made quite significant progress with what he called background enquiries. 'But we do know that Ronald Parker was in a relationship with Daisy Benson, sir. And as she's probably a prostitute, he might've paid her for his pleasure. We also know that Mavis Parker was not above meeting men at the skating rink. And Mrs Middleton thought that Mavis and her husband weren't getting on too well.'

'That's as maybe, Marriott, but we still don't know who murdered the man. And talking of Mavis Parker meeting men at the skating rink, have Catto and Lipton found out anything about this here Gilbert Stroud?'

'Yes, sir. They're in the office now.'

'Well, fetch 'em in, Marriott, fetch 'em in,' said Hardcastle impatiently.

'You wanted us, sir?' said Catto, as he and Lipton lined up in front of the DDI's desk.

'Of course I want you,' barked Hardcastle. 'Why haven't you reported yet about your observation last evening?'

'I thought you were busy, sir,' muttered Catto.

'I'm always busy. Now then, what happened?'

'We followed Gilbert Stroud, sir, and—'

'How did you know it was Stroud?' demanded Hardcastle.

'I spoke to him, sir,' said Lipton.

'You did *what*?' roared the DDI.

'Well, sir, we didn't know if the man who'd come out of the skating rink was actually Stroud, so I went up to him and suggested he was an old friend of mine called Tom Pickford. But he said he wasn't, and he told me that his name was Gilbert Stroud.'

'My God, Marriott, I've never heard the like of it. If you've compromised this business, Lipton, you'll have me to answer to.' Secretly, Hardcastle was quite impressed by Lipton's initiative, but had no intention of telling him as much. It was the sort of ploy he might have used himself in his younger days, but now, as a DDI, he had to take a more responsible and overall view. 'Anyway, what did you find out?'

'We followed Stroud, sir,' said Catto hesitantly, 'and er—'

'I should hope so. Spit it out, man. I haven't got all day.'

'No, sir. We followed him and he eventually entered a house in Caversham Road, Kingston, sir. I've written down the details and given them to Sergeant Marriott.'

'And did you check the voters' list?'

'Er, no, sir. I thought—'

'You should never think, Catto, you're not equipped for it. Right, get about your duties, both of you.'

'I told you he'd find fault, Gordon,' whispered Catto as the two DCs returned to their office opposite the DDI's.

'What did you say, Catto?' demanded Hardcastle.

'Er, nothing, sir,' replied Catto.

'Well, Marriott, at least we know where this Stroud lives,' said Hardcastle.

'I thought they did a good job, sir,' said Marriott, who was always keen to defend his charges, especially Catto, when they had been successful.

'I suppose so,' admitted Hardcastle grudgingly. 'I just hope they weren't spotted.'

'Do we pay him a visit, sir?'

'Not yet, Marriott. I want to know a bit more about him first. I'll put Wood on it. He's good at keeping observation. Is he here?'

'Yes, sir. I'll fetch him in.'

'Ah, Wood,' said Hardcastle, when Detective Sergeant Herbert Wood appeared in his office. 'I've got a job for you.' He explained about Gilbert Stroud and his apparent association with Mavis Parker. 'I want you to find out where this here Stroud works, Wood, but discreet mind.'

'Very good, sir,' said Wood.

'Start tomorrow morning.'

'He might not work on a Saturday, sir.'

'Everyone works on a Saturday, Wood,' said Hardcastle, 'but if he don't, then you'll have to take up the observation again on Monday.'

'Very good, sir.'

'And now, Marriott,' said Hardcastle, glancing at his watch, 'we'd better get our own skates on or we'll be late for the inquest.'

Hardcastle strode out to Whitehall and was confronted by a disabled ex-soldier playing a barrel organ. The man wore a grotesque skin-coloured mask, complete with a false moustache and dark glasses, and his free hand held a white stick. The mask was the latest example of an attempt by military hospitals to disguise appalling facial disfigurement from a sensitive public. Pausing only to drop a couple of coins into the man's cap, Hardcastle waved his umbrella at a passing cab and instructed the cab driver to take him and Marriott to the coroner's court in Horseferry Road.

An attendant pulled open the heavy door of the courtroom for Hardcastle and gave him a nod of recognition.

A couple of reporters from local papers lounged in the press box. The public gallery was occupied by a few individuals who seemingly had no interest in the proceedings, but who by their rough appearance were only concerned to find somewhere warm to languish on this cold March day.

There was a rustle of movement as the coroner entered and those in the body of the court scrambled to their feet.

The coroner spent a few moments in whispered conversation with his clerk, and then looked up.

'In the matter of Ronald Parker, deceased,' he said in a strained voice, glancing at the courtroom clock, and making a note in his ledger.

'Inspector Hardcastle,' cried the clerk in tones loud enough to have been heard by the DDI if he had been outside in the street.

'You are Divisional Detective Inspector Ernest Hardcastle of the A or Whitehall Division of the Metropolitan Police,' said the coroner. 'Is that correct?'

'It is, sir.'

'And are you the officer in charge of the investigation into the death of Ronald Parker?'

'I am, sir.'

'Perhaps you would afford the court the brief facts, Mr Hardcastle.'

'The body of Ronald Parker was recovered from the River Thames near Westminster Bridge at approximately eight forty a.m. on Monday the fourth of March this year, sir. It was secured in a sack and the deceased had been shot in the head. The body was later identified by Mr Harold Parker as that of his brother Ronald Parker.'

'Have your enquiries led you to discover the identity of any person or persons who might have been responsible for this death?'

'Not at this stage, sir.'

The coroner made a few more notes in his ledger. 'I shall adjourn this inquest until such time as the police have furthered their enquiries.'

An elderly man stood up behind the table reserved for counsel. 'I appear on behalf of the Parker family, sir, and make application for the release of the deceased's body.'

'Do the police have any objections, Mr Hardcastle?' asked the coroner.

'No objections, sir,' said Hardcastle, and sat down.

'I so order that the body be released,' said the coroner.

The solicitor gathered up his papers and left the court.

'Catch up with that solicitor, Marriott,' said Hardcastle, 'find out who briefed him to attend, and ask him to let us know the date of the funeral.'

'Yes, sir,' acknowledged Marriott, and when, minutes later, he was joined by Hardcastle on the pavement outside the court, he said, 'He was briefed by Harold Parker, Ronald's brother, sir, and he'll let us know when the funeral is to take place.'

'Good,' said Hardcastle, and hailing a cab said to the driver,

'Scotland Yard, cabbie.' He turned to Marriott. 'Tell 'em Cannon Row and half the time you'll finish up at Cannon Street in the City.'

'Yes, sir,' said Marriott wearily.

SEVEN

Detective Sergeant Wood was indeed a resourceful officer, and skilled at keeping a discreet observation. He arrived in Caversham Road, Kingston, at seven o'clock on the Saturday morning and conducted a preliminary survey of the street. Having concluded that it was not the easiest of areas in which to remain inconspicuous, he decided that a fixed observation post would be the only way in which he could safely keep a watch on Stroud's property.

He made his way to the nearby Kingston police station to enquire what, if anything, was known about the occupants of the houses immediately opposite Stroud's dwelling.

The constable on duty ran a hand round his chin. 'We know the man living at that one, Sergeant,' he said, pointing a pencil at one of the addresses in Wood's pocket book.

'D'you mean he's a villain?' asked Wood.

'Oh no, he's a respectable gent, Skip. A retired army officer by the name of Darke, Major Joseph Darke.'

It was eight o'clock by the time that Wood knocked at Major Darke's house. An elderly man came to the door, but before he could say anything, Wood produced his warrant card.

'Good morning, sir, I'm a police officer. Am I right in thinking that you are Major Darke?'

'That's correct,' said Darke.

'In that case, I wonder if you could assist me, sir.'

'Well, of course, Officer. You'd better come in.'

'Thank you, sir.' Wood removed the cloth cap he was wearing and followed the man into the hall.

'Is there some trouble, Officer?' Major Darke asked, once he had closed his front door.

'Not as far as you're concerned, sir.' Wood stuffed his cap into one of the pockets of the old raincoat he was wearing. 'Perhaps I'd better introduce myself: I'm Detective Sergeant Wood of the Whitehall Division.'

'Whitehall, eh? You're a long way from home, Sergeant. What's this all about?'

'A matter of national security, sir,' said Wood. 'I'm sure you'll appreciate that I'm not at liberty to say any more than that.'

'Ah, to do with the war effort, eh?'

'In a manner of speaking, sir. We have received information of a vital nature that requires me to keep a watch on one of the houses opposite. But I'm afraid I can't reveal which one. Neither can I tell you any more about it.' Wood was very good at making up stories to cover his enquiries.

'No, of course not, Sergeant. I quite understand. I was in the Boer War, you know, but unfortunately the chaps at the War House told me that I was too old for this one. I do know a bit about national security and I worked in intelligence in South Africa, sniffing out the Boer commandos, don't you know.' Darke fingered a striped necktie that Wood, had he been familiar with such things, would have recognized as the regimental tie of the East Surrey Regiment. 'So, what can I do to help?'

'If it wouldn't be an inconvenience, sir, I'd like to keep observation from your front room. It should only be for a short period.'

'No trouble at all, my dear fellow,' said Darke warmly, secretly glad to be involved in what he imagined as assisting in the defeat of the Hun. 'Come this way.' He showed Wood into the parlour where a fire was crackling in the grate. He saw Wood glance at an assegai mounted above the fireplace. 'That was a trophy I picked up at Spion Kop, Sergeant.'

'Very good, sir,' said Wood, although from what little he had heard about the South African conflict, he doubted that the Boers had used spears in their fight against the British.

'You'll notice that Mrs Darke insists on net curtains, so you'll be able to see without being seen, what?'

'That's splendid, sir, but I don't want to cause you or your good lady any trouble.'

'Good heavens, Sergeant, it's no trouble. Only too pleased to be able to do something to help. I'll get Mrs Darke to make you a cup of tea. Let me move this chair for you, so you can sit down and keep watch.'

'That's very kind, sir, and thank you.' Wood slipped off his
raincoat and settled down for what he hoped would not be too
long a period of time.

Ten minutes later the parlour door opened and a slender
grey-haired woman entered.

'Good morning, Sergeant, I'm Felicity Darke. I've brought
you some tea. If you'd be so good as to move that small table
nearer the window, I can put the tray down next to you.'

Wood leaped up and moved the table that Mrs Darke had
indicated, and took the tray from her.

'I've put a piece of fruit cake on there, too,' said Mrs Darke.
'I'm sure you could do with it.'

'Thank you, Mrs Darke, that's most kind,' said Wood.

For the next hour, Wood maintained a close watch on the house
occupied by Gilbert Stroud. He was just beginning to wonder if
his quarry did not go to work on a Saturday when he was rewarded
by the sight of a man emerging from the house. The man, who
fitted the description of Stroud furnished by Catto, began to walk
slowly down Caversham Road reading the newspaper that Wood
had earlier seen delivered.

Grabbing his raincoat, Wood moved quickly from his observation point into the hall. Major Darke appeared almost at once.

'I'm off, sir. Please thank Mrs Darke for the tea and cake.'

'It's a pleasure, Sergeant,' said Darke. 'I hope that you have
a successful conclusion to your enquiries, whatever they are, and
do make use of our parlour again if you need to.'

Putting on his raincoat and cap, Wood emerged from Major
Darke's house just in time to see Stroud turn into London Road.

Following at a discreet distance, he eventually saw Stroud turn
into Richmond Road and finally to Kingston railway station.

Fortunately there was no queue, and Wood risked moving close
enough to hear Stroud ask for a return to Waterloo. Having had
the foresight to buy a return ticket when he left London earlier
that morning, Wood was able to follow Stroud on to the
up-platform without wasting time at the ticket office. He watched
his quarry enter a third-class carriage, and got into the compartment next to him, secure in the knowledge that Stroud would
not alight at any of the intermediate stations.

*   *   *

It was a quarter past ten when the train arrived at Waterloo railway station in central London. Wood hurriedly alighted from his compartment, just as Stroud stepped down from his.

On the concourse, Wood thrust a halfpenny at a newsvendor and grabbed an early edition of that day's *Evening Standard*. Reading the newspaper as he walked, but keeping an eye on Stroud, Wood scanned the account of the previous night's raid on Maida Vale by three German Staaken-Zeppelin bombers. A residential building had been destroyed, killing twelve people, and four hundred houses were damaged. With a sigh at the futility of it all, Wood put the paper in his pocket and devoted his attention to finding out where Stroud was going.

But in Waterloo Road, he almost lost his man. Stroud leaped on to a moving bus and mounted the stairs to the top deck. Fortunately, a cab hove into view and Wood hailed it.

'D'you know where that number 1A bus goes?' he asked, pointing at the departing vehicle.

'I'm a cabbie, not a bloody bus driver, guv'nor,' protested the taxi driver.

'Never mind, follow it,' said Wood.

'Are you joking, guv'nor?' asked the driver, turning in his seat. 'That only happens in them Keystone Kops pictures.'

'No, I'm not joking,' snapped Wood. 'I'm a police officer. Get a shift on or we'll lose it.'

'Right you are, then, guv'nor. Follow that bus, like the man says,' muttered the driver, as he put the cab into gear and drove away as quickly as his antiquated cab would allow.

The bus carrying Gilbert Stroud crossed Waterloo Bridge and wound its way along the Strand. It stopped frequently during its journey, either to pick up or set down passengers, or because it was held up in traffic. Finally it stopped at Charing Cross and Stroud alighted, but remained at the bus stop.

'Is that it, guv?' asked the cab driver.

'No, hold on until he gets on another bus.'

'Right you are, guv.' The cab driver sniffed and wiped a hand across his moustache. 'At least this sort of lark makes a change from the usual,' he commented.

A few moments later, a number fifteen bus stopped, and Stroud climbed aboard.

'OK, follow it,' said Wood.

'Off we go again,' said the cabbie.

The bus passed Trafalgar Square and drove along Cockspur Street until finally Wood observed Stroud alighting in Haymarket.

Quickly paying off the cab, and remembering, just in time, to note its plate number – or his claim would be disallowed – Wood followed Stroud into Charles Street and saw him enter a building called Waterloo House.

He strolled past the elegant house, but could find no indication as to what took place within its walls. He crossed the road to where a policeman was standing.

'I'm DS Wood of A,' he said, showing the PC his warrant card. 'Any idea what goes on in that building?' He nodded towards Waterloo House.

'Other to say that it's some secret place to do with the government, Sarge, I don't really know,' said the PC. 'But that's why I'm stuck here on a protection post.'

'Right, thanks, mate,' said Wood, and began the long walk back to Cannon Row police station.

It was midday when Wood tapped on the DDI's door and entered.

'What news?' asked Hardcastle, leaning back in his chair and linking his hands across his waistcoat.

Wood gave the DDI a full account of everything that had occurred from the moment he had taken up observation in Major Darke's house to the point where he had seen Gilbert Stroud enter Waterloo House.

'But without going in, I couldn't find out what goes on in there, sir, but a local copper told me that it's something to do with the government and he's posted there to protect it, but he's no idea what it is.'

'Good work, Wood, well done,' said Hardcastle, breaking his usual rule of not complimenting his subordinates. 'Ask Sergeant Marriott to come in.'

'Yes, sir, thank you, sir.'

'Did Wood tell you what he'd found out, Marriott?' asked Hardcastle, once his sergeant had joined him.

'Yes, sir.'

'See what you can find out about this here Waterloo House that Stroud went into.'

'I've done it already, sir. I spoke to the CID at Vine Street, and it turns out that it's the headquarters of MI5.'

'God help us!' exclaimed Hardcastle. 'That's all I need. I suppose that means that Stroud is one of their people.' He was not happy at the prospect of getting involved with MI5 officers again. Their interference and obstruction into his investigation of Rose Drummond's murder in Hoxton in 1916 had left him not wanting to repeat the experience. 'So what's this fellow Stroud doing getting tied up with Mavis Parker?'

Marriott hesitated before answering, but eventually he said, 'It's beginning to look as though she's up to something, sir, and I suppose it means that we'll have to ask Special Branch.'

But Hardcastle did not reply immediately. He reached forward, picked up his pipe and spent the next minute filling it. Once he had lit it, he leaned back in his chair and gazed thoughtfully at the ceiling.

'Not at the moment,' he said, suddenly leaning forward, and pointing the stem of his pipe at Marriott. 'You know what those buggers are like, Marriott. I think we'll concentrate our attention on Mavis Parker because MI5 are obviously interested in her and it would be nice to beat that brainy lot at their own game, so to speak.'

'I see, sir.' But Marriott did not in fact see at all. 'What do you propose, then?'

'We'll keep a careful watch on Mrs Parker, Marriott, that's what we'll do. I want to know everything she does and everywhere she goes. And I want to know who she's seeing, because it's pretty plain from what Wood found out that she's not having an affair with Gilbert Stroud. Not unless MI5 officers can spare time for the occasional bit of jig-a-jig, even when there's a war on. No, Marriott, he's obviously befriended Mavis Parker for a reason, and I'm wondering if it has something to do with this new Sopwith aeroplane that she told Mrs Middleton about. She mentioned it the last time we saw her.'

'Are you suggesting that Mavis Parker might be spying, sir?'

'That's exactly what I'm suggesting, Marriott.'

'But isn't that the job of Special Branch, sir?' Marriott was concerned that his DDI appeared to be straying into territory that was rightly the preserve of the branch that was under the control of Superintendent Patrick Quinn and closely supervised by

Assistant Commissioner Basil Thomson. And indeed into matters
that were the concern of Colonel Vivian Kell's MI5.

'Special Branch hasn't told me anything, Marriott, which they
should've done seeing as how I'm responsible for investigating
Ronald Parker's murder,' said Hardcastle, 'and until they do, I
shall continue to investigate it to the best of my ability. It's only
common courtesy that I should've been told because they must've
known he'd been topped.' He placed his pipe in the ashtray. 'And
if we find out that someone's been spying, I'll let Special Branch
know. But not until after Parker's killer is standing on the hang-
man's trapdoor.'

'Who did you have in mind for this observation on Mrs Parker,
sir?' Marriott was extremely relieved that the DDI's plan would
not be his responsibility. He knew, from previous experience,
that the head of Special Branch would not view lightly any
interference in the work of his department and would undoubtedly go into a towering rage when he learned of it.

Hardcastle gave Marriott's question sparse consideration.
'Wood for one,' he said, 'and possibly Lipton. He seems to know
what he's about.'

'Will two men be enough, sir?' Marriott forbore
from suggesting Catto; he knew what Hardcastle's reaction
would be.

But then Hardcastle confounded him. 'I think we might also
use Catto, Marriott,' he said. 'He knows that area now, having
spent a while in Kingston.'

'When d'you want them to start, sir?'

'Monday,' said Hardcastle tersely. 'Fetch Wood in again.'

Wood had half guessed that his observation on Gilbert Stroud
would not be the end of the matter and was not relishing further
surveillance work. 'You wanted me, sir?'

'Yes, Wood.' Hardcastle explained precisely what he required
of him. 'Sergeant Marriott will give you all the details of where
this woman lives and works, and I want to know everything she
does. And if she meets another man, other than Stroud, that is,
I want to know all about him. There's a man called Mortimer
that she's apparently friendly with as well, but we don't know
anything about him yet, neither do we have a description of him.
And don't show out. Now, is all that clear?'

'Yes, sir.'

'You're to take Lipton and Catto for a start, but let Sergeant Marriott know if you need any more men.'

'Right, sir,' said Wood.

'Well, we'll see what that brings forth, Marriott,' said Hardcastle, once Wood had departed, reluctantly to set about his new task. 'And now I think it's time we had a pint. Then we'll call it a day.'

Alice Hardcastle was surprised to see her husband arrive home so early on a Saturday, particularly when he was investigating a murder.

'Have you solved it, then, Ernie?' she asked.

'Not yet, but there's nothing I can do until Monday.' Hardcastle settled down to read the evening newspaper, and was depressed to see that once again a whole page was given over to a gallery of photographs of officers recently killed in action. *Strange*, he thought, *how apparent it was that they were dead: there was that look about them.* He put aside the newspaper. 'Where are the children?'

'Kitty's up in the West End, doing some shopping, Maud's nursing and Wally's due in at any moment.'

'Has Kitty got herself another job, yet?' Alice had mentioned that the Hardcastles' eldest daughter was thinking about giving up her work as a conductorette with the London General Omnibus Company. Even though the war was not yet over, some men who were unfit for further active military service had been returning to take up their former employment.

'She's been talking about joining the Women Police Patrols, Ernie,' said Alice, fully aware of the reaction that would bring forth from her husband.

'She's *what*?' roared Hardcastle, allowing the newspaper to fall to his lap.

'You heard me, Ernie,' replied Alice mildly. 'You should take it as a compliment that she wants to follow in your footsteps.'

'Following in my footsteps be damned,' muttered Hardcastle. 'The Women Police Patrols are nothing but a bunch of prurient, interfering busybodies.'

'Really? I understood from the *Daily Mail* that they were doing good work among prostitutes. What's more, I read a suggestion in the paper's editorial the other day that women will one day be sworn in as constables, just the same as men.'

'I've never heard such rubbish,' exclaimed Hardcastle crossly. 'Women police officers? That'll be the day.' And with that contemptuous dismissal of what he perceived to be a ridiculous and untenable concept, he picked up his newspaper.

But Hardcastle's attempt to read the latest news was interrupted again, this time by the arrival of Walter, the Hardcastles' only son and the youngest of their three children. He was wearing his Post Office uniform, and had just finished a stint of delivering telegrams.

'Hallo, Pa. I didn't expect to see you home this early.' Walter tossed his uniform kepi on to a nearby chair.

'Nothing I can do until Monday, Wally,' said Hardcastle, casting his newspaper aside. 'And don't leave that cap on the chair, put it in the hall.'

'Been busy, Wally?' asked Alice.

'I delivered about ten telegrams this morning, Ma, all with the special mark on 'em.'

'What does that mean?' asked Hardcastle.

'They put a special mark on the envelope for telegrams containing bad news, and we're told not to ask if there's a reply. Anyway, like I was saying, ten this morning, all killed and injured, mostly from Wipers, I should think. At least that's what the lads at the office were saying.'

'It's Ypres, Wally,' corrected his father, even though the devastated Belgian market town was known to troops on the Western Front, officers and other ranks alike, as Wipers. 'I hope to God this damned war will soon be over. Still, now that the Americans are involved, thank the good Lord, they'll soon see off the Kaiser. That General Pershing's got his wits about him.'

'I still think I ought to volunteer,' said Walter.

'You know what happened when you tried to join the navy in January, Wally,' said his mother. 'They told you to carry on delivering telegrams because the war was nearly over.' Even so, she was desperately worried that, despite his failure to join the navy, Walter would sneak off to a recruiting office and succeed in enlisting in the army.

'I could've gone when I was fifteen,' Wally complained. 'Boy Cornwell won the Victoria Cross at Jutland when he was only sixteen.'

'Yes, and he was killed doing it,' said Alice.

'You couldn't have enlisted without my permission, Wally,' said Hardcastle, 'and you wouldn't've got it.'

'Well, I'm eighteen now, and I still think I ought to be doing something worthwhile.' Walter clearly refused to give up.

'Well, you are,' said Alice. 'It's important work you're doing, delivering telegrams to those poor people who've lost loved ones.'

'Are you going to stay with the Post Office once the war's over?' asked his father, attempting to deflect his son's oft-repeated desire to enlist.

'The postmaster said they won't be needing as many of us once men stop getting killed. I'm thinking of joining your lot, Pa.'

'Ye Gods, not you as well, Wally,' exclaimed Hardcastle. 'And by "my lot", I suppose you mean the Metropolitan Police,' he added sternly. 'It's a hard life, walking a beat for eight hours day and night in all weathers. And that's where you'll have to start.' He was not keen to have his son following him into the police force, but knew that once Walter had made up his mind, he was unlikely to be deterred.

'Well, if you did it, Pa, I'm sure I can,' said Walter, jubilantly turning his father's argument against him. 'Of course, I could join the City of London Police,' he added, knowing how that would annoy Hardcastle.

'Over my dead body!' exclaimed Hardcastle, as Walter disappeared into the kitchen in search of something to eat.

But it was Alice Hardcastle who had the last word. 'You know what Wally's like, Ernie. If he's made up his mind nothing will stop him.' She paused. 'Bit like his father really.'

Hardcastle finally gave up on the newspaper with the arrival of Kitty.

'Hello, Pa,' she said, taking off her uniform hat and coat.

'What's this I hear from your mother about you wanting to join the Women Police Patrols?'

'Make a change from the buses, Pa,' said Kitty. 'I thought it'd be a bit of a lark.'

'A lark?' exclaimed Hardcastle. 'Police work's not a lark, my girl.'

'Well, you seem to enjoy it, and at least I wouldn't have to help wounded soldiers on and off my bus,' rejoined Kitty, and flounced out to the kitchen.

EIGHT

Sunday saw Hardcastle in an irascible mood. Unable to get on with the enquiry into Ronald Parker's murder, and deliberately overlooking the list of jobs that Alice wanted done in the house, he walked down to Horace Boxall's shop at the corner of Kennington Road.

'Morning, Mr Hardcastle,' said Boxall. 'I see from the papers that you're dealing with another murder.'

'Never rains but it pours, Horace,' said Hardcastle gloomily.

'Your usual, is it, Mr Hardcastle?' enquired Boxall, turning to a shelf. 'That's eightpence altogether.' He placed a copy of the *News of the World* and an ounce of St Bruno tobacco on the counter. 'Terrible business, that bomb at Maida Vale last Thursday,' he said, pointing at the newspaper's photograph of the wrecked houses. 'Twelve killed and God knows how many injured, and all for what?'

'Yes, I heard about it,' said Hardcastle, putting down a shilling and collecting his fourpence change. 'Apparently there was a woman and two children killed, and her with a husband at the Front. It won't be much of a homecoming for him. Women half expect their husbands to be killed, not the other way round.'

Detective Sergeant Wood had decided that he would take Detective Constable Catto with him for the first day of the observation, and leave Lipton in reserve. He had been told by Hardcastle that Mavis Parker normally started work at the Sopwith Aviation Company at eight in the morning. Consequently Wood and Catto took up their observation in Canbury Park Road at just after seven o'clock on the Monday morning.

It was a difficult observation to maintain; both sides of the road were lined with dwelling houses and there was nowhere to hide. There was not even a bus stop at which the pair could loiter without attracting undue attention. Consequently, the two detectives were obliged to stroll up and down the street, ostensibly deep in conversation and trying desperately to appear nonchalant.

At twenty minutes to eight, Mavis Parker left her house and took the short walk to the factory, entering the gates on the corner of Elm Road ten minutes later.

'What do we do now, Skip?' asked Catto. 'The guv'nor said that she normally finishes at six. Do we hang about here all day?'

'No, we don't,' said Wood. 'We now spend the day ambling round Kingston seeing the sights, and grabbing a pint and a bite to eat. Then we'll get back here in time to follow her home from work.'

'But mightn't she go out at lunchtime, Skip?' Catto was worried that they might miss something important.

'I'll pretend I didn't hear that, Henry,' said Wood.

But what Wood and Catto had thought would be a prolonged observation, stretching perhaps for a week or more, looked as though it was going to be a remarkably short one.

At ten to six that evening, the two detectives stationed themselves near a greengrocer's shop on the corner of Queen Elizabeth Road whence they had sight of the factory gates.

Twenty minutes later, the day workers started to drift out of the factory, and Wood and Catto were forced to move closer for fear of missing Mavis Parker in the crowd.

But then they saw her, neatly dressed and arm in arm with another woman. Together the two women walked down Canbury Park Road, under the railway bridge in Richmond Road into Wood Street, and thence to Ceres Road where, finally, they entered the roller skating rink.

'That's where Gordon Lipton and I saw Gilbert Stroud last Thursday, Skip,' said Catto.

'Well, we're not interested in him any more,' said Wood tersely. 'And now, I suppose we hang about for another hour.' Although he was good at keeping observation, he disliked the task intensely, but was well aware of its value.

An hour later, Catto spotted the lone figure of Mavis Parker emerging from the rink. 'Here she comes, Skip,' he said, nodding towards the woman.

The waiting detectives had anticipated that their quarry would return home, but instead she turned the opposite way, towards Clarence Street. Reaching the corner, she paused and looked

around, casting furtive glances in all directions. But she failed
to take note of the following detectives who were apparently
engrossed in a display of pianos in the shop window on the
opposite side of the road.

Five minutes later, Mavis Parker was joined by a man who
came from the direction of the skating rink. He too glanced
around before kissing Mavis lightly on the cheek and taking her
arm. Together, they made for a tea shop a few yards along
Clarence Street where they sat at a table and the man placed an
order with a waitress.

'I wonder who the hell he is,' said Catto.

'No doubt we'll find out in due course, Henry,' said Wood, as
they settled down to wait.

For half an hour, Mavis Parker and her companion engrossed
themselves in deep conversation, drinking tea and consuming the
little cakes that were on a stand between them. Then the man
paid the bill and they got up to leave. Outside the tea shop, he
again pecked Mavis lightly on the cheek before making off in
the direction of London Road. Retracing her steps, Mavis Parker
began walking towards the skating rink.

Wood and Catto started to follow the man, but Wood ordered
Catto to overtake their prey and walk in front of him for a while.

'But how can I follow him from there, Skip?'

'Just do it, Henry,' said Wood, who knew much more about
surveillance work than did Catto, and crossed to the opposite
side of the road.

It was as well that Wood was experienced at shadowing
suspects; as he had anticipated, the man suddenly stopped, turned
and peered down the road in the direction from which he had
come.

Aha! thought Wood, *he's making sure he's not being tailed.
He must have something to hide.*

Apparently satisfied, the mystery man continued to walk towards
London Road, but then paused at a tram stop near the police station.
A few minutes later, a number 73 tram arrived. The man clambered
aboard and mounted the stairs to the upper deck.

Wood and Catto also boarded the tram, Catto just managing to
catch up with his sergeant in time, and they took seats where
they had a good view of the exits at both the front and rear of the
vehicle.

The tram wound its way up Kingston Hill, and at the stop near Queen's Road, the man descended the stairs and alighted. Walking swiftly away, he stopped several times and peered behind him, continuing to give the impression that he was fearful of being followed. Observed from a discreet distance by Wood and Catto, the man crossed the road and turned into Wolverton Avenue. From there he made his way into the staff entrance of Kingston Infirmary.

'Well, it looks like he's Mavis's fancy man and nothing more,' said Catto.

'I wouldn't be too certain, Henry,' said Wood, 'but there's one sure way of finding out.' Without further ado, and followed by Catto, he too entered the staff doorway of the infirmary.

'Can I help you?' The doorkeeper wore a blue uniform with a peaked cap, and his tunic bore a number of medal ribbons.

Wood had not been in the armed forces, although he recognized the doorman's ribbons as those awarded for service in the South African wars. He was, therefore, careful to avoid any reference to the army in case the doorman asked a question that he could not answer.

'I hope so, pal. The chap who just came in . . .'

'What about him?' asked the doorkeeper, fingering his heavy, drooping moustache.

'I could swear I was in the navy with him.'

'Who, Wilfred Rudd, the porter? I never knew he was in the Andrew. Was he one of your shipmates, then, chum?'

'Wilfred Rudd, you say?' said Wood, running a hand round his chin. 'Well I'm damned, that's not him, but I could've sworn it was. Oh well, sorry to have bothered you, mate.'

'That's was pretty smart, Skip,' said Catto, when he and Wood returned to the street.

Wood laughed. 'You pick up a few wrinkles when you've been at this game as long as I have, Henry,' he said.

'Reckon that's us done, then, Skip,' said Catto.

Wood emitted a grim, cynical laugh. 'That, I suspect, Henry, is only the beginning,' he said.

Detective Sergeant Herbert Wood was waiting outside Hardcastle's office door when the DDI arrived at eight o'clock the next morning.

'Come in and tell me why you aren't following Mrs Parker, Wood,' snapped Hardcastle, entering his office without pausing.

'Lipton and Catto are keeping observation on her at this very moment, sir, but I've a report to make.'

'Go ahead and report, then. I haven't got all day.'

Wood gave the DDI the details of what he and Catto had witnessed the previous evening.

'How old is this Wilfred Rudd?' Hardcastle filled his pipe and patted his pockets in search of matches.

'In his late thirties, sir,' said Wood promptly. He was not too certain of Rudd's age, but knew that Hardcastle disliked an inconclusive answer. 'Do you want me to make further enquiries at Kingston Infirmary, sir?'

'Not now you've shown out to the doorkeeper there,' said Hardcastle, and paused to light his pipe. 'Sergeant Marriott and I will look into the matter of Rudd. In the meantime, break off the observation on Mavis Parker. If she's up to what I think she's up to, we might just bugger it up. Get hold of Lipton and Catto and call 'em off.'

'Might be a bit difficult, sir.'

'It's not difficult at all, Wood. Use that telephone machine to speak to Kingston nick and tell 'em to send a plain-clothes officer up there to warn 'em off.'

'Very good, sir.'

'Did Mrs Parker go anywhere during her lunch break?' the DDI asked suddenly.

'No, sir.' Wood did not hesitate for a moment, knowing that Hardcastle would fly into a rage if he told the DDI that he had not bothered to find out.

'Very well. Ask Sergeant Marriott to come in.'

'Looks as though Bert Wood did a good job in tracking down this chap yesterday, sir,' said Marriott, as he entered the DDI's office.

'We'll have to pay a visit to this fellow's place of work, Marriott,' said Hardcastle, declining to comment on Wood's efficiency, 'and see what they can tell us about this Wilfred Rudd. Might be nothing more than some fancy man our Mrs Parker's picked up with.'

'According to Wood, sir, Rudd kept turning round as if he thought that he was being followed.'

'I know. Wood told me that. It could be that he's a married man, and was taking precautions in case he was being followed by an enquiry agent, Marriott,' said Hardcastle, never one to take things at face value. 'He might be a bit of a philanderer whose wife is on to him. We'll pay a visit to this here Kingston Infirmary this afternoon.'

'Who's the best person to see, sir?' asked Marriott, when he and the DDI arrived at the main entrance to the infirmary. 'The Lady Almoner?'

'Certainly not, Marriott. In my experience lady almoners are a bunch of aristocratic do-gooders,' said Hardcastle dismissively. 'They don't know A from a bull's foot when it comes to it. No, it's the matron we need to see. Matrons always know what's going on.'

Striding into the reception area, the DDI eventually found a nurse who directed them to the matron's office.

'What's her name, young lady?' asked the DDI, pausing as he turned away.

'Miss Morag McGregor,' said the nurse in hushed tones, as if in awe of the great woman.

'Have you ever noticed how often matrons are Scottish, Marriott?' said Hardcastle, tapping lightly on the matron's door.

'Come!' said a commanding voice from within.

Hardcastle pushed open the door, doffing his bowler hat at the same time.

'Yes?' snapped the matron, peering at Hardcastle over a pair of gold-rimmed pince-nez. She was immaculately uniformed, with a pristine white apron and a cap that was set squarely on her head. Altogether she represented the picture of an austere and unforgiving disciplinarian.

'We're police officers, madam. I'm Divisional Detective Inspector Hardcastle of the Whitehall Division and this is Detective Sergeant Marriott.'

'Well, come in, man.' The matron's forbidding countenance softened into a smile as she swept off her pince-nez. 'And tell me what I can do for you.' She skirted her desk and offered a hand. 'I'm Morag McGregor.'

Hardcastle shook hands. 'I'm conducting a murder enquiry, Matron, and I was hoping . . .'

'Sit down, Inspector, and you too, Sergeant.' The matron indicated a pair of hard-backed chairs in front of her desk. She lifted the fob watch that was attached to her apron by a black ribbon and peered at it. 'Five o'clock. I dare say you gentlemen would not be averse to a wee dram, eh? We Scots swear by it . . . for medicinal purposes only, of course,' she said, with a smile. And without waiting for a reply, she crossed to a cabinet and took out three tumblers and a bottle of Buchanan's Black and White whisky. Hardcastle was surprised; as a Scotch drinker himself, he knew that it retailed for nigh-on six shillings.

'Very kind, madam,' he murmured. 'Much appreciated.'

The matron poured a substantial measure of whisky into each of the tumblers. 'You'll not be taking water, I presume.' She posed the question in such a way as to brook no argument, and settled behind her desk once again. 'Slàinte!' she said, raising her glass.

'Good health, ma'am,' said Hardcastle.

'Now then, Inspector . . .' The matron placed her glass in the centre of her blotter. 'Be so good as to tell me how I may help you.'

Hardcastle explained about the murder of Ronald Parker and that his enquiries had led him to Kingston Infirmary in connection with a Wilfred Rudd who, he was given to understand, was working there as a porter.

'It's possible that there might be a matter of national security involved in my enquiry, madam,' he continued, 'so I'd be much obliged if you'd treat my enquiry in the strictest confidence.'

'You've no worries on that score, Inspector,' said Miss McGregor. 'I served on the Western Front for two and a half years, which is where I developed a taste for whisky. And I know how to keep my mouth shut. Now, what is it you want to know about this man?'

'As much as you can tell me,' said Hardcastle, taking another sip of his Scotch.

The matron struck a brass table bell on her desk and seconds later a young nurse appeared, bobbing in the doorway.

'Forester, go to Mr Donaldson's office and ask him to see me.'

'Now, madam?' asked Nurse Forester.

'Yes at once, girl, and be quick,' said the matron, with an impatient flourish of her hand.

It appeared to Hardcastle that Matron McGregor reigned supreme over the entire infirmary, a view that was confirmed minutes later when Mr Donaldson appeared in her office. His head was slightly bowed, and he was clasping his hands together in an almost supplicating manner.

'You wished to see me, Matron?' he asked, blinking through his spectacles.

'These gentlemen are police officers, Mr Donaldson,' said the matron. 'They're making routine enquiries about all the porters at this hospital.'

'Oh!' said Donaldson, nodding briefly in the detectives' direction and fluttering his hands. 'I'll need to fetch their records from my office, Matron.'

'Then, kindly do so, Mr Donaldson.' There was an edge of irritability in Miss McGregor's voice. 'And I should caution you, Mr Donaldson, that this enquiry is secret. It must not reach the ears of anyone else in the infirmary, no one at all. Is that understood?'

'Indeed, Matron.' Donaldson tweaked nervously at his moustache, and scurried away to get the appropriate dockets.

'I thought it best not to let Donaldson know *which* particular porter you were interested in, Inspector,' said the matron, once her door was closed behind the retreating functionary. 'This place is full of busybodies and tittle-tattlers. A drop more?' she asked, picking up the whisky bottle.

'Most kind, madam,' murmured Hardcastle, who by now was also in awe of the authority the matron wielded.

Miss McGregor had no sooner refilled the detectives' glasses than Donaldson reappeared clutching a sheaf of slim folders. He glanced at the whisky bottle, but was not offered any. Hardcastle noticed, however, that the matron was making no secret of the fact that she was imbibing. Doubtless, she was secure in the knowledge that if any word of it got round the infirmary there would be trouble for whoever had gossiped. Assuming, of course, that she was concerned about whether anyone knew that she enjoyed a tipple.

'Thank you, Mr Donaldson.' The matron held out her hand and Donaldson meekly handed over the bundle of folders. 'I'll let you know when I've finished with them.' She waved a hand of dismissal, and began to sort through the porters' dockets. 'Ah, here we are: Wilfred Rudd. He joined the staff as a porter about nine months ago, on the sixteenth of July 1917 to be precise. He was discharged from the army as unfit for active service on the twenty-ninth of June 1917.'

'Does it say which regiment he was with, madam?' asked Marriott.

'According to this he served with the Dorsetshire Regiment, but was gassed at the Somme. After a period in a base hospital, he was discharged from the army, as I said earlier.'

'Did Rudd produce any documents to support these claims of his, madam?' asked Hardcastle, who was always suspicious of an account of military service that had no documentary proof.

'It doesn't say so here, Inspector,' said the matron, looking up from the docket she was reading, 'but we tend to take the word of discharged soldiers. I know old soldiers, believe me, and I know a scrimshanker when I see one, and Rudd is not.' As it turned out, however, she was wrong in that assumption. 'It's hard enough for them to find employment without being interrogated about their war experiences. It's not only the physical wounds that have affected them, you see.'

'No, I suppose not.' Hardcastle stood up. 'Well, thank you for your assistance, madam, and thank you also for the whisky, most welcome. Oh, one other thing: do you have an address for Rudd?'

The matron glanced at the file. 'According to this, he resides at number seventeen Queen's Road. It says here that he occupies a bed-sitting room there.' She looked up. 'I take it that you don't wish to interview Rudd, Inspector.'

'No, madam, not at this stage, and certainly not here.'

'Is he a suspect in this murder of yours?'

'Not as far as I can see,' said Hardcastle, not wishing to tell the matron that he was, in fact, a strong suspect. 'But we have to look into the background of everyone whose name crops up in the course of our enquiries. And then we eliminate them, one by one.'

'Somewhat like a medical diagnosis, I suppose,' said the matron with a chuckle. 'One has to eliminate all the probabilities until only the possible remains.' She stood up and accompanied the detectives to the door of her office. 'Don't hesitate to call again if you think I can assist you any further,' she added, as she shook hands with Hardcastle and Marriott.

*   *   *

'We need to speak to the military about this fellow Rudd, Marriott,' said Hardcastle, the following morning. 'A word with Colonel Frobisher, I think, and there's no time like the present.' He put on his Chesterfield, and seized his hat and umbrella.

The two detectives walked the short distance down Whitehall to Horse Guards Arch where, as so often happened, the dismounted sentry mistook Hardcastle for an army officer in mufti. He came to attention with a crash of his left foot, and raised his sword in salute at the sight of the DDI's bowler hat.

Although not entitled to such a compliment, Hardcastle never-theless solemnly doffed his hat in acknowledgement. 'Wouldn't want to embarrass the poor fellow,' he muttered.

'Good morning, Inspector,' said Sergeant Glover, the APM's clerk. 'You'll be wishing to see the colonel, no doubt.'

'Is he here, Sergeant Glover?'

'Indeed, Inspector. He's always here early, and he's not all that busy. I'll show you in.' Glover knocked on the APM's door. 'Inspector Hardcastle, sir,' he said.

'Good day to you, Inspector.' Lieutenant Colonel Frobisher rose from behind his desk. 'It's not a social visit, I take it,' he said, with a twinkle in his eye. The APM knew perfectly well that the only occasion when Hardcastle called on him was to present him with some military problem that was usually difficult to solve. He was fairly sure that today would be no different.

'Good morning, Colonel.' Hardcastle and Marriott accepted Frobisher's invitation to sit down. 'I'm dealing with a murder, and the name of a former soldier has cropped up in the course of my enquiries.'

'Let me have the man's details, then.' With a sense that he was about to be faced with a time-consuming task, Frobisher drew a writing pad across his desk.

'Marriott.' Hardcastle glanced at his sergeant.

'His name's Wilfred Rudd, Colonel,' began Marriott, opening his pocket book. 'We've been told that he served with the Dorsetshire Regiment on the Somme where he was gassed. After a period in a base hospital, he claims to have been discharged as unfit for further active service on the twenty-ninth of June last year. He's now employed as a hospital porter at the Kingston Infirmary.'

Frobisher finished making notes, put down his pen and looked up. 'And I suppose you want me to confirm this for you, Inspector.'

'If it's at all possible, Colonel, yes,' said Hardcastle.

'It may take more than a day or two,' said Frobisher. 'I'm afraid the records of wounded take some time to filter through to the War House, particularly since the disaster of the Somme. There's a whole army of clerks dealing with nothing else but the consequences of that battle. There were so many casualties, you know.'

'So I understand,' said the DDI. In common with most people, he knew that by nightfall on the first day of the battle fifty-eight thousand had fallen, a third of whom were dead, and the carnage had not lessened by much since.

'Had this Rudd been killed in action, of course, there would've been a record of the notification sent to his next of kin. And that would've been done within a matter of days following his death. However, I'll do what I can. Is he a suspect in this murder of yours, Inspector?'

'It's possible,' said Hardcastle cryptically. 'Thank you, Colonel.'

'What now, sir?' asked Marriott, as they left Horse Guards.

'And now, Marriott,' said Hardcastle, 'we'll have to get a move on if we're to get to the cemetery in time for Ronald Parker's funeral.' He hailed a cab and ordered the driver to take them to Waterloo railway station.

NINE

When Hardcastle and Marriott arrived at Kingston Cemetery in Bonner Hill Road, they remained in their taxi. Hardcastle was not concerned about how much the fare would cost the Commissioner, but not wanting to be seen attending Parker's funeral, he deemed it a necessary expense.

At a quarter past eleven precisely, a glass-sided hearse, drawn by two black horses, turned into the cemetery. Led by a top-hatted funeral director on foot, it made its way slowly up the road towards the chapel, passing under an archway topped by a lofty spire. Following the hearse on foot was a small group of mourners, among them, Hardcastle noticed, were Mavis Parker, her brother-in-law Harold, a woman he presumed was

Harold's wife, and Mrs Middleton, the Parkers' next-door neighbour.

'Not much of a turnout, sir,' said Marriott.

'Didn't expect many,' said Hardcastle.

'And there's Mr Harvey, the gas company manager, sir,' continued Marriott, 'and George Quilter from Sopwith Aviation.' He nodded towards two soberly dressed men who were in conversation as they followed the main body of mourners.

'To be expected, I suppose,' said Hardcastle. 'Come to pay their respects.'

'But that's a surprise,' exclaimed Marriott. 'Look, sir, it's Daisy Benson, all tarted up.'

Although the late Ronald Parker's paramour was dressed in black from head to foot, complete with veil, her outfit did not disguise her attractive figure. She was walking slowly up the road towards the chapel, well behind the main party.

'I'm surprised she's got the nerve to turn up, Marriott.'

'Perhaps Ronald Parker was a bit more than just a client, sir. She might really have cared for him.'

'You going to be much longer, guv'nor?' asked the cab driver, turning in his seat and sliding back the glass partition.

'As long as it takes,' barked Hardcastle. 'Anyway, you're getting paid, and handsomely at that.'

In fact, it was another thirty minutes before Parker's coffin appeared from the chapel borne by half a dozen pall-bearers. After the usual obsequies it was lowered into a grave and the gravediggers began their task of filling in the pit.

Slowly, the mourners began to drift away towards the main gates.

'Well, that's that, I suppose,' said Hardcastle.

Last to emerge from the cemetery, and still maintaining a discreet distance from the main party, came Daisy Benson. But instead of following the others, she turned left. A little further up the road, she stepped into a Hispano-Suiza tourer, taking the seat beside the driver. Leaning across, she lifted her veil, embraced the man and kissed him.

'That's one expensive motor car, sir,' said Marriott.

'Yes, it is and I want to know where it's going,' said Hardcastle. 'Follow that car, driver.'

The cab driver turned in his seat. 'You some sort of copper, then?' he asked.

'Yes, I'm a Scotland Yard detective,' said Hardcastle, never averse to assuming such importance. 'Now, get going.'

'Blimey, guv'nor, right you are,' said the cabbie, and set off in pursuit of the vehicle carrying its unknown driver and Daisy Benson.

Twenty minutes later, the Hispano-Suiza came to rest in the driveway of a large house called The Beeches on Kingston Hill. Daisy and the man alighted and went into the house, arm in arm.

'How very interesting,' said Hardcastle, and addressing himself to the taxi driver, said, 'Kingston railway station, cabbie.'

The reply to the query about Wilfred Rudd that Hardcastle had lodged with the military police came much quicker than either Hardcastle or Frobisher had expected. At three o'clock that same afternoon, the DDI received a telephone call from Sergeant Glover to say that the APM had some important information for him.

Hardcastle and Marriott hurried back to Horse Guards and were shown into Frobisher's office immediately.

'Are you sure that you have the correct details of this man Rudd, Inspector?' asked the APM.

'The matron at the infirmary sent for the man's personal records, Colonel.'

'I see.' Frobisher brushed briefly at his moustache. 'According to army records, Inspector, your man Rudd is dead.'

'Dead?' exclaimed Hardcastle. *Everyone I'm interested in is turning up dead*, he thought, remembering that Daisy Benson's husband had also died. But he dismissed that fact as one of life's inevitabilities, considering that there was a war on.

Frobisher opened a docket that was in the centre of his desk. 'Private Wilfred Rudd, regimental number 14923 of the Dorsetshire Regiment was killed in action on the twenty-ninth of June 1917. He was one of a raiding party that was sent out in an attempt to capture one of the enemy.' The APM glanced up. 'It's something that is done from time to time, Inspector. A captured German soldier can often prove to be a very useful source of intelligence regarding the disposition of the enemy's forces.'

'Is that so?' said Hardcastle, who did not really understand the finer points of military strategy and tactics. 'But the matron was adamant that the details were correct.'

'Did she have any documentary proof that this man calling himself Rudd had served in the Dorsetshire Regiment?'

'Apparently not, Colonel. The authorities relied on the man's own statement. A bit slipshod in my view, but there it is.'

'I'm not surprised.' Frobisher tapped the docket with a forefinger. 'Mrs Molly Rudd, Wilfred Rudd's wife, was informed of her husband's death by War Office telegram on the fourth of July 1917.'

'Well, I'll go to the foot of our stairs,' exclaimed Hardcastle. 'I wonder what the bugger's up to.'

Frobisher smiled. 'There's an outside chance I might be able to help you there, Mr Hardcastle. On the day that Rudd was killed, a Private Eric Donnelly, a member of the same three-man raiding party, was reported missing believed killed. His body was not found, you see, although the bodies of Rudd and the third man were. That fact created some uncertainty about it and it was thought that Donnelly might've taken the opportunity, in the confusion of battle, to make himself scarce. It may be, therefore, that the man calling himself Rudd is in fact Donnelly and that he assumed Rudd's identity in order to desert.'

'I suppose it's a possibility,' muttered Hardcastle, furious that he had wasted so much time on a deserter. Not that that precluded Rudd from his list of suspects for the murder of Ronald Parker. If anything, now that it was known that the real Rudd was dead, it moved the bogus Rudd higher up that list.

'But I have to tell you that hundreds have been reported missing since the first of July 1916 – the day the offensive started in earnest – and are continuing to remain missing. I fear that some of them will never been found. For all we know, Donnelly might've been lost forever in the mud of Flanders. It's an awful and literally bloody battle.'

'You said that Rudd's wife was informed of his death on the fourth of July last year, Colonel,' said Marriott. 'Do you have an address for her?'

'I suppose it's in Dorset,' muttered Hardcastle, 'seeing as how he was in the Dorsetshire Regiment.'

Frobisher laughed. 'That doesn't follow at all, Inspector. The old concept of local men joining local regiments went out of the window a long time ago. Nowadays conscripts are sent to whichever regiment is short. And these days that's all of them.'

'Yes, of course,' said Hardcastle, remembering that Maud's

friend Lieutenant Charles Spencer had been gazetted to the North Lancashire Regiment, despite coming from Windsor.

'However,' continued Frobisher, glancing at his docket again, 'the address we have for Mrs Molly Rudd is in Gresham Road, Brixton.' He wrote the details on a slip of paper and handed it to Marriott.

'London!' exclaimed Hardcastle. 'Thank the Lord for that,' he muttered irreverently.

'Fetch Wood in here,' barked Hardcastle, when he and Marriott were back at the police station.

'Sir?' Wood buttoned his jacket as he entered the DDI's office.

'You're to come with me to Brixton, Wood. It concerns your observation when you tracked down Wilfred Rudd. I'll explain all about it on the way.'

The house in Gresham Road where Molly Rudd lived was three stories high with a basement area and a flight of steps leading to the front door. Pieces of concrete had broken away in places on the steps, and a ragged hedge fronted the property, the entirety of which was in poor repair. What had probably been a well-tended garden in years gone by was now covered in sodden cardboard boxes and an old mattress. The basement area had become one massive rubbish dump in which, among other things, were an old bath, a rusting bicycle frame and an abandoned bedstead.

'Nice place,' commented Hardcastle, as he and Marriott carefully ascended the crumbling steps.

'Yes, watcha want?' The grey-haired woman who opened the door in response to Hardcastle's knock was in her fifties and was wearing a black bombazine dress and a long apron. Her lank grey hair was tied back with a grubby piece of ribbon. She wiped her hands on a tea towel and gazed suspiciously at the two detectives.

'We're police officers, madam,' said Hardcastle, as he raised his hat. 'Am I addressing Mrs Molly Rudd?'

'No, you ain't,' said the woman. 'I'm Mrs Perkins, if it's any of your business. Watcha want, anyway?' she asked again.

'Strangely enough, a word with Mrs Rudd,' snapped Hardcastle, his temper beginning to shorten quite dramatically.

'Top floor, and mind you wipe yer feet.' Leaving Hardcastle

to close the door, Mrs Perkins disappeared into a room at the back of the house.

Hardcastle and Wood climbed the two flights of uncarpeted stairs to the top floor, the odour of boiled cabbage increasing with every upward step. The DDI tapped on a door to which was pinned a card bearing the name 'Mrs Rudd'.

The door was opened by a careworn woman probably in her thirties, but who looked older. She had a small child in her arms.

'Yes, what is it?'

'Mrs Rudd, I'm a police officer. Divisional Detective Inspector Hardcastle of the Whitehall Division and this is Detective Sergeant Wood.'

'Oh, and what do the police want with me? As if I ain't got enough trouble.'

'It concerns your husband, Mrs Rudd. Your *late* husband, that is.' Hardcastle was careful to avoid raising the woman's hopes that Wilfred Rudd might still be alive. Since the war had begun, it was not unusual for men, originally thought to have perished, later to turn up alive and well.

'You'd better come in, then, though I don't know what I can tell you other than he was killed on the Somme last year.'

'So I understand, madam.' Hardcastle and Wood followed the woman into a sparsely furnished room. Apart from a table, two chairs, and a bed, there was little else. The floor was partially covered with a threadbare rug, leaving untreated wooden boards exposed around it. The table bore the remains of a meagre meal.

'What's this about my Wilfred, then,' asked the woman, settling herself on the edge of the unmade bed, 'apart from him having got hisself killed and leaving me to bring up a child on a war widow's pension that ain't enough to feed a sparrow? It ain't no wonder I has to take in washing.'

'We have come across a man who we believe is pretending to be your husband, Mrs Rudd,' said Hardcastle. 'He claims to have been discharged from the Dorsetshire Regiment on the day that your husband was reported killed in action.'

'The cheeky sod. Who is this man, then?'

'That's what we're attempting find out, Mrs Rudd,' said Wood.

'If you have a photograph of your late husband, it would help to clear up this mystery,' said Hardcastle.

'Just a minute.' Molly Rudd laid her child in the centre of the bed, and crossed to the table. Opening a drawer she took out an unframed studio portrait of a man in khaki service dress, puttees smartly wound, forage cap squarely set, and a swagger cane beneath his left arm. His right hand was resting on a torchère. 'That's my Wilf,' she said, handing the picture to Hardcastle, 'taken just before his embarkation in 1914. Three years he was out there afore he got hisself killed, and never a single day's leave, neither.'

Hardcastle handed the photograph to Wood. 'Is that the man you saw, Wood?'

Wood made a careful study of the photograph before giving it back to the DDI. 'That's definitely not the man I saw, sir.'

'Thank you, Mrs Rudd,' said Hardcastle, returning the picture of Wilfred Rudd to his widow. 'That solves the problem as far as I'm concerned.'

'And you say you don't know who this man is, what's pretending to be my Wilf, Inspector.'

'Not at the moment, Mrs Rudd, but you may rest assured, I'll soon find out. We think he might be a deserter.'

'A *deserter* is he? Well, it's nothing but barefaced cheek if you ask me,' exclaimed Molly Rudd disgustedly. 'I hope he gets hisself shot at dawn. There's my Wilf laying down his life for King and Country, and some dirty rat runs for it and then pretends to be him.'

'Don't you worry, Mrs Rudd,' said Wood. 'As soon as we find him, we'll hand him over to the provost.'

'I'm sorry to have bothered you with such distressing enquiries, Mrs Rudd,' said Hardcastle, 'and I'm sorry about your husband,' he added in a murmur, as usual stumbling over expressing words of condolence.

'What now, sir?' asked Wood, once he and the DDI were in the street again.

'Now, Wood, we find this here Mr Rudd, or whatever his name is, and we feel his collar.'

On the Thursday morning, Hardcastle decided to waste no more time in dealing with the matter of Wilfred Rudd, or whoever he was. Having cast a cursory glance over the crime book and finding nothing to arouse his immediate interest, he paused only to summon Detective Sergeant Wood. The two officers took a taxi to Waterloo railway station and thence a train to Norbiton.

'I'll not bother the matron again, Wood,' said Hardcastle, who was still in awe of the great woman, and pushed open the door of the staff entrance at the Kingston Infirmary.

The doorkeeper looked up from his five-day-old copy of the *Sporting Times*, an enquiring look on his face.

'Can I help you, sir?'

'Yes, you can tell me where I can find Wilfred Rudd,' said Hardcastle.

'He ain't here this morning, guv'nor. He's on the night shift, starts at eight o'clock.' The doorkeeper glanced at Wood, and recognition dawned. 'Here, wasn't you the gent what was asking about him the other day? You said as how you thought you was in the Andrew with him.'

'That's right,' said Wood.

The doorkeeper chuckled. 'Brought your father with you today to have a glim at old Wilf just to make sure, have you?'

'I'll thank you to keep a civil tongue in your head, unless you want me to have a word with the matron,' snapped Hardcastle. 'Bloody cheek of the man,' he muttered as he turned on his heel.

'Where to now, sir?' asked Wood, barely able to keep a straight face, and impatient to relay to his colleagues the exchange between the doorkeeper and the DDI.

'We'll pay him a visit at this here place of his he's got in Queen's Road. Any idea how we get there, Wood?'

'Yes, sir.' Wood had obtained the address from Marriott and looked it up on the street guide, knowing that, at some stage, Hardcastle would want to know. 'It's only a short stride down this road, sir, across Kingston Hill, and Queen's Road is almost opposite.'

Hardcastle set off at a brisk pace, determined to waste as little time as possible on someone who would probably turn out to be a deserter and nothing more. Nevertheless, he did not lose sight of the fact that Rudd might be Ronald Parker's murderer.

The house where, according to the matron, Rudd had rooms, was a large dwelling.

Quickly ascending the steps, Hardcastle rapped on the front door. Eventually, it was opened by a woman who regarded the two men on the doorstep with undisguised disdain.

'Whatever it is you're selling, I don't want it. And if you've come here to read me bits out of the Bible, I don't want to hear

it. I give up religion after my Tom was killed on the Somme.'
And with that short tirade, she made to close the door.

But Hardcastle placed a firm hand on the door and held it ajar.
'We're police officers, madam,' he said. 'And I want to see Wilfred
Rudd who, I'm told, lives here.'

'How do I know you're rozzers?' demanded the woman, unim-
pressed by Hardcastle's announcement. 'For all I know you might
be some of them walk-in burglars what you reads about in the
paper.'

The DDI produced his warrant card, and the woman appeared
satisfied.

'I take it you're the landlady,' said Hardcastle.

'Indeed I am, and this is a respectable house. Up one flight,
first door on the right,' said the woman, 'but he's probably
sleeping on account of him working nights across at the
infirmary.'

'That's all right,' said Hardcastle, 'we'll wake him up.'

When they reached Rudd's room, Hardcastle pushed open the
door without bothering to knock, so hard that it crashed against
the wall.

'Here, who the hell are you?' The man in the bed was obviously awake, but had not, so far, risen.

'Eric Donnelly?' asked Hardcastle, taking a chance on using
the name that Colonel Frobisher had suggested might be that of
a deserter.

The man acted with lightning speed. Twisting his body, his
hand went under his pillow and he produced a revolver.

But Hardcastle did not hesitate. With no concern for his
personal safety, he launched himself at the man, flattening him
on to the bed and seizing his right wrist. There was a loud explo-
sion as the revolver was discharged, but the bullet missed
Hardcastle and flew into the ceiling. After a second or so, a piece
of ornamental moulding crashed to the floor.

Wood leaped to the DDI's assistance, grabbing the revolver
and wrenching it from the man's hand. He dropped the weapon
on the floor, kicking it out of harm's way, and produced a set of
handcuffs.

'I took the precaution of drawing these from the nick before
we left, sir,' he said breathlessly, as he quickly shackled one of
the man's hands to the railed bedhead. 'Just in case.'

'Very thoughtful of you, Wood,' said Hardcastle mildly, as he stood up and smoothed his jacket.

'What on earth's happened?' The woman who had admitted the two detectives now stood in the doorway of Rudd's room.

'Nothing to worry about, madam,' said Hardcastle. 'This chap just tried to murder me, that's all. Do you possess a telephone, by any chance?'

'Yes, we are connected,' said the landlady, and glanced at the ceiling where the bullet had struck, and then at the sizeable piece of plaster on the floor. 'And who's going to pay for that, might I make so bold as to ask?'

'I dare say the Commissioner of Police will,' said Hardcastle. 'In due course,' he added, well aware that such claims often took months to be settled. 'Wood, borrow this lady's telephone contraption and ask the local station to send a conveyance for our prisoner.'

'Perhaps you'd show me where the instrument is, madam,' said Wood.

'Come this way,' said the landlady. 'And I hope you're going to pay for the call.'

'Now then,' said Hardcastle, picking up the revolver and removing the remaining rounds from the chamber, 'I'm a police officer. Are you Eric Donnelly?'

'I'm Wilfred Rudd.'

'Is that a fact?' But it was clear to Hardcastle that his question had unnerved Rudd. He sat down on the only chair in the room and fixed his prisoner with a steely gaze. 'In that case, tell me why a hospital porter needs to keep a loaded firearm under his pillow.'

'For protection,' said Rudd churlishly. 'I never knew who you was, coming barging in here without so much as a by-your-leave.'

'Well, for a kick-off, I'm arresting you for attempted murder, Rudd, or whoever you are. And I rather fancy that that'll only be the start.'

'I wasn't never going to kill you,' said Rudd lamely. 'Like I said, I never knew who you was.'

'You'll have a chance to explain that to a jury at the Old Bailey,' said Hardcastle, as Wood came back into the room. 'Well?'

'They're sending a van, sir.'

'Very kind of 'em,' muttered Hardcastle. 'Get this man what calls himself Rudd downstairs.'

TEN

Detective Sergeant Wood and a local constable had accompanied Rudd to Kingston police station. Deeming it not to be his function to accompany prisoners unless absolutely necessary, Hardcastle walked back to Kingston Hill where he hailed a cab to take him.

'I'm DDI Hardcastle of A,' he announced to the sergeant on station duty when he arrived at the police station in London Road.

'All correct, sir,' said the station officer.

'That's as maybe,' muttered Hardcastle. 'Where's my prisoner? The man who calls himself Rudd.'

'In the charge room, sir,' said the sergeant, as though that was the logical place for Rudd to be.

Still handcuffed, Rudd was seated on one of the benches in the charge room. He glanced at Hardcastle with a surly expression, but said nothing.

'I'm told you were in the Dorsetshire Regiment, Rudd.' Hardcastle took a seat on the opposite side of the room.

'So, what if I was?'

'And you told the infirmary authorities that you were discharged as unfit for active service on the twenty-ninth of June last year.'

'That's right.'

'Well, now, that's a very strange thing.' Hardcastle took out his pipe and began to fill it.

'What's strange about it, copper?' snarled Rudd.

'Because according to the military police Private Wilfred Rudd was killed on that day, and his grieving wife was sent a telegram to that effect. We know that because we've seen her.'

Rudd was momentarily taken aback by the DDI's statement, but quickly recovered.

'They must've got it wrong. There's always a hell of a mix-up after a battle. No one knows who's dead, who's missing, or who's done a runner.'

'So if we get Mrs Rudd here, she'll recognize you, will she?'

'I've changed a lot. The war does that to people.' Rudd stared defiantly at the DDI.

'What's your regimental number, then?' asked Hardcastle suddenly.

'I can't rightly remember, what with the gassing and that. It affects your memory, you know,' said Rudd, making a vain attempt to hide the fact that he did not know the real Rudd's number.

'I was always told that soldiers never forget their regimental number,' commented Hardcastle mildly.

'Never mind all that. I tell you, I'm Wilfred Rudd, and I'm no deserter. You can't keep me here.'

'Can't I? You seem to have overlooked the fact,' said Hardcastle, applying a match to his pipe, 'that I've arrested you for attempted murder and unlawful possession of a firearm.'

'I was issued with it,' muttered Rudd, 'so it ain't unlawful.'

'I doubt that an infantryman would've been issued with a revolver,' observed Hardcastle. 'More likely to have been a Lee-Metford rifle or something similar, I'd've thought. So where did you get the revolver? Nick it off a dead officer, did you?'

'I ain't saying nothing,' said Rudd.

'Anyway, even if you were issued with it, you're not entitled to keep it once the army has discharged you. It doesn't entitle you to attempt to kill me with it, either.'

'Well, like I said, I never meant to kill you. You scared the living daylights out me, barging in like what you did.'

'Really?' said Hardcastle, standing up. 'Well, just so that we can clear up the question of who you really are, I shall have you transferred to my police station in London and get the provost to come and take a gander at you.' He paused at the door. 'What's your wife's name, Rudd?'

'I can't rightly remember. Like I said, the gas does strange things to the brain. There's a lot of things I can't remember.'

'Well, that don't somehow come as a surprise,' said Hardcastle. Leaving the man who called himself Rudd in the charge room, he found DS Wood in the front office.

'Wood, get on that telephone thing and ask Sergeant Marriott to arrange an escort to bring Rudd up to Cannon Row.'

'Very good, sir. Are you charging him with attempted murder?'

'Not at this stage, Wood,' said Hardcastle thoughtfully. 'You see, he'd probably go down for about ten years penal servitude for that, but if the military find that Rudd *is* the deserter called Donnelly they'll shoot him at dawn. Much cheaper from the point of view of the public purse, and it would save you and me wasting our time at Surrey Assizes. A much more satisfactory outcome altogether, don't you think?'

'Yes, sir. But we know he's not Rudd because his missus showed us a photograph of the real Rudd, and it wasn't the bloke in the charge room.'

'Very true,' said Hardcastle, 'but he doesn't know that. Make sure you bring that revolver with you, and when we get back to the nick get it across to Inspector Franklin. With any luck, he might find it matches the round taken out of Ronald Parker's head.'

It was two o'clock that afternoon before the escort arrived at Cannon Row police station with Rudd.

Hardcastle and Marriott had lunched on their usual fourpenny cannon and a pint at the Red Lion public house, but Hardcastle decided that there was nothing to be gained by interviewing their prisoner. Instead, he paid another visit to the APM's office at Horse Guards.

'I've taken the man calling himself Wilfred Rudd into custody on a charge of attempted murder, Colonel,' he announced.

'Good Lord!' Frobisher looked up in surprise. 'May I ask who he attempted to murder, Inspector?'

'Me,' said Hardcastle, 'with what looks very like a service revolver.'

'Good Lord!' exclaimed Frobisher again. 'I hope you weren't hurt, Inspector.'

'He'd've had to be quicker than he was to catch me out, Colonel. However, he refuses to disclose his real identity, but if he's the Eric Donnelly you suggested he might be there's the problem of getting someone to identify him.'

Colonel Frobisher leaned back in his chair, a thoughtful expression on his face. 'Yes, that could be difficult,' he said. 'Obviously, it would mean finding someone who knew both Rudd and Donnelly, but the battalion they served with is still in France.'

'We're satisfied that he's not Rudd, Colonel, both from what you told me, and from having visited Rudd's widow. She showed me a photograph of her late husband and it's definitely not the man I've got in my police station.'

'Well, that's something,' said Frobisher. 'How long can you hold this man?'

'For as long as it takes,' said Hardcastle. 'I doubt that there's anyone prepared to swear out a writ of habeas corpus on his behalf.'

'Yes, I understand. Nevertheless, you'll doubtless wish to have this matter cleared up as soon as possible. I'll get on to the depot of the Dorsetshire Regiment in Dorchester and see if there's anyone in this country who knows what Donnelly looks like. I'll be in touch as soon as possible.'

'I'm much obliged, Colonel.'

Lieutenant Colonel Frobisher was as good as his word. The following morning, Hardcastle received a call from the APM to say that there was a Sergeant Mooney in his office who had at one time been Donnelly's platoon sergeant. But, continued Frobisher, Mooney had been wounded in the same battle that had cost Wilfred Rudd his life, and was now a firearms instructor at the depot battalion.

'I'll send him straight across to the police station, if that would be convenient, Inspector.'

'Admirable, Colonel, and I'm much obliged to you.'

Fifteen minutes later, there was a knock on Hardcastle's door and the station-duty constable appeared.

'There's a Sergeant Mooney of the Dorsetshire Regiment downstairs, sir. He says he's been sent here by Colonel Frobisher.'

'Show him up here, lad,' said Hardcastle. 'And on your way out ask Sergeant Marriott to come in.'

The soldier who entered the DDI's office was immaculate from head to toe. His uniform was pressed, the creases razor sharp. His cap badge glistened, as did his boots, and his puttees were impeccably wound. Beneath his left arm was a silver-headed swagger cane.

'Inspector 'Ardcastle, sir?' he asked, snapping to attention and throwing up a quivering salute. 'Sarn't Mooney, Depot Battalion, the Dorsetshire Regiment, thirty-ninth of foot, sah!'

'Take a seat, Sergeant,' said Hardcastle. 'This is Detective Sergeant Marriott,' he added, as Marriott entered the office.

'Sarn't.' Mooney nodded in Marriott's direction.

'I'm told that you know Private Donnelly by sight, Sergeant Mooney. Is that correct?'

'Know him, sir? I'm not likely to forget the leery little bastard. He's got bad blood in him, has that one. When he come out to France, he was in the Bullring for a few weeks, and he struck a canary and got hisself twenty-seven days in the glasshouse. That was after he come out of the sick bay. Apparently he fell down the guardroom steps and done hisself a bit of harm, so I heard,' added Mooney with a chuckle.

'Bullring? Canary? What on earth are you talking about Sergeant Mooney?' Hardcastle was, yet again, completely mystified by the soldier's excursion into the esoteric argot of the military.

'Ah, yes.' Mooney tugged at his moustache. 'The Bullring's what they call the training camp at Étaples in France, sir,' he said, pronouncing it Eat-apples. 'It's where the infantry does their training when they first come out to the BEF, and the canaries is the sergeant-instructors. They call 'em canaries on account of wearing yellow armbands.'

'But why was he given twenty-*seven* days?' queried Hardcastle. 'That seems a strange sentence.'

'Ah, well, the colonel at the Bullring's a bit of a tartar, sir. He knows that twenty-eight days is the minimum sentence what entitles a defaulter to a few days' remission for good behaviour. But twenty-seven days don't qualify. So the colonel always hits 'em with twenty-seven, and then they do the full whack, so to speak.'

Hardcastle nodded approvingly. 'That colonel sounds like a man after my own heart, Sergeant Mooney. Now, perhaps, you'd come with Sergeant Marriott and me and have a look at this man I've got locked up in one of our cells.'

'It'll be a pleasure, sir,' said Mooney. 'Best place for him.' He seemed to have made up his mind that Rudd was indeed the deserter Donnelly.

'Open up Rudd's cell, Skipper,' said Hardcastle to the station officer, as the three men arrived in the front office.

'Very good, sir.' The station officer seized a large bunch of keys and led the way into a dank passageway. He slid open the wicket of number three cell, peered in, and then unlocked the door.

The man calling himself Wilfred Rudd was stretched out with his hands behind his head, on the narrow wooden bench that did service as a bed. But he looked up in alarm at the sight of Sergeant Mooney and scrambled to his feet.

'Aha, Donnelly, you idle son of a whore's Saturday night coupling on the kitchen table, we meet again,' said Mooney.

'What's he doing here?' demanded the prisoner, addressing himself to Hardcastle.

'Sergeant Mooney's come to tell us who you are,' said Hardcastle, and turned to the army sergeant. 'Perhaps you'd be so good as to identify this man formally, Sergeant Mooney.'

'That, sir, is Private Eric Donnelly, of the Dorsetshire Regiment, and a bloody disgrace to the old thirty-ninth of foot, so he is.' Mooney took a pace closer to Donnelly. 'My only regret, laddie, is that I'll not be at the Tower of London one fine morning when they put a few rounds into you for cowardice and desertion in the face of the enemy.'

Donnelly sank down on to the bench and put his head in his hands.

'Thank you, Sergeant Mooney.' Hardcastle turned to the station officer. 'You can lock Donnelly up again until I decide what to do with him, Skipper,' he said.

'My adjutant told me that Colonel Frobisher said that you'd be charging Donnelly with attempting to murder you, sir,' said Mooney, as they returned to Hardcastle's office.

'I don't really think he intended to kill me, Sergeant Mooney,' said Hardcastle airily. 'As I told my Sergeant Wood only yesterday, the best he'd get for that is ten years in the nick.' He forbore from mentioning that Donnelly was still a suspect for Ronald Parker's murder. 'It's a much better and cheaper solution if the army shoots him.' He paused. 'D'you think they will?'

'Without a doubt, sir. Leaving his dead comrade on the field of battle and then slinging his hook is despicable, sir, and that's a fact. Field Marshal Sir Douglas 'Aig won't find no problem in confirming a sentence of death. Not that it'll be down to him, I s'pose,' he added thoughtfully, 'because they'll likely court martial Donnelly here in the Smoke. Don't matter, though; either way they'll top the bastard.'

'What now, sir?' asked Marriott, once Sergeant Mooney had left the police station to return to Dorchester.

'We wait until we hear from Mr Franklin about the tests he's doing on the revolver we seized from Donnelly when Wood and me nicked him, Marriott.' Hardcastle thought about that for a moment or two. 'Go across to the Yard, Marriott, and see if Mr Franklin can tell us anything now.'

But fifteen minutes later, Marriott returned with disappointing news.

'Inspector Franklin said that the weapon you seized from Donnelly, sir, is definitely not the revolver that was used to murder Parker.'

'Sod it!' exclaimed Hardcastle. 'What did Mr Franklin say about the revolver?'

'It's a service issue, sir. He could tell because it's got the broad arrow on it. As you suggested, Mr Franklin thought that Donnelly probably picked it up on the battlefield when he ran. I wonder when he got back here from France.'

'No doubt the army will be interested to find out *how* he got back here, Marriott, but I'm damned if I am.' And with that, Hardcastle immediately lost interest in Donnelly. 'Get on to Colonel Frobisher and tell him he can have the prisoner and the sooner the better. You'd better arrange for the revolver to be returned to him, as well.'

'Yes, sir.'

'And now, Marriott, we're back to the beginning with this damned murder. It's too bloody frustrating for words, that's what it is.'

Saturday morning found Hardcastle ill-tempered and dissatisfied. He had convinced himself that Eric Donnelly, alias Wilfred Rudd, was responsible for Ronald Parker's murder. But now it appeared that he had done nothing more than pick up with Mavis Parker at a time when she was vulnerable and she and her late husband had been experiencing some difficulty in their marriage. And he wondered whether the death of the Parkers' child from diphtheria had had something to do with her straying from the straight and narrow of acceptable married life. On the other hand, working in the paint shop of Sopwith Aviation had perhaps introduced her to new friends and, to her, an exciting and liberated new world.

'It's high time we had another word with Mavis Parker, Marriott,' said Hardcastle, taking out his watch and peering at it.

'But she's working today, sir, and doesn't finish until six o'clock. What's more, she might be going out, seeing that it's a Saturday.'

'I dare say, Marriott, but she'll go home first to change into her glad rags. I don't know of any woman who'll go out for the evening in the clothes she's been to work in.'

'D'you want to see her today, sir?'

'Certainly, Marriott. We've wasted enough time already on this enquiry.'

'Very good, sir.' Marriott had promised to take his wife Lorna out for a meal. She had arranged for Meg Lewington, the sergeant's wife who lived next door to their Regency Street quarters, to look after the Marriotts' two children James and Doreen. It looked as though Lorna would be disappointed yet again, but that, regrettably, was the lot of a policeman's wife.

'In the meantime, Marriott, what've you found out about the owner of the Hispano-Suiza that Daisy Benson couldn't wait to jump into after Parker's funeral?'

'A check with the licensing people shows the owner of the vehicle to be a man called Vincent Powers, sir. I've set Wilmot to finding out what he can.' Fred Wilmot was one of the older detective constables at Cannon Row, and could be relied on to carry out an enquiry that was both discreet and thorough.

'We'll have wait and see what he turns up, I suppose.'

Fred Wilmot was very good at finding out things. For the task that Marriott had set him, he had attired himself in an outfit that was well worn, but hinted at the gentility of a man who had fallen on hard times.

Early on the Saturday morning, he approached the house called The Beeches on Kingston Hill with the intention of carrying out a preliminary survey, but luck was with him. A young maid was outside the gates polishing the brass nameplate of the house.

'Good morning, miss,' said Wilmot, touching his worn cap, and approaching the girl with a feigned limp.

'Hello,' said the girl, pausing in her work. 'I've not seen you around here before.'

'I suppose the gent who lives here isn't in need of a good handyman, is he?' Wilmot was an accomplished carpenter, a trade he had followed prior to joining the police. 'I've been given me ticket from the navy after getting me leg busted up at Jutland, and I haven't been able to find much in the way of work.'

'I don't think there's any vacancies for that sort of post,' said the girl, casting a nervous glance at the house. 'But you wouldn't want to work here anyway.'

'Why's that? Isn't the mistress good to the staff, then?'

'There ain't no mistress, leastways not permanent. There's just the master and he ain't good to us. He's got a very nasty temper and I'm thinking of packing it in, even though jobs in service is hard to come by, especially without a character. And Powers wouldn't give me one.'

'Is that his name?' asked Wilmot innocently.

'Yes, Mr Vincent Powers, that's who he is.'

'What have you done to upset him, then?'

The girl moved a little closer. 'He's too free with his hands, is that one,' she said, emphasizing her point by holding up her hands with the fingers spread. 'I'll tell you this straight, mister, two or three times he's tried to get me into his bed. That's when he ain't entertaining some tart what he's brung in and who we're supposed to call "madam". Well, what with him being in the theatre an' all, I s'pose he's got the pick of the chorus, as you might say.' She lowered her voice. 'It's happening all the time and only this morning one of his fancy women left the house in a taxi. Seven o'clock it was, and she'd been here all night. It ain't decent.'

'The master's an actor, then, is he?'

'So he says. He reckons he's in that show at the Alhambra in Leicester Square at the moment. *The Bing Boys on Broadway* it's called. I'd love to see it, but getting a free ticket out of him is like getting blood out of a stone.'

At midday, Wilmot arrived in the DDI's office.

'It's about Vincent Powers, sir.'

'What have you found out about him, Wilmot?'

'He's an actor, sir.'

'How did you know that? Wearing a dickey without a shirt, was he? That's how you can usually tell an actor.'

'Not quite, sir.' Wilmot laughed and went on to recount the conversation he had had with the maid at The Beeches, and related the story of the woman who had left in a taxi that morning.

'Any idea who this woman was, Wilmot.'

'No, sir. I asked the girl what she looked like, but the description wasn't any help. It'd fit any one of a dozen ragtime girls.'

'It could've been Daisy Benson, I suppose,' said Hardcastle thoughtfully. 'Although from what you said, it could've been anyone. All right, Wilmot, you can leave it there. Sergeant Marriott and I will look into it when we have time.'

ELEVEN

'There she is, Marriott.' Hardcastle had stationed himself near the greengrocer's shop opposite the factory gates at a quarter to six that same evening. Mrs Parker had emerged at just after six o'clock and turned towards her house in Canbury Park Road. The two detectives followed at a discreet distance.

Once Mavis Parker had entered her house, Hardcastle and Marriott waited a few yards down the road. At twenty past six, the two of them marched up the path and the DDI hammered on Mrs Parker's door.

'Yes?' At first, the woman failed to recognize the two CID officers, but then she said, 'Oh, it's you, Inspector. I was just going out.'

'I won't hold you up for long, Mrs Parker, but there are a few questions that I need to ask you.'

'You'd better come in, then,' said Mavis, and somewhat reluctantly showed them into the parlour.

'I've made enquiries at the Ministry of National Service, Mrs Parker,' said Hardcastle, immediately getting to the nub of the matter, 'and they told me that a letter was sent to your late husband on Monday the eighteenth of February this year. That letter informed Mr Parker that he'd been exempted from military service due to ill health.'

Mavis Parker looked extremely guilty at this announcement, but endeavoured to cover it up. 'Oh, um, well, I don't know anything about that.'

'Are you sure that Mr Parker didn't mention anything about having received such a letter?' asked Marriott.

'If he did get it, he didn't say anything to me about it.' Mavis Parker seemed flustered by the question.

'Do you know where your husband kept his correspondence, letters, bills and that sort of thing?' queried Hardcastle, who was finding it hard to believe that Parker would not have told his wife about such a letter. *Unless, for some reason, he had not seen it.*

Mavis Parker did not immediately answer the question and covered her confusion by asking one of her own. 'Why are you so interested in this letter, Inspector?'

'Very simply, Mrs Parker,' said Hardcastle, 'because someone murdered your husband, and I intend to find out who that person was. The ministry assured me that the letter was sent, but you told me that your husband was attempting to get to Holland in order to avoid military service. That, to my way of thinking, seems to imply that he didn't see this here letter, and I want to know why.'

'He sometimes put letters and bills in the drawer of the kitchen table,' said Mavis. 'I'll go and have a look. Not that I think he ever got it, because I'm sure he would've told me if he had.'

'Go with Mrs Parker, Marriott,' said Hardcastle, 'in case she needs some help. She might not know what a letter from the Ministry looks like. And he might've put it anywhere. I've known of people hiding things in the strangest of places.'

Marriott had worked with Hardcastle for long enough to understand that the DDI wanted him to take his time, and to delay Mrs Parker's return for as long as possible.

Once Marriott and Mrs Parker had left the room, Hardcastle began a quick search of the parlour. Being an experienced detective, he did not look in the most obvious places first. He examined the back of the pictures, the underside of the two occasional tables in the room, and finally lifted the top lid of the upright piano.

There, tucked in between a couple of the strings, he found an envelope marked 'On His Majesty's Service'. Carefully removing it with the tips of his fingers, he saw that it was addressed to Mr Ronald Parker and had already been opened. Inside the envelope was a letter which he imagined to be the original of the carbon copy he had been shown by Mr Makepeace, the official at the Ministry of National Service. But he did not remove the letter from the envelope, aware that it might bear the fingerprints of whoever had opened it. And that, according to Parker's widow, was unlikely to have been Parker himself. But it might well have been his killer.

By the time that Mavis Parker and Marriott returned to the room, Hardcastle was, once again, seated on the sofa.

'No luck, I'm afraid . . .' began Mavis, but then paused as she saw the envelope that the DDI was holding between finger and thumb. 'Oh, have you found it?'

'Yes, I've found it, Mrs Parker.'

'Where was it?'

'Curiously enough, it was in the top of the piano.'

'Whatever made you think of looking there, Inspector?' said Mavis, avoiding the DDI's gaze.

'My old father always used to put things in the top of the piano,' said Hardcastle, 'particularly when he didn't want anyone else to find them. But we all knew that that's where he hid them, because when we played chopsticks on it, it sounded strange. He never found out that we knew though.'

'How funny,' said Mavis. 'I'd never have thought of looking there.' But her attempt at innocence was belied by the flush rising steadily from her neck. She held out her hand. 'May I have it?'

'I'm afraid not, Mrs Parker. You see it could be valuable evidence in the matter of your husband's murder.' Hardcastle put the letter in his inside jacket pocket. 'I'll let you have it back in due course.'

'What sort of evidence?' Mavis Parker was obviously loath to let the letter out of her possession.

'I don't know. I'm only a simple policeman, Mrs Parker,' said Hardcastle blithely, 'but our scientists like to have a look at these things. You'd be surprised what they can find out these days.' In fact, it was his intention to hand the letter to Inspector Collins in the hope that there might be some useful fingerprints on it.

'Oh, really?' responded Mavis lamely.

'How long have you known Wilfred Rudd?' asked the DDI suddenly.

'Who?'

'Wilfred Rudd, the hospital porter.'

'Oh, Wilfred.' Mavis played for time. 'Of course, but I think
you've got that wrong. Mr Rudd is an army officer, or was. He
told me that he'd been wounded and discharged from the army.
He was in all the battles, you know. He told me he'd got the
Military Cross.' She put a hand to her mouth. 'Oh, goodness,
you don't think he murdered my poor Ronald, do you?'

'It's a possibility I'm considering,' said Hardcastle, although
in the face of Detective Inspector Franklin's findings that Rudd's
revolver was not the murder weapon, he had to admit that it was
unlikely. He had also dismissed the likelihood that Rudd had
acquired a second weapon; he did not for one moment think that
he was that clever, and a search of his room at Queen's Road
had failed to find any other firearms.

'But surely, I mean, being an officer . . .'

'He was not an officer, Mrs Parker, he was a private soldier
named Donnelly who had deserted in the face of the enemy and
taken the identity of a dead comrade called Wilfred Rudd. He is
now in military custody awaiting court martial, and will doubtless
be shot at dawn.'

'Oh no!' Mavis paled and for a moment appeared to be on
the point of swooning.

'How did you meet him, Mrs Parker?' asked Marriott.

'At a dance at the Surbiton Assembly Rooms, about two months
ago.'

'And what did your husband think about that?'

'He didn't know,' said Mavis quietly.

'What did he think you were doing?'

'Roller skating. I often went skating with some of the girls
from Sopwiths.'

'Is that where you met Gilbert Stroud?'

Mavis Parker raised her eyebrows in surprise. 'How did you
know about him?' she asked. That Hardcastle knew about Stroud
clearly disconcerted her greatly.

'We find out all sorts of things when we're investigating a
murder, Mrs Parker,' put in Marriott. 'It's a very serious crime.'

'Second only to treason,' said Hardcastle mildly, 'but the
penalty is the same for each.'

But the DDI's last comment seemed to have no great effect
on Mrs Parker, and he wondered why.

*   *   *

'What did you make of Mrs Parker, sir?' asked Marriott, when he and Hardcastle were back at Cannon Row police station.

'Either she knows nothing, or she's in over her head, Marriott. But given that Stroud of MI5 is taking an interest in her, I rather think it's the latter.'

'So, what's the next move, sir?' Marriott was concerned that the DDI was encroaching even further on the preserve of Special Branch, and from what he had heard of its head, the formidable Superintendent Patrick Quinn, that was an extremely dangerous thing to do. 'D'you think we should talk to Special Branch, sir?' he asked, giving voice to those thoughts.

'Certainly not, Marriott,' said Hardcastle vehemently. 'They don't know anything about solving murders over there. Mr Quinn told me as much when we got involved in the murder of Rose Drummond.'

'More observations, then, sir?'

'Yes, but not on weekdays, Marriott. The most I suspect she does after work is to go skating. I'm interested in what she gets up to on a Sunday.'

'According to Daisy Benson, she goes to church on Sundays, sir.'

'She won't be there all day, Marriott,' said Hardcastle, 'not unless she's possessed of some sort of religious mania. If she's meeting anyone secretly, it'll be on a Sunday afternoon, you mark my words.' He glanced at his watch. 'Are Lipton and Catto still here?'

'Yes, sir.'

'Good.' Hardcastle walked to the open door of his office. 'Lipton, Catto, come in here,' he bellowed. And when the two detective constables appeared, he said, 'I've got a job for you two tomorrow.'

'It's my day off, sir,' complained Catto unwisely.

'It's cancelled,' said Hardcastle bluntly. 'It's a murder enquiry we're dealing with here, not a picnic in the park. There's no time for days off.'

'What's the job, sir?' asked Lipton quickly, in an attempt to stop Catto pursuing his complaint and incurring a wrath that was likely to descend upon them both.

'I need you to follow Mavis Parker. I want to know what she gets up to of a Sunday, and who she meets, because I'm damned sure she's meeting someone we haven't come across yet. It might even be this Mortimer fellow that the manageress at the skating rink told us about. Now, I'm told she goes to church on Sunday mornings, so you'd better be ready to start first thing. And if she picks up with someone, I want to know who he is and where he lives.'

'D'you want us to follow Mrs Parker as well as this man, sir?' Catto was concerned to get his assignment right for fear of bringing forth another reproof. But in that he failed.

Hardcastle emitted a sigh of exasperation. 'I know where Mrs Parker lives, Catto. So if she does meet a man, you follow him and leave her to her own devices, so to speak. There, that plain enough for you?'

'Yes, sir,' said Catto, still furious that the day at Brighton that he had proposed to spend with a young woman whom he had recently met would not now take place. But it was not the first time it had happened. All the girls he had met in the past had proved to be intolerant of his erratic working hours, and that meant he probably would not see his latest conquest ever again. There were times when Catto despaired of ever getting married; marriage was recognized as the only means of escape from the Spartan accommodation afforded by the police section house in Ambrosden Avenue.

'Right, Marriott,' said Hardcastle, once Lipton and Catto had departed, 'it's nine o'clock. I think we'll have an early night. My regards to Mrs Marriott.'

'Thank you, sir, and mine to Mrs H.' Marriott did not think, however, that Lorna would be grateful for the DDI's regards, as it was he who had been responsible for cancelling her evening out. His task, when he got home, was to attempt to placate her.

Marriott had judged his wife well, and found her in an unforgiving mood.

'It's really too much, Charlie,' said Lorna, the moment Marriott stepped through his front door. 'I'd got everything arranged with Meg Lewington to look after the children and then you go off on some wretched enquiry.'

'I couldn't really help it, love. You know what Ernie Hardcastle's like when he gets the bit between his teeth. And it is a murder we're dealing with.'

'Well, he ought to have more consideration,' rejoined Lorna. 'I'll bet he doesn't mess up his own evenings out.'

'I'm afraid he does, love, frequently,' sighed Marriott. 'I sometimes think he lives, eats and sleeps the Job.'

'Yes, but he doesn't have two small children.' Lorna refused to give up. 'Jimmy and Doreen were looking forward to having Meg look after them. Mind you, I think she reads them lots of stories and lets them stay up too late. Which is what you should be doing.' She shook her head at the unfairness of it all. 'But I suppose you'll be an inspector one day,' she added with a sigh.

'Maybe,' said Marriott.

'You're late this evening, Ernie.' Alice was alone in the parlour, engaged in her self-imposed task of knitting socks and mufflers for the soldiers on the Western Front. Once a week, she and a few friends would meet in a room at Bethlem Hospital at the end of Kennington Road. There they would parcel up their knitwear and leave it for collection by the Army Post Office staff.

'I had to go to Kingston,' said Hardcastle, without elaborating.

'I could do with a glass of sherry, Ernie.' Alice knew better than to ask questions about her husband's work. She put down her knitting on a side table and stretched her arms.

'The children out, are they?' Hardcastle poured his wife a glass of Amontillado and a whisky for himself.

'As usual,' said Alice. 'They don't seem to spend much time at home these days. But Maud should be in shortly. Her young man's taken her out to supper.'

Hardcastle had no sooner sat down with his whisky and the evening newspaper than he heard the front door opening. There was a whispered conversation in the tiny hall, followed by giggles from Maud and laughter from Charles Spencer. And then the couple appeared in the doorway.

'Good evening, sir.' Spencer crossed the room and shook hands with Hardcastle. 'Mrs Hardcastle.' He nodded briefly in Alice's direction.

'Have you had a nice evening, dear?' asked Alice.

'A *very* good evening,' said Maud with a mischievous smile. 'Charles took me to the Cafe Royal, and we saw that Mr Churchill having dinner with some of his friends.'

'Didn't realize he had any,' muttered Hardcastle, who was not a supporter of the Liberal party.

'I wonder if I might have a word with you, sir.' Spencer, looking rather self-conscious, fingered the top button of his tunic.

'Perhaps we could go into the kitchen, Ma, and make some sandwiches,' suggested Maud.

'But I thought you'd just had supper . . .' Alice began, but then her womanly intuition took over. 'Yes, of course. I'm sure your father could do with a bite to eat. He only got in a few minutes ago.'

The women left the room, Alice remembering to close the door firmly behind her.

'Well, what is it, Charles?' asked Hardcastle.

'I would like to ask permission for your daughter's hand in marriage, sir,' said Spencer, nervously beginning his well-rehearsed speech.

'Good God!' exclaimed Hardcastle. He put his unlit pipe in the ashtray and stared at the young man opposite him. 'You'd better sit down and have a glass of whisky, m'boy,' he said, playing for time. As the father of two girls, he had known all along that there would come a day when a young man would pose this very question, but now that it had happened he was quite unprepared for it. He busied himself pouring whisky for the young army officer.

'I proposed to Maud this evening, sir, and she accepted.'

'Yes, I imagine she would have done,' said Hardcastle, knowing that he ought to be asking some pertinent questions, but right now he could not think of any. He was never at a loss when questioning a suspect or a witness, but this, to him, was an entirely different situation. 'She's only twenty, you know.' It was the only observation he could think of at the moment.

'Yes, I know, sir, but she's very mature for her age, and she's a jolly good nurse.'

'I suppose I should ask you about your prospects.' Hardcastle changed tack as he handed Spencer a tumbler of whisky, and took a substantial mouthful of his own.

'As a matter of fact, I'm rather keen on staying in the army, sir, and I intend to apply for a regular commission when this show is over. Although the army will be drastically reduced after the war's ended, my colonel thinks I should stand a very good chance. In fact, he told me that I'm likely to be promoted to captain next week, so I suppose that's a good sign.'

'Yes, I imagine it is.' Hardcastle certainly knew about promises of promotion, but also knew how often they remained unfulfilled. 'But supposing they turn you down for a regular commission?'

'It was my intention to read for the bar until this lot with Fritz started, but I'm afraid it rather got interrupted,' said Spencer, with a boyish grin. 'But if the army turns me down that's what I'll do.'

'The law's a bit of a tricky profession to start with. Not much money in it until you're established.' But then Hardcastle laughed. 'I could find you cross-examining me one day at the Old Bailey, I suppose.' He took another sip of whisky. 'Oh, dammit, man, of course you can marry my daughter.' He crossed the room and shook Spencer's hand vigorously. 'My congratulations, Charles. And now, I suppose we'd better fetch the women in and break the news to Mrs Hardcastle.'

'I think she might already know, sir,' said Spencer.

Hardcastle opened the parlour door. 'Alice, Maud, come back in here.'

Maud was first through the door. 'Well, Pa, what did you say?'

'Say?' said Hardcastle impishly. 'Say about what?'

'Oh, Pa, you know perfectly well.'

'Yes, I do.' Hardcastle embraced his daughter and kissed her on the cheek. 'I hope you'll both be very happy. God knows, there's little enough happiness in the world at the moment.'

Alice crossed the room, took Charles Spencer's hand in both of hers, and kissed him lightly on the cheek. 'Congratulations, Charles. I'm delighted that Maud has found such a charming young man to be her husband. And I'll be very pleased to welcome you as a son-in-law.'

'It's a shame we don't have any champagne,' said Hardcastle, but given that the cheapest was at least seven shillings a bottle, it was an expense he could not afford, even on an occasional basis. Apart from anything else, German submarine activity in the Channel had ensured that only essential supplies were shipped. The sparkling wine that was produced in Champagne was regarded as an unnecessary luxury and very few cases of it got through.

'It so happens that I have some, sir.' Spencer darted out into the hall. 'I managed to persuade an American officer chum of mine to part with a bottle,' he said, as he came back. 'He's just returned from the Front for a spell of furlough in London, and he picked up a case after the show near Butte de Mesnil in Champagne itself. I had to promise him that he'd be my best man, although I suspect he'll be back in the United States come the wedding. I'm afraid it's a bit on the warm side,' he added, brandishing the bottle.

'It sounds as though you'd got this all planned, Charles,' said Hardcastle, warming to his future son-in-law.

'Strategy and tactics are all part of an infantry officer's job, sir,' said Spencer.

For once, Hardcastle forbore from launching into a diatribe about what he saw as the inadequacies of the military. 'You'd better find some glasses, Maud,' he said, as Spencer twisted the cork from the champagne.

'When do you propose to get married, Charles?' asked Alice.

'Not until after the war's over, Mrs Hardcastle.'

'D'you think that'll be soon?' asked Hardcastle.

'Yes, I do,' said Spencer firmly. 'From what we've heard from some of the Germans that have been taken prisoner they're sick to death of the whole business. In fact, they're surrendering in their thousands. What's more, the Royal Navy has interfered so much with their food supplies that half the population of Germany is starving.'

'Yes, I read that in the paper the other day,' said Hardcastle. He took a glass of champagne from his future son-in-law and raised it. 'Here's to your future happiness, both of you.'

TWELVE

D etective Constable Henry Catto was still in a disagreeable mood about his cancelled leave day when he and Lipton took up their observation early on the Sunday morning. There was a butcher's shop near Queen Elizabeth Road, and it was from there that the two detectives were able to see anyone coming out of Mavis Parker's house.

'I still don't know what's so urgent about this murder that the guv'nor had to cancel my day off,' complained Catto, stamping his feet and turning up his collar against the chill March wind. 'I don't know why people can't get murdered in the summer. I'm bloody freezing.'

'Yeah, tough luck,' said Lipton unsympathetically, hands deep in his overcoat pockets.

'I wonder how long we're going to be hanging about here,' said Catto.

'As long as it takes,' said Lipton.

'But what if she doesn't go out today, Gordon?'

'Then we'll be back here next Sunday, I suppose.' Lipton was no more enamoured of their boring duty than was Catto, but at least the DDI had not cancelled his day off. Next Sunday, however, *would* be his day off and he hoped that discovering what Mavis Parker did on a Sunday would be resolved today.

At twenty minutes to eleven their long wait was finally rewarded. Mavis Parker came out of her house and set off at a brisk pace towards Lipton and Catto. Quickly moving away from their vantage point, they pretended interest in a shop window further down the road.

As befitted a recently widowed woman, Mrs Parker was clothed all in black. On her coat, of a length to reveal only button boots, was a small black glass and pearl mourning brooch, and her straw hat bore a veil that covered her face. A handbag was hooked over her left arm and she held what looked like a prayer book or a Bible in one hand and an umbrella in the other.

'Looks like she's off to church, Gordon,' said Catto.

'That's a very shrewd observation, Henry,' said Lipton caustically.

Mavis Parker turned into Queen Elizabeth Road, and Lipton and Catto followed. A couple of hundred yards further on, she entered the John Bunyan Baptist Church.

'I reckon we've got time for a cup of tea somewhere, Gordon,' said Catto.

'Firstly, Henry, I've no idea where you'd get a cup of tea round here on a Sunday morning, and secondly we don't know what time the service will finish. And what if she comes out early? Being recently widowed, she might have a fainting fit and have to go home. If you're prepared to tell the DDI that we lost her, I'm not.'

'P'raps you're right,' said Catto grudgingly.

'Of course I'm right,' snapped Lipton.

It was another hour and a half before the congregation started to emerge. The minister stood at the church door and shook hands with those of his parishioners who paused to exchange a few words. When Mrs Parker stopped, the minister held her hand and spoke to her at some length, presumably commiserating about the death of her husband. Twenty minutes later, she was back indoors.

'Now what?' demanded a thoroughly disgruntled Catto. 'I'm starving hungry.'

'We wait.' Lipton had originally been junior to Catto, but since passing the written examination for detective sergeant their status had been reversed, and he was now the senior man. It would, however, be months, if not years, before he was promoted to third class sergeant, even though he had 'acted up' on occasion. Consequently, he was very conscious of the fact that if this observation, for which he was responsible, went wrong, it could well put his promotion in serious jeopardy. The DDI was known to be very unforgiving when it came to what he described as 'dereliction of duty'.

'What about that pub over there?' suggested Catto, pointing at the Canbury Arms.

'We wait,' said Lipton again.

For an hour and a half, the two observers loitered in Canbury Park Road, strolling up and down, chatting and generally attempting to appear inconspicuous. And trying to keep warm.

Then, at just past two o'clock, they saw Mavis Parker come out of her house and walk towards Richmond Road. In place of her sober churchgoing outfit, she now wore a green coat with a brightly-coloured knitted scarf slung casually around the shoulders, and a small green beret, but she had kept the button boots she had been wearing previously. A handbag and an umbrella completed the outfit.

'She soon dispensed with her widow's weeds,' said Catto, and he and Lipton began to follow the woman.

'It's the war,' said Lipton. 'People can't be bothered too much any more.'

Mavis eventually arrived in Canbury Gardens and spent several minutes gazing at the river. A hardy young man, attired in a singlet and shorts, was sculling rapidly towards Teddington Lock and he seemed to hold Mavis's attention all the while he was in her sight.

'I hope she's not going to jump in and commit suicide,' said Catto.

'I've come to the conclusion, Henry,' said Lipton, 'that you're a bloody pessimist.'

Five minutes later, a man strolled up to Mavis and they embraced.

'I wonder who he is,' queried Catto unnecessarily.

'That's what we're here to find out,' said Lipton, becoming increasingly intolerant of Catto's inane remarks.

Arm in arm, Mavis Parker and her male companion walked back to the Lower Ham Road where the man ushered her into a Morris Oxford two-seater tourer. He spent a few minutes putting up the hood before taking a starting handle from inside the car. Inserting it in the radiator, he swung it vigorously until the engine burst into life. Mounting the driver's seat, he leaned across and pecked Mavis lightly on the cheek.

'That's torn it!' exclaimed Catto. 'We'll never get a taxi here,' he added, looking around in the hope of finding one.

'All is not lost, Henry. Get the details of the number plate.'

Catto produced his pocket book and pencil, and began to write.

'Discreetly, for God's sake, Henry,' cautioned Lipton. 'You don't want them to see you taking their number.'

'Oh, right,' said Catto, and turned his back while he finished writing.

'And write this down, Henry: late thirties, five foot seven, moustache, leather motoring coat, brown tweed cap worn back to front, and goggles.'

'Is that the man you're describing?' queried Catto.

'Of course it is, you idiot. The last time I saw a woman with a moustache was at the circus. And she had a beard as well.'

'Who's got a beard?'

'Shut up, Henry, and just get on with it,' said the exasperated Lipton. 'I sometimes wonder whether you're serious or just playing the fool all the time.'

The man fiddled about with the car's controls and he and Mavis set off towards Richmond.

'She doesn't waste any time, Gordon,' commented Catto. 'First of all there was Wilfred Rudd, now there's this bloke. And to think she only planted her husband last Wednesday.'

'Well, there's nothing more we can do today,' said Lipton. 'We might as well go home.'

'But what if they come back?' asked Catto.

'If they do, it's unlikely they'll come back to this exact spot,' Lipton said. 'Anyway, they could be hours. It might even be tomorrow morning before they come back.'

However, neither of the detectives had seen the man watching them from behind a tree.

Lipton and Catto were waiting outside the DDI's door when he arrived promptly at eight o'clock on Monday morning.

'What are you two hanging about for?' barked Hardcastle, entering his office and hanging up his hat and coat. He dropped his umbrella into the hatstand with a resounding clatter as the ferrule hit the metal tray.

'It's about yesterday's observation, sir,' said Lipton, as they followed the DDI.

'Well?' Hardcastle settled himself behind his desk and began to fill his pipe. 'And shut that bloody window, Catto,' he said. 'I can't hear myself think with those trains going in and out.'

Catto darted across to the window. 'It's stuck, sir,' he said.

'Well unstick it for God's sake,' growled Hardcastle, and turned to Lipton. 'Well?'

Lipton outlined what they had learned of Mavis Parker's movements the previous day, finishing with a description of the man with whom she had left Canbury Gardens.

'Who does this car belong to, Lipton?'

'I did a check with the London County Council's register, sir. It took me some time to wake up the night watchman and—'

'Cut out the frills and get on with it,' said Hardcastle sharply.

'Yes, sir. It's a 1914 Morris Oxford registered to a Mr Lawrence Mortimer,' said Lipton.

'That must be the L. Mortimer the manageress at the skating rink told Sergeant Marriott and me about,' said Hardcastle. 'In that case, you needn't bother with keeping observation there again.'

'The address the county council has for him is a Westminster one, sir.' Lipton hurried on with his report. 'It's a block of apartments called Ashley Gardens in Thirleby Road. I've written down the details, sir.' Lipton proffered a slip of paper bearing the full address.

'I don't need that, Lipton,' said Hardcastle, waving away the piece of paper. 'Find out all you can about this here Lawrence Mortimer.' He stared at the two detectives. 'Well, what are you waiting for?' But then he changed his mind. 'Wait!'

'Sir?' Lipton turned at the door.

'On second thoughts, I think this is a job for Sergeant Wood. Send him in.'

'You wanted me, sir?' said Wood, as he entered a moment or two later.

'I've got a job that demands your special talents, Wood.'

'Yes, sir?' Wood was not in the remotest fooled by the DDI's blandishments; he had heard them too often in the past.

Hardcastle gave Wood the broad outlines of what Lipton and Catto had seen the previous day. 'I want you to find out all you can about this man Lawrence Mortimer, but you must be very circumspect, Wood. I don't want him to have the slightest idea that we're interested in him, so to speak. Lipton will give you a description of the man.'

'Very good, sir.'

At ten o'clock, Hardcastle donned his hat and coat and picked up his umbrella. Crossing the corridor, he put his head round the door of the detectives' office.

'Time we were getting round to the inquest, Marriott,' he said.

'Coming, sir.' Marriott grabbed his overcoat and bowler hat, and followed the DDI down the stairs.

Five minutes after Hardcastle and Marriott arrived at the coroner's court in Horseferry Road, the coroner took his seat and the jury of seven men was sworn in.

The two detectives seated themselves next to Dr Bernard Spilsbury.

'I hope this damned coroner fellow isn't going to make a day of it, Hardcastle,' said Spilsbury. 'I've three cadavers waiting for me on the slab back at St Mary's.'

'In the matter of Ronald Parker, deceased,' announced the coroner in dry tones. 'Inspector Hardcastle?'

'Sir?' Hardcastle stood up.

'Have you made any progress, Mr Hardcastle?'

'I regret to inform the court, sir, that despite extensive enquiries, I am, as yet, unable to discover who was responsible for the death of Ronald Parker.'

'Do you think that such a person might be identified in the foreseeable future?'

'At this stage of my enquiries, sir, no,' said Hardcastle. In fact, he never gave up, but was trying to avoid an appearance before the coroner once a week.

'Very well. Take the oath.'

Hardcastle crossed to the witness box, took the New Testament in his right hand and recited the oath without reference to the card on the ledge of the box.

'Sir, as I said at the first hearing, Ronald Parker's body was found in the River Thames near Westminster Bridge at approximately eight forty a.m. on Monday the fourth of March this year. It was tied up in a sack and the victim had been shot in the head. The body was later identified by Mr Harold Parker as that of his brother Ronald Parker of Canbury Park Road, Kingston upon Thames.'

'Any questions?' asked the coroner, glancing at the jury.

'No, sir,' said the foreman.

'Dr Spilsbury?' The coroner looked enquiringly at the pathologist.

Bernard Spilsbury gave his evidence in succinct medical terms, and attributed death to a gunshot wound to the back of the head.

Again the coroner satisfied himself that the jury had no questions. 'Very well,' he said, 'you may retire to consider your verdict.'

It took but twenty minutes.

'Are you agreed upon a verdict?' asked the coroner when the jurymen filed back into court.

'Yes, sir,' said the foreman. 'We find that Ronald Parker was murdered by person or persons unknown.'

'So be it,' said the coroner. 'I shall record your verdict. That is all. The court is adjourned.'

'Well, that's it over, I suppose, sir,' said Marriott.

'Over!' exclaimed Hardcastle. 'I've only just begun, Marriott.'

Detective Sergeant Herbert Wood set about his task immediately. His first call was to the London County Council's offices in

Spring Gardens, a turning off The Mall. There he discovered that the previous owner of Lawrence Mortimer's car was a Mr Marcus Sawyer of Dordrecht Road, Acton.

Wood boarded an Underground train at Trafalgar Square and, after a change at Holborn, eventually alighted at Shepherds Bush. He walked the rest of the way to Dordrecht Road, hoping that after such a tortuous journey he would find Mr Sawyer at home.

A maidservant answered the door and cast a discerning eye over the detective.

'Yes?'

'Is Mr Sawyer at home?' asked Wood.

'Who shall I say it is?' asked the maid.

'I'm a police officer, miss.'

'I see. Wait a moment.' Leaving Wood on the doorstep, the maid disappeared into the house. Moments later, she returned. 'Come this way, please,' she said, and showed Wood into the parlour. 'The policeman, sir,' she announced.

Sawyer was about fifty, wore a black jacket and striped trousers, and had a beard and a moustache. He was standing in the centre of the room, reading a docket.

'Sarah tells me you're a police officer,' he said, allowing the monocle to drop from his eye as he closed the file he was holding.

'Yes, sir. Detective Sergeant Wood of the Whitehall Division.'

'And what can I do for you, Sergeant,' said Sawyer as he shook hands. 'Does it concern some case I'm dealing with?'

'Case, sir?' queried Wood.

'Yes, I'm a solicitor. I presumed you wished to see me on some official matter.'

'No, sir, it's to do with the car you once owned.'

'Oh, I see. You'd better sit down, and tell me what you wish to know.'

Wood referred to his pocket book. 'I understand that you sold a Morris Oxford tourer to a Mr Lawrence Mortimer of Ashley Gardens, Thirleby Street, Westminster, on the fourth of October 1917, sir.'

'That's correct, Sergeant, but it was all perfectly above board.' Sawyer walked across to a bureau in the corner of the room. 'I can show you all the documentation,' he said, opening the bureau's flap.

'That won't be necessary, sir, but we're rather interested in Mr Mortimer.'

'Why is that?' Sawyer closed the bureau and turned.

'I'm afraid I'm not at liberty to say, other than it might concern a matter of national security.'

'Ah, you interest me, Sergeant. What can I tell you, then?'

'I wondered what sort of opinion you formed of Mortimer, sir.'

Sawyer placed his forefingers in the top pockets of his waistcoat and gazed thoughtfully at a picture on the wall behind Wood.

'A strange sort of chap,' he said, redirecting his attention to Wood. 'To be perfectly honest, I don't think he knew a damned thing about cars. He didn't ask the sort of questions that most people would ask, like how many miles it did to the gallon, or how long I'd owned it and why I was selling it. Neither did he quibble about the price. I rather thought that any potential purchaser might try to knock me down a bit, and I'd purposely raised the price a little in anticipation of some bargaining. But he just wrote me a cheque, there and then.'

'Do you happen to recall which bank his cheque was drawn on, sir?'

Sawyer went back to the bureau and sorted through some paper. 'Yes,' he said eventually, 'I made a note of the cheque details in case it was returned "No Account", but it was in fact paid. It was Williams Deacon's Bank at their Victoria Street branch.'

'Did he, by any chance, happen to say what he did for a living, sir?' asked Wood.

'Yes, he mentioned that he was a commercial traveller of some description and needed a car for his business. I think he said that he sold corsets. It seemed a damned odd thing for a chap of his age to be doing, especially with a war on. Couldn't understand why he wasn't at the Front.'

'How old was he, then, sir?'

'Nearing forty, I'd've thought. On reflection, perhaps he was a bit younger.'

'He didn't happen to mention the company he worked for, I suppose.'

'Not that I recall, and I certainly didn't bother to ask him. All I wanted to do was dispose of the Morris. I've bought a rather splendid new Vauxhall. Perhaps you saw it on your way in; that's it outside. Are you interested in cars, Sergeant?'

'Yes, I am, sir, but I can't afford one. What would people say if they saw a policeman driving about in his own car?'

Sawyer laughed. 'They'd probably say you were being paid too much.' He paused and laughed again. 'Or that you were up to no good.'

'I'm much obliged to you for your assistance, sir,' said Wood, rising to his feet. 'I'll not take up any more of your time.'

THIRTEEN

Wood stopped off at a pub and treated himself to a ham sandwich and a glass of light ale. He returned to Westminster at about two o'clock and made his way to Thirleby Road. According to the address held by the motor vehicle licensing authority, the apartment in Ashley Gardens occupied by Lawrence Mortimer was on the first floor.

But Wood had no intention of calling there. Instead, he rang the bell of the apartment immediately beneath it.

'Good afternoon, sir?' said a trim housemaid, as she opened the door.

'Is your mistress at home?' Wood deliberately asked for the lady of the house assuming, correctly as it happened, that her husband would be at work. 'I'm a police officer, but please tell her that there's no cause for alarm. I'm merely making some routine enquiries.'

'If you care to step inside, sir, I'll enquire if the mistress is at home.'

After a short delay, the maid reappeared and conducted Wood into a sumptuously furnished sitting room.

'My maid Ethel tells me that you're a police officer.' The young woman standing by the window was wearing a bottle-green silk day dress with close fitting, full-length sleeves. She regarded Wood with a forbidding expression, as though his intrusion had just disturbed whatever she had been doing. Her long hair was parted in the centre and braided into a plait that was draped over the front of her left shoulder. The cigarette in a long holder that she had in her right hand lent her a raffish air that rather shocked

Wood; he was unaccustomed to seeing women smoking. But his
first impression of severity was immediately dispelled by
the woman's welcoming smile as she crossed the room with a
rustle of silk. 'Please sit down.'

'Thank you, ma'am. I'm Detective Sergeant Wood of the
Whitehall Division.'

'And I'm Felicity Talbot. How may I help you, Sergeant?' The
woman sat down opposite Wood, hitched her skirt slightly, and
crossed her legs to reveal trim ankles, a glimpse of art silk stock-
ings and glacé kid court shoes.

'It's nothing really important, Mrs Talbot.' Wood paused. 'It
is *Mrs* Talbot, is it?'

'Oh yes, I'm well and truly married.' Placing her cigarette
holder in an ashtray, Felicity Talbot smiled and twisted her
wedding ring, as if to lend credence to her marital state.

'We've received a complaint of noise, unnecessary noise, that
is, from one of the residents in these apartments, Mrs Talbot. It's
all really a waste of time, but the police are duty bound to follow
up such matters.'

'Really?' Mrs Talbot appeared surprised. 'I can't say I've ever
heard any untoward noise, and my husband has never mentioned
anything either. When he's here.'

'As I thought,' said Wood. 'And the people on either side of
you are quiet, are they?'

'We never hear them.'

'And the people upstairs, immediately above you, they're quiet,
too?'

'We wouldn't know there was anyone there, Sergeant. As a
matter of fact, we hardly ever see Mr Mortimer. He lives there
by himself, you know. We've occasionally passed the time of
day when we've happened to meet, but that's all.'

'I see. A businessman, is he?'

'I don't really know, but I rather got the impression that he's
a man of private means.' Felicity Talbot laughed; it was a tinkling
and engaging laugh, and she picked up her cigarette holder and
put a fresh cigarette in it. 'Well, I say that because he seems to
go in and out at odd times. I don't mean in the middle of the
night, or anything like that, of course. Not that I'd know about
that; I'm always in bed rather early. And I sleep like a log.' She
paused to light her cigarette. 'Is he the resident that the complaint

was about?' she asked, expelling smoke towards the ceiling. 'Or was he the one complaining?'

'Oh no, it wasn't him,' said Wood. 'But I can't reveal the source of the complaint, you'll understand, particularly as it seems to be groundless. These things lead to bad feeling among neighbours.'

'Of course.' Felicity Talbot paused, as if a sudden thought had occurred to her. 'Would you care for a cup of tea, Sergeant?'

'That's very kind, ma'am,' said Wood, 'but I don't want to put you to any trouble.'

'It's no trouble. It's probably made already. The girl usually brings it in about now.' Mrs Talbot leaned across to press a bell push. 'Would you bring us the tea, Ethel,' she said, when the maid appeared. 'Your job must be very interesting, Sergeant Wood,' she continued, while they were waiting for the tea. 'Have you investigated any murders?'

'One or two,' said Wood, without mentioning that he was investigating one right now.

'How exciting. Do tell.'

'I'm afraid they're all rather mundane,' replied Wood. 'Mainly what we call domestics. Husband kills wife and that sort of thing.'

'Good heavens.' Mrs Talbot put a hand to her mouth, rather affectedly. 'How fascinating, but not here in Ashley Gardens, I hope.'

'No, ma'am,' said Wood, grateful that, at that moment, the maid appeared with the tea.

'You can leave it, Ethel, I'll pour it,' said Mrs Talbot. 'It's so nice to have someone to talk to,' she continued, as she busied herself pouring the tea into bone china cups. 'It gets rather lonely here during the day and my husband works long hours. Milk and sugar?' But before Wood could ask what her husband did, she volunteered the information. 'He's a major in the Royal Flying Corps, but he's stationed at the War Office now, thank God, helping to prepare plans for the new service.'

'The new service?' Wood gave the impression of being puzzled by the comment.

'It's no secret,' said Felicity. 'They're busy drawing up plans to put the RFC and the Royal Naval Air Service into one organization next month. I believe it's to be called the Royal Air Force.'

'Well I never,' said Wood, who was well aware of the proposal, but always believed in encouraging conversation however banal.

'This Mr Mortimer, the man upstairs, seems to be a motoring enthusiast, you know,' Mrs Talbot continued. 'He bought a new car – well, I don't think it was new – a couple of months ago. He once offered to take my husband and me out for a spin, but Robert, that's my husband, declined. He said he didn't trust the fellow.' Felicity laughed her same gay laugh again. 'I think he thought that Lawrence Mortimer had designs on me.'

Wood laughed too. 'Well, if, as you say, he doesn't go out to work, I suppose he has to do something to wile away the time.'

'I don't know why he isn't in the army. My husband said that Mr Mortimer is the sort of man that women give white feathers to. But maybe he's engaged in some sort of secret war work that he doesn't dare to talk about.'

It's probably a case of him not daring to admit that he sells corsets, thought Wood, as he rose to his feet. 'Thank you for the tea, Mrs Talbot. I'm sorry to have wasted your time on what seems to have been a pointless enquiry.'

'Not at all, Sergeant Wood. As I said just now, it's nice to have a bit of company from time to time.' Felicity Talbot stood up and extended a hand. 'But it seems an awful waste of a detective's time to be following up on trifling enquiries about people disturbing their neighbours. I'd've thought that they'd've sent an ordinary policeman.'

'Not necessarily, ma'am,' said Wood, surprised at the woman's perspicacity. 'In wartime it's always possible that a simple enquiry of that sort could lead to something far more serious.'

'Golly!' exclaimed Mrs Talbot, 'I'd never thought of that.'

Wood stepped out into Thirleby Road just in time to see a man turn sharply and walk swiftly away. But he was not so quick that Wood failed to recognize him. It had begun to rain and Wood put up his umbrella and hurried out to Victoria Street in search of a bus to take him home.

Arriving at Cannon Row on Tuesday morning, Wood made straight for the DDI's office.

'Learn anything, Wood?' asked Hardcastle.

Wood explained in some detail what he had discovered from his visits to Marcus Sawyer in Acton and Felicity Talbot in Ashley Gardens.

'Interesting,' said Hardcastle, when Wood had finished. 'I

suppose it's possible that he is engaged in some sort of secret war work, but I'm not buying it.' Clearly, he had made up his mind that Lawrence Mortimer was up to no good. 'I mean to say, no self-respecting man claims to be a corset salesman if he ain't.'

'There was one other thing, sir,' said Wood. 'When I came out of Ashley Gardens, I spotted Gilbert Stroud of MI5. He legged it a bit sharply, but not before I'd recognized him.'

Hardcastle took his pipe from the ashtray and lit it, leaning back in his chair. 'Well now, ain't that a curious thing, Wood? In my book, that means that Lawrence Mortimer is likely to be up to something that interests MI5. And that interests me.'

For some time, Hardcastle sat mulling over what Wood had reported. Then he shouted for Marriott.

'I presume you've heard what Wood discovered about Mortimer, Marriott,' said Hardcastle when his sergeant had joined him.

'Yes, sir.'

'In that case, I think we'll pay a visit to the War Office, Marriott, and have a word with this here Major Robert Talbot of the Royal Flying Corps.'

'What do we hope to learn from him, sir?' Once again, Marriott was mystified that the DDI was changing the direction of the enquiry.

'If Lawrence Mortimer is up to no good, and I rather think he is, then we can rely on the major to be factual about anything he knows, Marriott, which is probably more than his wife knows. And being an army officer, Major Talbot's likely to be a reliable and discreet informant.' And without further ado, Hardcastle put on his overcoat and hat, and seized his umbrella. With Marriott in tow, he set off for the War Office, further down Whitehall.

'All correct, sir.' The policeman on the fixed point outside the War Office saluted as Hardcastle and Marriott approached.

'I doubt it; there's a bloody war on,' muttered the DDI, as he ascended the four steps and pushed open one of the double doors.

'Can I help you, sir?' asked the elderly custodian as he approached the DDI, but then recognition dawned. 'Ah, it's Inspector Hardcastle, ain't it? I remember you coming here a few times a couple of years back, sir.'

'You've got a good memory,' said Hardcastle.

'You has to keep your wits about you in this job, guv'nor,' replied the custodian. 'Now then, who did you want to see today?'

'Major Robert Talbot of the RFC,' said Hardcastle.

'Major Talbot, ah yes. Him what's working on this new air force nonsense. Not that I think it'll ever come to anything. After all, when this lot's over they'll be going back to cavalry like what we had in South Africa. That General French commanded the first cavalry brigade out there and routed the Boers at Colesberg. Never needed no airy-planes to sort that lot out.'

'That's all very interesting,' said Hardcastle, 'but where can I find Major Talbot?'

'Ah yes, Major Talbot. Half a mo, guv'nor.' The custodian spent a few moments thumbing through a directory. 'Now, let me see. Ah, there he is,' he said, jabbing the page with a finger. 'I'll get one of the messengers to take you up, sir.'

Hardcastle and Marriott were eventually shown into a small office on the top floor of the War Office.

'The police is here to see you, sir,' announced the messenger.

Robert Talbot was a young man, probably in his mid-twenties, and was seated behind a desk. He was in his shirtsleeves, and his distinctive RFC 'maternity' tunic, bearing pilot's wings and the ribbons of the Distinguished Service Order and the Military Cross, was thrown casually over a chair.

'Whatever it is, I didn't do it,' said Talbot, with a laugh. 'Now then, what can I do for you?' He stood up, skirted the desk and shook hands.

'I'm Divisional Detective Inspector Hardcastle of the Whitehall Division, Major, and this is Detective Sergeant Marriott.'

'Is this a coincidence, I wonder? Oddly enough, my wife had a visit from the police yesterday afternoon, Inspector.'

'Yes, I know, Major. Detective Sergeant Wood is one of my officers.'

'Ah! Am I to take it that you're interested in Lawrence Mortimer, then? Reading between the lines, I rather thought that this business about people in our apartment block creating a disturbance was all my eye and Betty Martin. After all, detectives don't usually take an interest in that mundane sort of thing, do they? From what Felicity told me, I got the impression that your man seemed more interested in Mortimer than in noisy neighbours. Sorry, do take a pew.' Talbot swept up his tunic, slipped it on – but left it unbuttoned – and indicated a couple of chairs.

'Your wife sounds like a very astute woman, Major,' said Marriott.

'Not at all, old boy. It was me who worked out that there was more to your chap's enquiry than met the eye. Felicity's only interested in the newest dance craze to cross the Atlantic. I think her latest fad is something called the Monkey Hunch, whatever that is when it's at home. Not that I have any time for dancing what with all this business about creating something to be known as the RAF. According to the latest bumf to float up from downstairs, "Boom" Trenchard wants me to be called a squadron leader instead of a major. Still, I suppose it'll all come right in the end. But I've got my doubts, particularly as it's supposed to come into being on All Fools' Day.'

'You're quite right, Major,' said Hardcastle. 'We are interested in Lawrence Mortimer. And if I might speak in confidence—'

'Of course, Inspector. Anything said between these four walls stays here.'

'We have reason to believe that Mortimer might not be the corset salesman he claims to be.'

'Mortimer a *corset* salesman?' Talbot threw back his head and guffawed. 'Not Pygmalion likely!'

'What do you think he does for a living, then, Major?'

'Frankly, I don't know, Inspector, but he's a bit of a shady cove, coming and going at odd hours. Whatever it is that he does, it's not a regular job. But you obviously think he's up to no good.'

Hardcastle weighed carefully what he was about to say next. 'Between you and me, Major, I rather fancy him for a murder.'

'Ye Gods! Do you really? By Jove, that's a turn up.'

'It might be as well not to alarm your good lady by telling her that, Major, and it is only a suspicion at the moment. I'm not suggesting that he's a Jack the Ripper, rather that I think he might've murdered a man for a specific reason.'

'I see. What can I do to help?'

'Just keep your eyes open, Major, that's all,' said Hardcastle, as he and Marriott stood up. 'Don't confront him, or ask questions or anything like that. Apart from anything else, I don't want him alerted to our interest, but if you happen to notice something odd, perhaps you'd let me know at Cannon Row police station.'

'Gladly, Inspector,' said Talbot, shaking hands once again.

Marriott was still puzzled by the interview with Major Talbot when he and Hardcastle reached the street.

'We don't seem to have achieved much by talking to the major, sir,' he said.

'On the contrary, Marriott,' said Hardcastle. 'We've cast our bread on the waters. Anyone like Major Talbot who's won a DSO and a Military Cross flying one of them wood and string contraptions on the Western Front will have developed a sharp eye. He'll tell us if he spots anything that's likely to be useful to us.'

Hardcastle settled himself behind his desk, took his pipe from the ashtray, but after a moment's thought replaced it.

'Well, Marriott, so far we've got Lawrence Mortimer taking Mrs Parker out for a spin in his motor car on a Sunday morning. Marcus Sawyer, the solicitor, told Wood that Mortimer claimed to be a corset salesman. Frankly, I don't buy it and nor, would it seem, does Major Talbot. I think it's time we had Mortimer in for a few questions. I want to know how and where he met Mrs Parker, and what he's up to.'

But at that precise moment a knock on Hardcastle's door effectively took that decision out of his hands.

'Good morning, sir.' The smartly dressed man who stood on the threshold was well known to Hardcastle, and his arrival usually presaged something unsettling.

'Bless my soul, Marriott, if it ain't Detective Sergeant Aubrey Drew of Special Branch. I wondered how long it would be before you turned up, Drew.'

'It's Detective *Inspector* Drew now, sir,' said Drew, with a grin.

'Good gracious!' exclaimed Hardcastle. 'What did you have to do for that, Mr Drew? Catch twenty spies, or can you get away with just collaring ten these days?'

'Something along those lines, sir.' Drew glanced at Marriott. 'Good morning, Charlie.'

'Good morning, sir,' said Marriott, acknowledging, at least in Hardcastle's presence, the fact that Drew was now an inspector.

'From what I know of Special Branch, Marriott, one should

always beware of the smile on the face of the tiger.' Hardcastle glanced back at the SB inspector. 'I don't somehow think you just called in to tell us of your good fortune, Mr Drew,' he said.

'Indeed not, sir. Mr Quinn sends his compliments and would be obliged if you'd see him as soon as is convenient.'

'Is it raining, Mr Drew?' asked Hardcastle,

'No, sir,' said Drew, slightly puzzled by the question.

'But one never knows when a sudden squall might occur,' said Hardcastle enigmatically, as he seized his bowler hat and umbrella. He knew that when a superintendent asked a divisional detective inspector to see him as soon as was convenient, it meant immediately. And it usually meant trouble, but just how much trouble he was soon to discover.

FOURTEEN

Leaving the police station, Hardcastle crossed the courtyard and mounted the steps of New Scotland Yard, finally reaching the office of the head of Special Branch.

'Good morning to you, Mr Hardcastle. I shan't keep you a moment.'

Superintendent Patrick Quinn, head of Special Branch for the past fifteen years, was standing behind a huge oak desk set across the corner of the room. He was a tall Irishman of severe countenance, with a grey goatee beard, an aquiline nose and black, bushy eyebrows. For a moment or two, his piercing blue eyes studied the inspector who now stood in front of his desk, before returning to the dossier he had been reading. Eventually closing it, he placed it in the centre of his desk, sat down and surveyed Hardcastle afresh.

'Well now, Mr Hardcastle, I've received disturbing reports that you've been interfering in matters that are rightly the preserve of my Branch.' Although Quinn spoke with a soft Mayo accent, his voice, nonetheless, conveyed an element of menace.

'Not intentionally, sir, I assure you,' said Hardcastle, even though he was aware that his tenacious pursuit of Parker's murderer might have been ruffling some of Scotland Yard's feathers.

'Mrs Mavis Parker of Canbury Park Road, Kingston upon Thames,' said Quinn.

Hardcastle did not immediately reply, thinking that Quinn was about to continue. 'Yes, sir, I'm investigating the murder of her husband,' he said eventually.

'I'm well aware of that, Mr Hardcastle, but why have your men been following her about?'

'When a woman's husband is murdered, sir, I've often found that the widow might've had something to do with it. I was hoping that she might lead us to the killer.' Hardcastle paused. 'If, of course, she was not the murderess herself.' He was at a loss to know how Quinn knew of the observations he had set up. But it was not long before he found out.

'D'you really think that Mrs Parker is capable of shooting a man in the back of the head, tying him up in a sugar sack and throwing him in the river, Inspector?' Quinn asked sarcastically.

'Perhaps not, sir.' Hardcastle was taken aback that the head of Special Branch knew so much about the murder of Ronald Parker.

'No, perhaps not indeed. Those two idiots you sent to carry out surveillance on her last Sunday morning could've seriously compromised a very important operation in which officers of this Branch and MI5 are involved. Standing about, openly writing down the details of Mortimer's car number plate and his description was just about the most crass piece of police work I've come across.'

'If you don't mind me asking, sir, how did you know about that?' Hardcastle was thoroughly shaken by Quinn's continuing revelations.

'Your men were being watched, Mr Hardcastle,' said Quinn, 'but they were too busy engaging in their amateurish antics to realize that they, too, were under surveillance. You should familiarize yourself with the Latin tag *Quis custodiet ipsos custodes*? Loosely translated,' he continued, seeing the look of bewilderment on Hardcastle's face, 'Who will watch the watchers? Or, as I've heard some translate it: Big fleas have little fleas on their backs to bite 'em, and little fleas have smaller fleas, and so on, ad infinitum.'

'I didn't realize, sir,' said Hardcastle lamely. There was little else he could say in the face of Quinn's blunt assessment of the A Division officers' shortcomings.

'Obviously. Well, I can tell you this: throughout your men's cack-handed performance they were being observed by an officer from MI5. He was the same agent, a Captain Gilbert Stroud incidentally, whom another of your officers followed all the way from his home in Kingston to his office in Waterloo House.'

'But I still have to find the murderer of Ronald Parker, sir,' Hardcastle protested mildly.

'I'm aware of that, Mr Hardcastle, but some things take precedence even over murder. Lawrence Mortimer has been under surveillance by officers of Special Branch and MI5 for some considerable time.'

'I see, sir.'

'I'm not sure you do, Mr Hardcastle.' Quinn sighed and opened the dossier in front of him. 'I suppose I'd better acquaint you with the details of the operation, in the strictest confidence, you understand,' he said, staring at Hardcastle with a forbidding expression on his face, daring him not to breathe a word of what he was about to hear.

'Yes, sir,' muttered Hardcastle.

'There is little doubt that Mortimer is a German intelligence agent, but we need more information before he can be arrested,' Quinn continued. 'In fact, we need to catch him *in flagrante delicto*. We now know that he was sent here to garner information about British aeroplanes, and those produced by the Sopwith Aviation Company in particular. But he's only recently begun to take an interest and he befriended Mrs Parker in order to achieve his goal. Mrs Parker quite properly informed her works manager, a Mr Quilter, and he in turn informed us. As a result, Mrs Parker has been working closely with MI5 and ourselves, and has been feeding Mortimer false information that purports to be about prototype aeroplanes.'

'Good grief!' exclaimed Hardcastle, and after a pause, added, 'There is the question of the letter, sir.'

'What letter?'

'A letter was sent from the Ministry of National Service informing Ronald Parker that he was exempt from military service. But it looks as though Parker didn't get it.'

'I really can't explain that, Mr Hardcastle,' said Quinn. 'We

wanted Parker out of the way in case he got too interested in
what his wife was doing. Apparently, he was one of these inquisi-
tive fellows who wanted to know everything his wife was doing.
Consequently when Parker announced that he was going to
Holland it solved the problem. That he didn't receive the letter
was fortuitous.' He paused. 'Of course, we didn't foresee that
he'd be murdered, but the result is the same: he's out of the way.'

'So, where does that leave me with regard to his murder, sir?'
Hardcastle was a hardened and experienced detective, but even
he was astounded that the murder of Parker was regarded as a
satisfactory solution to the sudden and unforeseen problems of
a Special Branch investigation.

'You may continue with your enquiries, Mr Hardcastle, but
neither you nor your officers are to go anywhere near Lawrence
Mortimer or Mavis Parker again. Is that clearly understood?'

'Yes, sir,' said Hardcastle, wondering how he was to conduct
a murder enquiry without speaking to the victim's widow or to
a man he regarded as the principal suspect.

'To that end, Mr Hardcastle, I am assigning Detective Inspector
Drew to your enquiry in order that he might assist you in avoiding
any accidental contact that might further jeopardize this
operation.'

'Very good, sir.' Hardcastle had the distinct feeling that Drew
was being attached to his enquiry for the sole purpose of keeping
a careful eye on everything he did. And to report it to his chief.

'That's all,' said Quinn, closing the dossier.

Aubrey Drew was waiting outside Superintendent Quinn's
office when Hardcastle emerged.

'I understand that I'm to be attached to your enquiry, sir. Is
there anything in particular you want me to do?'

'Yes, Mr Drew, make sure you keep out of my bloody way,'
snapped Hardcastle. It was unfair that his fury at Quinn's treat-
ment of him should be visited on Drew, but he was still seething
at having been spoken to like a trainee detective.

'Come in the office, Marriott, *now*!' bellowed Hardcastle, as he
passed the door to the detectives' office.

'Sir?' Marriott hurried after the DDI.

'Mr Drew has been attached to us for the duration of our
enquiry into the murder of Ronald Parker.'

'Why's that, sir?' Marriott was completely mystified at this latest twist.

'I'm not allowed to tell you, Marriott. It seems that the likes of you and me ain't to be trusted. However, now that we've got time on our hands, we'll take an interest in this here Vincent Powers what's taken a fancy to Daisy Benson.'

'Is there anything I can do in that connection, sir?' asked Drew. He had a high regard for Hardcastle and was embarrassed that Superintendent Quinn had put him in the difficult position of virtually monitoring every movement that the DDI made. It was made no easier that Hardcastle was senior to him in rank.

'Come to think of it, Mr Drew, it so happens there is.' Hardcastle explained what was known so far of both Daisy Benson and Vincent Powers. 'I should think that you're quite good at passing yourself off as a stage-door Johnny, Mr Drew. I'd be obliged if you'd see fit to make a few enquiries at the Alhambra Palace in Leicester Square and see what's known of the man.'

'I'll certainly do what I can, sir.' Although such enquiries were outside his remit, Drew felt that he had to make some contribution to Hardcastle's enquiry, if only to placate him. 'I'll get on to it straight away, sir.'

Once Drew had left, Hardcastle invited Marriott to take a seat.

'Now that Mr Drew's out of our hair for a bit, Marriott, m'boy, I can tell you what's what.' And despite Quinn's caveat about secrecy, Hardcastle proceeded to tell his sergeant all that he had learned from the Special Branch chief, being careful to leave out those parts of the conversation that had left the DDI feeling like a complete Dogberry.

'That sort of puts the kibosh on our enquiries, guv'nor,' said Marriott. 'How can we possibly find out who killed Parker without talking to his missus?'

'There are ways and means, m'boy,' said Hardcastle mysteriously. 'In the meantime, we'll adjourn to the Red Lion for a pint and a fourpenny cannon. I've got a nasty taste in my mouth that I need to get rid of.'

It was four o'clock when Aubrey Drew returned to Cannon Row police station.

'I had a very interesting discussion with the stage-door keeper at the Alhambra, sir. However, Powers isn't there any longer.'

'Take a seat, Mr Drew, and tell me what you've found out.'
Hardcastle reached forward and took his pipe out of the ashtray.

'It would seem that Vincent Powers is a South African, but he
was not at all liked by the rest of the cast. The play is called
The Bing Boys on Broadway and I was told that Powers was
understudying George Robey, but seemed to think that he
should've been treated as if he were the star. As a matter of fact,
the stage-door keeper described Powers as a pompous arse. From
what I could gather, he has only been in this country for a matter
of weeks. At least, that's when he first appeared in the show. But
no one seemed to know where he'd come from, other than to
suggest it was probably South Africa, or precisely when.'

'You said he was no longer at the Alhambra, Mr Drew. Why
is that?'

'According to my information, sir,' said Drew doubtfully, 'and
I have to admit that it's somewhat tenuous, his first appearance
as Robey's understudy was in a Wednesday matinee. But
he wasn't a patch on Robey and was booed off the stage. The
management had to give the audience its money back.'

'Not surprising, Mr Drew,' said Hardcastle. 'They call George
Robey the Prime Minister of Mirth and to coin an apt phrase,
he'd be a hard act to follow.'

'Frankly, sir, I have a problem believing that story. It was, I
suspect, second-hand backstage tittle-tattle.'

'You're probably right, Mr Drew. It seems unlikely that a man
could arrive out of the blue, so to speak, and straightaway land
a part as George Robey's understudy. Did anyone know if Powers
got another part anywhere after he was sacked?'

'No, sir, but I've got one or two contacts in the theatrical world
and I'll see what I can find out.'

'Good, but make it sooner rather than later, eh?'

The following morning found Hardcastle devouring his usual
gargantuan breakfast without which, he claimed, he could not
face a day's work. Despite the shortages occasioned by the war,
Alice Hardcastle still managed to serve him two fried eggs,
several rashers of bacon, a few pieces of fried bread and a couple
of sausages. This was followed by two slices of toast and marma-
lade, washed down with three cups of tea. Hardcastle half
suspected that such supplies were made available to his wife

because she was married to a senior police officer, but he thought it unwise to enquire too deeply into such matters.

Breakfast was interrupted by a clatter from the hall as the morning newspaper was pushed through the letter box.

'About time,' muttered Hardcastle, rising from the table. He walked into the hall and returned with a copy of the *Daily Mail*. 'That paper boy gets later every day. I don't know what the world's coming to.' He continued to grumble until settling himself at the table again.

'I'm very glad I don't work for you, Ernest Hardcastle,' said Alice. 'Do you carry on like that all day at your police station? If you do, I feel sorry for the men who have the misfortune to work for you.'

Hardcastle adopted a stoic indifference to his wife's comments, knowing that it could develop into an argument he could not win, and propped the newspaper against a bottle of tomato ketchup.

'Mind you don't knock that bottle over, Ernie. You haven't put the cap on, and as the price of it has gone up to one and tenpence a bottle, I can't afford to waste any.'

'It says here that we fired eighty-five tons of phosgene gas near St Quentin and killed two hundred and fifty Germans,' said Hardcastle, studiously avoiding any discussion about what he regarded as domestic trivia. 'That'll teach 'em. Mind you, now that the Russians have packed it in, the Germans are sending all their troops from the eastern front to the west. Still, now we've got the Americans on our side, they'll soon finish off the Hun.' Hardcastle had no idea, however, that the following day would see the start of a massive German counter-attack on the Somme that would result in the enemy pushing forward four and a half miles and capturing 21,000 British troops. He folded the newspaper and took it with him into the hall. Donning his hat and coat and picking up his umbrella, he pecked his wife on the cheek. 'See you tonight, love.'

Alice heard the front door slam with a feeling of relief. Her husband was always in an irascible mood when he had a difficult murder to solve. What she did not know was that Hardcastle was still smarting from Superintendent Quinn's condescending and critical remarks of the previous day.

*　　*　　*

Hardcastle's mood had not lightened by the time he arrived at the tram stop. If anything, it had been worsened by the lateness of the tram – fifteen minutes – and the surliness of its conductor when Hardcastle complained about the service.

'You might not have noticed, guv'nor,' the conductor had said, 'but there's a bloody war on.'

Alighting at Clock Tower, better known to the world as Big Ben, Hardcastle marched down Cannon Row and into the police station.

'All correct, sir,' said the station officer, as the DDI swept in.

'Anything been put in the crime book overnight?' Hardcastle asked.

'Yes, sir. A man was arrested attempting to break into one of the houses in Lower Belgrave Street last night. He was spotted on top of the portico by a patrolling PC.'

'Good,' said Hardcastle. 'Anything else?'

'Not one for the crime book, sir, but a man, name of George Huggins, was caught in the grounds of Buckingham Palace. The Buck House inspector took the usual action under the Lunacy Act and deemed him of unsound mind.'

'Quite right,' said Hardcastle. It was standard police practice to deal with such trespassers in that way, rather than generating unwanted publicity for the Royal Family by suggesting that intruders were potential assassins.

'Huggins will appear before the justices in lunacy in three days' time,' continued the station officer. 'He reckoned he'd made a mistake and thought he was breaking into one of the big houses in Grosvenor Gardens.'

'Well, he was right, wasn't he? You've quite made my day, Skipper,' said Hardcastle, and was still chuckling when he arrived at the top of the stairs.

'Good morning, sir.' Detective Inspector Drew was waiting outside Hardcastle's office door.

'Good morning, Mr Drew. Come in and take a seat. What news?'

'I've found out a little more about Vincent Powers, sir. As I'd anticipated, he wasn't an understudy to George Robey at all, but merely had a non-speaking walk-on part. And, as I thought, the story about the audience being given its money back because of Powers' poor performance was all my eye and Betty Martin. The truth of the matter is that the safety curtain jammed and the performance had to be cancelled.'

'Yes, that's a much more likely reason,' said Hardcastle. 'Why was he sacked, then? I presume he did get sacked.'

'Indeed he was, sir. Apparently he got a bit fresh with one of the girls in the chorus and she complained to the producer. The producer told Powers that extras were two a penny and showed him the door.'

'Seems our Vincent Powers is something of a ladies' man, Mr Drew.'

'So it would seem, sir. However,' continued Drew, 'I spoke to my contact at *The Stage*, the acting profession's trade periodical, but they've no record of Powers having placed an advertisement with the paper. It's the sort of thing that a resting actor will do, especially if he arrives from abroad. In fact, no one in the acting business seems to have heard of him, apart from the people at the Alhambra. Anyway, my contact has promised to let me know if he hears anything.'

'Thank you, Mr Drew. It sounds to me as though this man is nothing more than someone who puts these tales about in order to impress a woman. But he has a large house on Kingston Hill, an expensive motor car, and employs servants. If the stage is not his main source of income, I wonder where his money comes from. I think that Marriott and I will have another word with Daisy Benson about Powers and then waste no more time on him.'

FIFTEEN

'Why are we so interested in this Vincent Powers, sir?' asked Marriott as he and Hardcastle left Kingston railway station. 'Surely he's just another of Daisy Benson's clients.'

'Very likely, Marriott,' said Hardcastle, as he engaged a cab from the rank outside the station, 'but anybody who was acquainted with Ronald Parker, however loosely, might just lead us to his murderer. And Daisy, it seems, knew both Parker and Powers; that's the connection. It's one of the principles of criminal investigation to tie up loose ends. I'd've thought you would've known that, Marriott.'

'Yes, I see, sir,' said Marriott, following the DDI into the cab. It was yet another of his chief's little homilies on murder that he received from time to time. But he still could not see the point of pursuing Powers. However, he would be the first to admit that Hardcastle's enigmatic whims often produced a satisfactory result.

As the two detectives alighted from the cab in Gordon Road, a man left Daisy Benson's house.

'Ah, Mr Smith, we meet again,' said Hardcastle jocularly, as he recognized the man he had seen on his last visit, and whom Daisy had said was a lodger. 'Don't be late for work at the income tax office.'

Smith laughed nervously and scurried down the road without a word or a backward glance.

There was some delay before Mrs Benson answered the door. And when she did, she was barefooted and wearing nothing but a peignoir, and her long hair was loose around her shoulders.

'Oh, it's you, Inspector. I do apologize for my appearance, but I've just had a bath.' But despite the excuse, Daisy Benson seemed more embarrassed by Hardcastle's arrival than was justified.

'May we come in?' asked Hardcastle, as he raised his hat. 'We just bumped into one of your, er, paying guests,' he said. 'Works at the tax office, I think you said.'

'Oh, yes, that was Mr Jones. He comes and goes at odd hours,' said Daisy, clearly flustered. 'You'd better come in, Inspector.' She showed them into the parlour.

'It's a cold day, Mrs Benson,' said Hardcastle. 'Wouldn't you like to get dressed before we have our little chat?'

'Yes, of course. I won't keep you a moment.' With undisguised relief, Daisy Benson hurried from the room.

'She seems a busy woman, Marriott.' There was an element of sarcasm in Hardcastle's voice as he warmed his hands in front of the fire and then sat down.

When Daisy Benson returned she was wearing a peach-coloured day dress, and her hair was swept up and secured with a comb at the back.

'Now, Inspector, you said you wanted to talk to me.' Daisy seemed more relaxed now that she was decently attired.

'I'll not beat about the bush, Mrs Benson. How much did Ronald Parker pay you for his favours or, for that matter, Mr Jones? Or even Mr Smith?'

Daisy gazed at Hardcastle, a stunned expression on her face and her colour rose rapidly. 'Ooh, you are a wag, Inspector,' she said eventually, in a desperate attempt to make light of the DDI's blatant accusation. 'Are you suggesting that I'm a loose woman?'

'As I said just now, Mrs Benson, we met one of your lodgers on our way in. You said his name was Jones, but the last time we were here you said his name was Smith.'

'They come and go so often that I get them mixed up,' said Daisy lamely, not realizing that her comment was capable of misinterpretation. She put her hand down the side of a cushion and produced a fan with which she proceeded vigorously to cool herself. 'I've got a Mr Smith *and* a Mr Jones staying here.'

'And what about Vincent Powers?' asked Marriott quietly.

'Who?'

'Don't pretend you don't know who I'm talking about, Mrs Benson. We saw you get into his car after Ronald Parker's funeral last Wednesday. It was a Hispano-Suiza if I remember correctly, and the two of you seemed very affectionate.'

'Oh, *that* Mr Powers, yes. He's a friend of mine.'

'So it would appear,' said Hardcastle. 'So friendly, in fact, that you stayed the night at his house.' That was supposition on the DDI's part, but from what Wilmot had told him he thought it was a safe assumption.

'Well, I am a widow, after all, Inspector,' said Daisy defensively, 'and I don't see that there's anything wrong in having a man friend. I'm what you might call a free spirit.'

Hardcastle took out his pipe and held it up. 'D'you mind if I smoke?' he asked.

'Not at all. I like the aroma of tobacco smoke.' Daisy seemed relieved now that Hardcastle appeared to be veering away from the subject of Vincent Powers, but in that she was mistaken.

'I'm going to be quite honest with you, Mrs Benson . . .' began Hardcastle, once his pipe was satisfactorily alight. 'I could arrange to have this house kept under observation and it would not take me long to prove that you're engaged in prostitution . . .' He held up his hand as Daisy appeared about to protest. 'But I don't intend to do anything about it provided you're willing to cooperate with me.'

'What is it that you want of me, then, Inspector?' Daisy leaned back against the cushions of the sofa on which she was sitting and her shoulders slumped in an attitude of capitulation.

'I want you to tell me all you know about Vincent Powers. Furthermore, you are not to say anything about this to Mr Powers, or I most definitely will come after you.'

'I don't know about you, Inspector, but I could do with a drink. D'you fancy one?'

'No thank you, but don't let me stop you.' Hardcastle imagined that Daisy Benson's sudden need of a drink was merely a device to allow her to marshal her thoughts.

Daisy crossed to a small cabinet. With a shaking hand, she poured an inch of gin into a glass and topped it up with water from a jug that was standing on a nearby table.

'I met Vincent at the Kingston Empire,' she said, sitting down again. 'It was one of those variety shows with lots of turns, jugglers and escapologists, and that sort of thing. Oh, and there was a woman dressed as a soldier singing songs popular with the troops—'

'Can we get to the point, Mrs Benson?' interrupted Hardcastle.

'Oh, yes, of course. Well, Vincent was the chairman introducing the acts. He wasn't very good at it, though. He kept forgetting who he was supposed to introduce and had to keep looking at his script. But he did manage to cover it up well.'

'When did this performance take place, Mrs Benson?' asked Marriott.

'It was the second week in February I think,' said Daisy. 'He was only there for the one week. I love those shows and one of my friends had treated me to a seat in a box, so that I was close to where Vincent was sitting at the side of the stage. I was there on the Friday, and he kept looking at me and winking. Well, after the last but one act, he slipped me a note asking me to meet him after the show for a drink in the lounge at the Kingston Hotel. It's almost next door to the theatre.'

'And presumably you took up his offer.'

'Yes, I did. Why not? He seemed a nice man and funny too, when he remembered his lines. Anyway, he not only bought me a drink, but dinner as well.'

'Was he staying at the hotel, Mrs Benson?' asked Marriott.

'Yes, as a matter of fact, he was.'

'And you stayed the night with him, I suppose,' suggested Hardcastle.

'Why not? I'm a single woman now. In fact, we're both single people.' Daisy raised her head and stared defiantly at Hardcastle, as if to imply that there was no impropriety in her liaison with Powers.

'Where did he go after the show at the Kingston Empire finished?'

'I think he said something about looking for a part somewhere. He mentioned that he was really a Shakespearian actor, but had taken the job of chairman at a variety show as a stopgap.'

'He seems to be a rich man,' said Hardcastle, dismissing Powers' claim to be a classical actor as an attempt to impress. 'Surely he doesn't depend on the theatre for an income if he's only working from time to time.'

'He has a private income,' said Daisy, finishing her gin and crossing to the cabinet for a refill. 'At least, that's what he said.'

'I understand that he's a South African,' said Marriott, as the woman resumed her seat. 'Is that where his money comes from?'

'I suppose it must do. He told me that he's got business interests there. He said something about having mined diamonds in some place called Kimberley and making a lot of money. But he really wanted to be an actor and that's why he came to England. He said there's not much in the way of decent theatres in South Africa. Not that I would know.'

'Did you mention any of this to your friend Ronald?' asked Hardcastle.

'I might've said something about it,' said Daisy in an offhand manner as she glanced out of the window.

'I think the fact of the matter is that you told Ronald Parker quite a lot about Vincent Powers, Mrs Benson,' said Hardcastle. 'And did you tell Powers about Ronald Parker?'

'Yes. I told Vincent that I had this good friend Ronald, and that he was a company director and very rich.' Daisy Benson smiled. 'I wanted to make Vincent jealous, you see, and I think I did. He was certainly much more attentive after that. And very generous.'

'Are you seeing Powers again?'

'Is there any reason why I shouldn't?' demanded Daisy, with a toss of her head.

'Well, don't forget what I said. You're not to breathe a word to him about our conversation.'

'If you say so.' Daisy Benson was clearly irritated by

Hardcastle's admonition, but was in no doubt that he meant what he had said about prosecuting her if she failed to keep her word.

'We'll see ourselves out, Mrs Benson,' said Hardcastle, as he and Marriott rose to leave. 'And thank you for your assistance.'

'Oh, it's my pleasure, Inspector,' said Daisy, but her response had a sarcastic and hollow ring to it.

'D'you think she is running a knocking shop, sir?' asked Marriott, as he and Hardcastle walked down Gordon Road towards the railway station.

'I neither know nor care, Marriott, and I doubt that the subdivisional inspector at Kingston would waste time on it with a war on and Sopwith Aviation on his patch.'

'Back to the office, then, sir?'

'Not until we've had a word with the manager of the Kingston Hotel, Marriott.'

'It struck me as odd, sir,' said Marriott, 'that a man who's got a house on Kingston Hill and a motor car should take rooms at a hotel in the same town.'

'Not odd at all, Marriott,' said Hardcastle. 'He saw an opportunity to bed a willing woman and didn't want to waste time taking her back to Kingston Hill. I'll put money on it having been a last minute booking and for one night only.'

The Kingston Hotel was an old-established hostelry that had opened its doors some forty years previously. It boasted 25 bedrooms, a large assembly room, a billiard room, public coffee rooms and a coffee lounge for ladies.

'I want to speak to the manager,' announced Hardcastle, marching up to a man seated behind a desk on which was a small sign indicating that it was the concierge's station.

'He's very busy, sir. Is there something I can assist you with?'

'No,' said Hardcastle. 'I'm a police officer and I need to see him now.'

'Very good, sir. If you care to wait a moment, I'll see if he's free.' The concierge picked up a telephone and asked for the manager's office. After relaying Hardcastle's request, he replaced the receiver. 'The manager will be with you directly, sir,' he said.

The man who appeared from a door at the rear of the reception area was tall and immaculately attired in morning dress.

'I understand that you're from the police,' he said in somewhat condescending tones.

'I'm Divisional Detective Inspector Hardcastle of the Whitehall Division and this is Detective Sergeant Marriott. I'm investigating a murder, so perhaps we could go somewhere less public.'

'Yes, of course, Inspector,' said the manager, becoming immediately more conciliatory. 'My name is Webb, by the way, Horace Webb,' he added, as he led the way into his office. It was a comfortably furnished room with a large desk and easy chairs. Hardcastle wondered how many times it had witnessed an uncompromising interview between the manager and those of the hotel's guests who were a little tardy in settling their accounts.

'I understand that a Mr Vincent Powers stayed here during the second week in February, Mr Webb,' said Hardcastle.

'Powers, Powers,' said Webb reflectively. 'I can't say that I recall the name. One moment.' He lifted the receiver of his telephone and posed the question to the person who answered. After a moment or two's pause, he replaced the receiver. 'You're quite correct, Inspector. Mr Powers took a room for one night only on the eighth of February last. I'm told he was a theatrical gentleman.' There was an element of disdain in Webb's statement, as though accepting members of the acting profession as guests was an imposition that hotels like this one had to tolerate. 'It's one of the drawbacks of being situated almost next door to the Kingston Empire,' he added, confirming the impression he had conveyed.

'Just the one night, you said?'

'That's correct, Inspector.'

'Told you so, Marriott,' said Hardcastle in an aside to his sergeant.

'Did he have anyone staying with him, Mr Webb?' asked Marriott, even though Daisy Benson had admitted spending the night there with Powers.

'Someone staying with him?' Webb sounded shocked at the very idea. 'I'm told that the reservation was for the one gentleman, although he did order dinner for two in the brasserie.'

'I've been told that he shared the room with a lady that night,' said Hardcastle, purely out of devilment. 'A lady who was not his wife.'

'I'm sure that you were misinformed, Inspector,' protested Webb. 'This is a most respectable establishment.'

'As a matter of fact, it was the lady who spent the night here with Mr Powers who told me,' said Hardcastle mildly. 'What's more we believe her to be a prostitute,' he added, just for the fun of it.

Webb's mouth opened and then closed. 'I, well, I'm . . . I mean that I'm shocked that such a thing could have taken place in this hotel, Inspector.'

'It's of no consequence, at least not to me,' continued Hardcastle, now thoroughly enjoying the hotel manager's discomfort. 'My real interest is in Vincent Powers.'

'Oh my God, you're not suggesting that he's a murderer, surely? You did say you were investigating a murder.'

'I'm not suggesting anything, Mr Webb. I'm just interested in the man because it's possible that he has vital information that could assist the police in their enquiries,' responded Hardcastle blandly.

'Oh, I see.' Webb appeared relieved. 'How can I help you, then?'

'Is there a member of your staff, a floor waiter perhaps, who provided room service for Mr Powers?'

'I'll find out.' Once again, Webb turned to his telephone and conducted a brief conversation. A few minutes later, a waiter appeared in the office.

'You wanted me, sir?'

'Yes, Hubbard, perhaps you can assist this police officer. He's making enquiries about a Mr Vincent Powers who was a guest here on the night of the eighth of February.'

'Oh, I do remember that gentleman, sir,' said the waiter warmly.

'Why particularly do you remember him, Mr Hubbard?' asked Hardcastle.

'He was a very generous gentleman, sir,' said Hubbard, glancing nervously at the manager. 'I took him a bottle of champagne, the Pol Roger 1906 – that costs seventeen shillings and sixpence a bottle here in the hotel – and caviar, sir. He tipped me a five-pound note and asked me to ensure that he wasn't disturbed, sir.'

'What time was this?'

'About ten o'clock, sir. In the evening, of course.'

'Was there a young lady in the apartment, Mr Hubbard?' asked Marriott.

'I didn't see one, sir, but Mr Powers did ask for two glasses when he ordered the champagne.'

'Thank you, Mr Hubbard,' said Hardcastle. 'You've been most helpful.' He turned to the manager after Hubbard had been dismissed, and added, 'I'll not trouble you further, Mr Webb.'

'I hope you don't think that this hotel makes a habit of allowing loose women on its premises, Inspector.' By the tenor of his response, Webb was very concerned about his licence and the reputation of his establishment.

'Your secret's safe with me, Mr Webb,' said Hardcastle.

But he could only guess at how uncomfortable for the unfortunate Hubbard would be his interview with Webb, for failing to report that two glasses had been ordered with champagne destined for a room occupied by one man.

'Did we really learn anything from yesterday's talk with Daisy Benson, sir?' The following morning, Marriott was discussing the case with Hardcastle in the latter's office at Cannon Row police station. 'Or from what Hubbard, the floor waiter at the hotel, told us?'

'I think we did, Marriott,' said Hardcastle thoughtfully. He sat back in his chair, puffing contentedly at his pipe. 'There are two things that interest me. Firstly, Powers has a lot of money and I don't think that this story about diamond mines in South Africa holds much water. It's all flimflam in my opinion and I think that Powers is a villain, a confidence trickster most likely. Secondly, Daisy Benson said that she'd mentioned Ronald Parker to Powers, but I think she told him an awful lot about Parker. God knows why, though. So, I ask myself, is there a connection between Powers and Parker?'

'What sort of connection were you thinking about, sir?' By now, Marriott was completely mystified by the DDI's line of reasoning, the more so as he kept harping on the fact that Daisy Benson knew both men: Powers and the victim.

'I don't know, Marriott, and it's probably nothing. After all, I can't see an unfit, mild-mannered gas company clerk getting mixed up with Powers except through Daisy Benson, and she's the only link. And as she seems to have a lot of so-called lodgers, I don't think there's much to be gained from pursuing it. It's a coincidence.'

But Hardcastle's contradictory arguments with himself were interrupted by the arrival of Aubrey Drew.

'Sorry to intrude, sir.'

'What is it, Mr Drew?'

'Superintendent Quinn would like a few words at your convenience, sir.'

'Any idea what it's about, Mr Drew?'

'I'm afraid not, sir. Mr Quinn doesn't generally confide in the messenger,' said Drew, risking a grin.

'I suppose I'd better see him now, then. In the meantime, Mr Drew, there is something that you might be able to do for me.'

'What's that, sir?'

'This man Powers . . .' Hardcastle went on to explain what he and Marriott had learned from their interviews with Daisy Benson and the staff of the Kingston Hotel. 'Seeing as how you're an accomplished Special Branch inspector with fingers in all sorts of pies, so to speak, do you know any South African diplomats? I suppose they must have some sort of office here. But it would have to be someone who might be able to shed some light on whether there's any truth in this diamond story that Powers is putting about, or whether he was known there as an actor.'

'I do have one or two contacts at the legation who might be able to help, sir.' Drew glanced at his watch. 'I'll get up to Morley's Hotel right now. It's only a short walk.'

'What's Morley's Hotel got to do with it?' Hardcastle wondered if this was yet another Special Branch smokescreen designed to cover the truth.

'It's where the South African legation people have taken rooms, sir, pending the acquisition of proper accommodation for their high commission.'

'Is that so? Well, I can't be expected to know what happens on Bow Street's ground,' grumbled Hardcastle, mildly irritated by what Drew had just told him. Although it was true that Morley's Hotel was on E Division, it was immediately adjacent to Trafalgar Square and, therefore, only a matter of a couple of yards outside Hardcastle's area of responsibility. He was, nevertheless, annoyed at being unaware that South African diplomats had offices there.

'Any idea why your guv'nor is so interested in Vincent Powers, Charlie?' asked Drew, once Hardcastle had left for his interview

with the head of Special Branch. 'As far as I can make out, the
man's only a jobbing actor with a good conceit of himself.'

'Not really, Aubrey,' said Marriott. 'From what he was saying
just now, I thought he'd given up on Powers, but he does sometimes come up with an idea that solves a murder for him. In fact,
it's more often than just sometimes.'

'I've asked to see you, Mr Hardcastle, because I think it is necessary to tell you that yesterday evening my officers arrested
Lawrence Mortimer for spying. It has been established that his
real name is Gerhard von Kleiber and he holds the rank of
Hauptmann in the German Army.'

'That must be a very rewarding result, sir.'

'Yes, it is. Mrs Parker informed us that she was meeting von
Kleiber at the roller skating rink in order to hand him some of
the falsified documents prepared by MI5. It was most fortunate
that when he was detained by my officers he also had photographs
of the naval installations at Portsmouth Harbour in his possession.' In a rare display of humour, Quinn chuckled and then
added, 'And one of the photographs he took at Portsmouth was
of Nelson's flagship HMS *Victory*. I just hope that he thought it
was one of our latest dreadnoughts. However,' he continued,
becoming serious once more, 'I've not brought you here to tell
you that. It means that you're now free to interview Mrs Parker
at any time you wish.'

'Thank you, sir, that'll be a great help.' Hardcastle paused at
the door. 'What will happen to Mortimer, sir?'

'He'll be shot early one morning at the Tower of London, Mr
Hardcastle,' said Quinn, as though a trial was a mere formality.

'Shot, sir? Not hanged? I thought spies were hanged.'

'No, von Kleiber will be shot. It's one of the privileges of
being an army officer. By the way,' continued Quinn, dismissing
Kleiber's fate as a mere bagatelle, 'you can send Mr Drew back
immediately.'

'Very good, sir.' Hardcastle thought it unwise to explain that
he had just sent Drew on an errand unconnected to his proper
duties. But he was saved from doing so by Quinn's next remark.

'On second thoughts, tomorrow morning will do.'

SIXTEEN

Detective Inspector Charles Stockley Collins, the fingerprint expert, was waiting for Hardcastle when he returned from his interview with Quinn.

'I've got the results of my examination of the letter about Parker's exemption that you found in his piano, Ernie, such as they are.'

'Anything that's likely to help me, Charlie?'

'I took dabs from Parker's body when he was taken into the mortuary and I can tell you that they're definitely not on the letter.'

'So he hadn't seen it,' reflected Hardcastle. 'That would explain why he told his wife that was he trying to get to Holland.'

'But there are four other sets on the letter, as yet unidentified.'

Hardcastle thought about that for a moment. 'Well,' he said, 'the most likely other people who could have handled it are Mrs Parker, Makepeace at the Ministry of National Service and maybe his clerk or whoever put it in the envelope. But the fourth set . . .?' He sighed at the endless options. 'Possibly they belong to the murderer, but I doubt that I'd be that lucky.'

'What would you like me to do, then, Ernie?'

'Could you get one of your assistants to take the prints of Makepeace and his clerk? The Ministry of National Service's offices are in St James's Square. And then there's Mrs Parker at Kingston, but they might be on record.'

'Not in my collection they're not, Ernie,' said Collins adamantly, as though Hardcastle had accused him of an oversight.

'No, I didn't suppose they would be, but I think I might know where they are,' said Hardcastle mysteriously. 'But I'm not allowed to tell you, Charlie,' he added, with a laugh.

Collins laughed too, but saw through Hardcastle's secrecy immediately. 'Have you been mixing with Special Branch again, Ernie?'

'Something like that,' said Hardcastle.

'All right, Ernie, leave it with me.'

*　　*　　*

It was late afternoon when Drew returned.

'I got an answer of sorts about Powers, sir.'

'Sit down, Mr Drew.' Hardcastle closed the docket he was reading and pushed it aside.

'I don't know whether this will be of any assistance, sir, but my contact at the South African legation was very interested in Vincent Powers. Although the name of Powers was not familiar to him, he drew my attention to a man called Jan de Ritzen who is wanted by the South African Police for the murder of a British officer in Kimberley. And a warrant for his arrest has been issued in Bloemfontein.'

'What does any of this have to do with Powers, Mr Drew?' asked Hardcastle. 'Although Daisy Benson said that Powers had mentioned something about mining diamonds in Kimberley.'

'That more or less confirms what I was told, sir,' said Drew. 'From the description of Powers and his way of life that I was able to give my contact, he seemed to think that de Ritzen and Powers might be one and the same. When diamonds were first discovered in Kimberley there was a rush and all manner of people turned up hoping to make their fortune. It seemed that de Ritzen was one of the men who made a great deal of money. But "The Rush", as it was called, also attracted a large number of undesirables, including a small army of prostitutes.'

'Can we get to the point, Mr Drew,' said Hardcastle impatiently.

'Apparently there was some dispute between de Ritzen and the British officer, a Captain Angus Sinclair of the Black Watch, over a quantity of diamonds that Sinclair maintained were his. Apparently, British officers were allowed to stake a claim after the war was over, and Captain Sinclair made such a claim. But there was a heated argument over whether de Ritzen's diamonds were his own or Sinclair's. Apparently their claims bordered each other. However, that proved to be of little consequence compared with a later argument that arose between the two over a prostitute named Dolores de Wet, a white Afrikaans woman. Both men were having intimate relations with the woman, and to cut a long story short de Ritzen is alleged to have murdered Sinclair in a drunken rage of jealousy before fleeing South Africa with a quantity of diamonds. He has not been seen since.'

'There's not much evidence there to prove that Powers and de Ritzen are the same man, though, is there?'

'The only other connection, sir, is that de Ritzen was very keen on amateur dramatics and often talked of one day becoming a professional actor, going to Cape Town and opening a theatre. However, the police in Cape Town made enquiries, but could find no trace of him.'

Hardcastle leaned back in his chair, placed his hands behind his head and contemplated his nicotine-stained ceiling for some time. Then he shot forward. 'If Powers *is* de Ritzen,' he said, 'it's also possible that he murdered Ronald Parker, although I can't see what reason he could have had for killing him except jealousy. And if he's murdered once over a woman, he might've done it again. In my book, Mr Drew,' he said, 'once a murderer always a murderer. A leopard don't change his spots, so to speak.'

'I suppose that's a possibility, sir.' Although Drew was a very good Special Branch officer, he would have been the first to admit that he did not know a great deal about the finer points of murder investigation.

'By the way, Mr Drew, Superintendent Quinn wants you back again tomorrow morning. I suppose you've heard that Lawrence Mortimer was arrested for spying yesterday.'

'Yes, I did know that, sir.'

'Thought you might,' murmured Hardcastle. 'But there is something you can do for me. I've no doubt that Mortimer's fingerprints were taken when he was arrested, but is it likely that Mrs Parker's fingerprints were also taken when she was set up to trap Mortimer? I imagine it would've been done for the purposes of elimination when the documents Mrs Parker handed to Mortimer were examined.'

'I'd say it was highly likely, sir. I'll find out for you. I imagine that you'd like to know as soon as possible.'

'Yes, I would. Perhaps if there is such a set, you could hand them to Detective Inspector Collins of the Fingerprint Bureau, together with Mortimer's.'

'I'll get on to it straightaway, sir,' said Drew. 'I presume it's something to do with the letter you found in Ronald Parker's piano.'

'There's not much as misses you Special Branch fellows, is there, Mr Drew?'

'We like to think so, sir,' said Drew.

Hardcastle went home and for most of that Thursday evening mulled over the possibility that Powers was, after all, the murderer of Ronald Parker. But he could not think of any motive other than that Powers had had an affair with Daisy Benson. And the only connection between Powers and Ronald Parker was that Parker had also shared Daisy's bed. However, it was more than likely that Daisy had abandoned Parker in exchange for Powers' opulence. There was not much competition between a gas company clerk and a man who lavished dinner, champagne and caviar on his paramours in fine hotels.

Bearing in mind what Detective Inspector Drew had said about de Ritzen being wanted for a murder that had arisen over a prostitute, it was possible that history had repeated itself. But that would only hold good if Powers *was* de Ritzen.

Hardcastle was still fretting over the matter when he arrived at Cannon Row police station on the Friday morning. But at nine o'clock he made a decision.

'Marriott!' shouted Hardcastle.

'Yes, sir?' Marriott hurried across the corridor to the DDI's office.

Hardcastle recounted what he had learned from Aubrey Drew the previous day. 'It's possible that Powers is our man for Parker's murder after all, Marriott. If he ain't, we might still have him for Captain Sinclair's murder in South Africa if he turns out to be de Ritzen.'

'But what if Powers is *not* de Ritzen, sir?'

'We'll cross that bridge when we come to it, Marriott.'

'Is there a warrant out for this de Ritzen, sir?'

'I'm told there is, Marriott,' said Hardcastle, without mentioning that the warrant was in Bloemfontein. 'So, get up to Bow Street as soon as they open for business and swear out a search warrant for Vincent Powers' address on Kingston Hill. Once you've done that, we'll get down there and see what's what. Oh, and let Kingston nick know, and ask them to send a couple of officers up to assist.'

* * *

Apart from Hardcastle's interest in Powers, other events were
unfolding on that Friday morning. Some fifty miles away at
Aldershot, Private Eric Donnelly of the Dorsetshire Regiment
was tried by general court martial. Two days later, he was
executed by a firing squad in the yard of the feared military
prison at North Camp. Sergeant Mooney would doubtless have
been disappointed that Donnelly had not met his end at the
Tower of London.

It was close to three o'clock that afternoon when the two detectives alighted from a taxi outside Powers' house.

'Mr Hardcastle, sir?' asked a uniformed sergeant who, together
with a constable, was waiting in the road a few yards down from
the house. 'We were told you might need some assistance.'

'Wait out here until I've gone in, Sergeant, and then come up
to the front door and stay there,' said Hardcastle. 'I'll call you
when I need you.' Mounting the steps, he rapped loudly with the
heavy lion's-head knocker.

'Good afternoon, sir,' said the housemaid, bobbing as
she answered the door.

'Good afternoon. Is Mr Powers at home?'

'I'll enquire, sir. May I say who it is?'

'We're from the London Theatrical Casting Agency, miss.'
Hardcastle told the lie with a reassuring smile. He knew that if
he and Marriott were to be announced as police officers, Powers
– if he was de Ritzen, the killer of Sinclair and Parker – would
disappear, probably through a rear window, never to be seen
again. Worse still he might confront them with a gun, and
Hardcastle had no desire to repeat what had happened when he
arrested Eric Donnelly alias Wilfred Rudd.

'Please come in.' Having admitted the two detectives, the maid
disappeared into a room at the rear of the large hall.

Moments later, a man emerged from the back room. A shade
over six foot tall, he was of portly appearance, and had a florid
countenance and flowing hair not unlike that of the Shakespearian
actor he had claimed to be when he met Daisy Benson.
Hardcastle's estimation of Powers' age, when he had caught a
brief sight of him driving Daisy Benson away from Ronald
Parker's funeral, put him at about forty. Closer examination
confirmed that original estimate.

'Good afternoon, gentlemen. I am Vincent Powers.' The man spoke with a deep and resonant voice, but there was no disguising his South African accent. 'Violet tells me that you're casting agents.' He opened his arms in an expansive gesture of welcome that added to his theatrical persona.

'That's not quite correct, Mr Powers, we're police officers,' said Hardcastle.

'*Police officers!*' Clearly outraged, Powers shouted the words, all pretence at bonhomie vanishing in an instant. 'What the hell d'you mean by coming into my house by telling lies to my maidservant? I shall make a very strong complaint. In any case, I can't possibly imagine what the police would want of me.'

'I have a warrant issued by the Bow Street magistrate to search these premises,' said Hardcastle mildly. He withdrew the warrant and flourished it under Powers' nose.

'*A search warrant?*' Powers became even more incensed. 'This is a scandal. Who is your superior?'

'Sir Edward Henry, the Commissioner of Police,' said Hardcastle, beginning to enjoy himself as he deliberately fuelled Powers' tantrum. 'His office is at New Scotland Yard, but I doubt he'd be too interested in the protests of a bit-part actor. However, I am Divisional Detective Inspector Hardcastle of the Whitehall Division, Mr Powers, and I suggest you calm yourself.'

'How dare you to have the effrontery to tell me how to behave in my own house.' Powers, now even more red in the face than hitherto, continued to address Hardcastle as though delivering an impassioned monologue to the gallery at the Old Vic. 'Under no circumstances will I allow you to search my house, and that's final.' He took a pace towards the two detectives and opened his arms wide, as if to prevent them from going any further into his property. 'I demand that you leave at this very moment.'

That suited Hardcastle. 'Vincent Powers, I am arresting you for obstructing police in the execution of their duty.' He laid a hand on Powers' arm as a token of the man's detention. 'Fetch them two officers in here, Marriott.'

Marriott went to the front door and admitted the two policemen.

'This man is under arrest, Sergeant,' said Hardcastle. 'But he's to stay here while Sergeant Marriott and me conducts a search of this here house.'

The maidservant, standing at the back of the hall, had witnessed the arrest of her master with an open mouth and undisguised pleasure.

'Where is Mr Powers' study, Violet?' Marriott asked the girl.

For a moment or two, the maid dithered, but she had told DC Wilmot that Powers was not a pleasant man to work for, and that, coupled with the unwelcome sexual advances her employer had made to her, decided her.

'I'll show you, sir.' The maid led the two detectives upstairs.

'You're dismissed, you slut,' screamed Powers at the maid's retreating back. 'Pack your bags and go. And you'll get no character from me,' he added.

'Shut up, you,' said the uniformed sergeant, roughly pushing Powers into a leather-upholstered watchman's chair near the back of the hall.

The study was sumptuously furnished. A large oak desk stood across one side of the room and there was a three-foot high Ratner safe on the wall opposite.

'Where does Mr Powers keep the key to the safe, miss?' asked Hardcastle.

'In the top right-hand drawer of the desk, sir,' said Violet promptly.

Hardcastle tried the drawer, but was not surprised to find that it was locked.

'And the key to that drawer is under the corner of the rug, sir,' said Violet, before Hardcastle could ask, thus confirming his long held view that servants knew everything that went on in a household.

Marriott folded back the corner of the rug and handed the key to Hardcastle.

The DDI opened the drawer, found the key to the safe, and seconds later had it open. With a shout of triumph, he withdrew a passport and a revolver.

'What was it that Greek chap said, Marriott?' asked Hardcastle, as he studied the passport. 'Archie someone, wasn't it?'

'Archimedes, sir, and "Eureka!" is what he said, meaning "I've found it."'

'Exactly so, Marriott. Well, m'boy, here we have a South African passport in the name of Jan de Ritzen that contains a photograph that looks astonishingly like Vincent Powers.' He opened the chamber of the revolver and satisfied himself that it was not loaded. 'And unless I'm very much mistaken,' he added, 'this is the weapon that killed Ronald Parker.'

The two CID officers descended to the hall where Powers, still seated in the watchman's chair, was being closely guarded by the two uniformed officers.

'Vincent Powers, otherwise known as Jan de Ritzen, I am arresting you for the murder of Captain Angus Sinclair of the Black Watch upon an unknown date at Kimberley in the Union of South Africa.'

In an attitude of defeat, Powers collapsed against the back of the chair and stared at Hardcastle. 'Well, that's it, I suppose,' he said.

'I am also arresting you on suspicion of having murdered one Ronald Parker on or about the fourth of March this year.'

'I've never heard of anyone called Ronald Parker,' protested Powers, sitting upright again.

'Yes, well, we'll see about that, my lad,' said Hardcastle, unable to keep the delight from his voice, having, at last, solved the murder of the man found floating in the River Thames nearly three weeks previously. 'He certainly knew about you from Daisy Benson, one of your many whores.'

Marriott turned to the maid. 'Does your master have a telephone here, Violet?' he asked, anticipating Hardcastle's next instruction.

'Yes, sir, it's in the drawing room. If you'll follow me, it's this way.'

'I've arranged for transport from Kingston police station, sir,' announced Marriott, when he returned to the hall a few minutes later.

'Excellent.' Hardcastle rubbed his hands together.

Once Powers was safely lodged in Kingston police station, and having informed the station officer that an escort would be sent to convey the prisoner to Cannon Row, Hardcastle turned to Marriott.

'Well, Marriott, that looks like that.'

'Perhaps we should have a drink to celebrate, sir. The lads here tell me that there's a decent pub just up the road. The Fighting Cocks, it's called.'

'Don't be ridiculous, Marriott,' said Hardcastle with a wave

of his hand. 'We'd have to pay for our beer in there. No, we'll
wait till we get back to civilization.'

The escort brought Vincent Powers to Cannon Row police station
at eight o'clock that evening. Hardcastle immediately set about
interviewing him in the small room at the front of the building.

'Well now, de Ritzen . . .' Hardcastle and Marriott settled
themselves in chairs on the opposite side of the table from the
South African more familiarly known to them as Powers. 'I shall
shortly charge you with the murder of Ronald Parker. Is there
anything you wish to say about that?'

'I told you before,' protested Powers, 'that I don't know anyone
of that name.'

'Yes you do. Daisy Benson, the woman you bedded at the
Kingston Hotel on the night of Friday the eighth of February last
and subsequently at your house, told you that Ronald Parker was
someone who'd enjoyed her favours and was continuing to do
so,' said Hardcastle, speculating that this might well have been
the case. 'What's more she told you that she wouldn't stop seeing
him. But you don't like anyone sharing your women, do you? I
suggest that you were so insanely jealous that you murdered him,
just like you murdered a British officer called Captain Angus
Sinclair for taking an Afrikaans whore off you in Kimberley.'

Since his arrest, Powers had recovered his equanimity and sat
staring blandly at Hardcastle. 'I've not the faintest idea what
you're talking about, Inspector,' he said eventually, running a
hand through his flowing hair. 'I certainly don't recall any such
conversation with this Mrs Benson you talk of. In fact, I'm quite
sure I do not know a woman called Daisy Benson.' He waved
an imperious hand as though dismissing the suggestion as a
figment of Hardcastle's imagination. 'Furthermore, I'm warning
you that I am a very rich man and I shall brief the finest lawyers
available to defend me against this ridiculous trumped-up charge.
Until then, I have nothing more to say to you.' The South African
folded his arms, leaned back in his chair and afforded Hardcastle
his best withering gaze.

'Take him through to the charge room, Marriott,' snapped
Hardcastle furiously. 'I'll be along shortly to charge him.'

*   *   *

Hardcastle arrived at the police station at his usual time of eight o'clock on Saturday morning. After inspecting the crime and charge books, and muttering about the inability of his detectives to get out and catch thieves, he settled in his office and lit his pipe. For the next hour, he studied the *Police Gazette*, read his detectives' reports – some of which he sent back for resubmission – and prepared his notes about the arrest of Jan de Ritzen, alias Vincent Powers.

Finally, he ran his eye over the previous day's edition of *Police Orders*, and muttered an oath when he read that Divisional Detective Inspector Edward Brady of Y Division had been promoted ahead of him. Brady was his junior in age, service and seniority. Then he read the entry again, just to make sure that his eyes were not deceiving him. He knew of Ted Brady's reputation and had often wondered how he had got as far as being given charge of the detectives on that outlying division, let alone to go even farther. But he presumed that Brady had friends among the higher echelons of Commissioner's Office, as New Scotland Yard was correctly styled.

He called for Marriott. 'Send a couple of men down to Powers' house to do a proper search. Better make it Wood and Wilmot. When you've done that, come back here.'

'Yes, sir.' It was clear to Marriott that his chief was not in the best of moods this morning.

'And find out what's known about this bloody South African warrant.'

'It would seem, sir,' said Marriott, when he returned thirty minutes later, 'that the Foreign Office hasn't received an arrest warrant for de Ritzen from the South African government. That means, of course, that a warrant won't have been issued by the Bow Street magistrates for his arrest, which they would've done if the South African warrant had been lodged.' It was his job to concern himself with such matters and advise his chief accordingly, and he had not needed the DDI to tell him.

'That don't matter a jot, Marriott,' said Hardcastle, dismissing with a wave of his hand what he considered to be a minor point of legal bureaucracy, 'because I've already charged Powers with the murder of Ronald Parker. The Chief Metropolitan Magistrate won't worry about the South African warrant yet. He'll remand him in custody for eight days anyway for the murder of Parker.

That'll give the Boers plenty of time to sort out a fugitive offender's warrant. All we need then is for the Foreign Office to get
off their backsides.'

'But if the police in South Africa get him back, sir, surely
that'll mean that we won't be able to proceed against him for
Parker's murder?'

'Ah, but the South Africans ain't got him in their custody,
Marriott, we have,' said Hardcastle, gently tapping the top of
his desk with the closed fist of his hand for emphasis. 'Possession
is nine points of the law and I ain't letting Powers go without
a fight. Mind you, the South Africans will hang him anyway,
so it don't make much difference in the long run.' He glanced
at his watch, briefly wound it and dropped it back into his
waistcoat pocket. 'Time we was getting ourselves up to Bow
Street.'

SEVENTEEN

I t was nigh on eleven o'clock before Sir Robert Dummett, the
Chief Metropolitan Magistrate, had finished dealing with
the usual parade of prostitutes and drunks that, by long-
standing custom, always appeared first in the register.

'Vincent Powers, Your Worship. Charge of murder,' cried the
policeman-gaoler, as the South African was escorted into the dock.
There was a feverish flurry of excitement in the press box as
journalists began to make notes. It was a rare occurrence for a
prisoner accused of murder to appear in the court.

'Is your name Vincent Powers and do you reside at The
Beeches, Kingston Hill in the County of Surrey?' asked the clerk
of the court.

'It is and I do,' replied Powers loftily, and swept the court
with his gaze, as though appraising a first-night theatre audience.
'And I am completely innocent of this ridiculous charge.'

'Now is not the time to enter a plea,' said the magistrate mildly.

'You may sit down,' said the clerk.

Ignoring the prisoner, Dummett turned to Hardcastle as he
stepped into the witness box. 'Good morning, Inspector.'

'Good morning, Your Worship.'

'Are you in a position to proceed, Mr Hardcastle?'

'Not at this stage, Your Worship.'

'In that case, I'll delay taking a plea. Do you wish to make an application?'

'I respectfully ask for a remand in custody, sir, on the grounds that Powers might interfere with witnesses, and that he might attempt to flee the country,' said Hardcastle blandly, not that he thought the former to be the case, but as he was not testifying on oath it did not matter too much. 'There is some evidence that the prisoner was responsible for the murder of one Ronald Parker on or about the fourth of March this year, but further enquiries need to be pursued before depositions can be taken. I also have it on good authority that a warrant, in the name of Jan de Ritzen, exists in South Africa for Powers' arrest on a charge of murdering a Captain Angus Sinclair of the Black Watch at Kimberley on an unknown date. Having examined the prisoner's passport, I am satisfied that Vincent Powers and Jan de Ritzen are one and the same, sir.'

'There is no such warrant before the court,' observed Dummett mildly, confirming what Hardcastle already knew. 'Is there?' he asked, leaning forward to address the clerk of the court.

'No, sir,' said the clerk.

'That is correct, Your Worship,' said Hardcastle. 'An urgent communication has been sent to the Foreign Office requesting that they expedite the matter.' He glossed over the fact that Marriott had merely made enquiries earlier that day, and spoke as if the requisite legal process was already well in hand. But he knew that nothing would happen before Monday morning anyway.

'Very well, Mr Hardcastle.' Dummett glanced at his ledger and then at the prisoner. 'Vincent Powers, you are remanded in custody until Monday the first of April.'

'I protest most strongly,' exclaimed Powers.

'Your protest is noted,' said Dummett, making the necessary note in his ledger.

'Begging your pardon, Your Worship,' interrupted Hardcastle, 'but the first of April is Easter Monday.'

'Ah, so it is, Mr Hardcastle, so it is. We'll make that the second of April, then.' Dummett scribbled a few more words in his ledger and looked up. 'Don't want to spoil my chances of receiving white gloves for the sake of a remand, eh?' he added with a smile. Although the court always sat on Easter Mondays, there were rarely any cases brought before it on that day. Traditionally, in such an event, the magistrate was presented with a pair of white gloves.

'Indeed not, sir,' said Hardcastle.

'Next case,' said the magistrate.

'And now we need to get a move on, Marriott,' said Hardcastle, when he and his sergeant were back at Cannon Row. 'Get that revolver we seized from Powers across to Mr Franklin *tout de suite*. I want him to tell me that it was the weapon that killed Parker.' He rubbed his hands together. 'We're beginning to get somewhere at last,' he added.

'Very good, sir,' said Marriott.

'And I wonder how Mr Drew got on with the fingerprints of Mrs Parker.'

'No doubt he'll let us know as soon as he gets a result, sir.'

'I hope the Foreign Office hurries up with getting in touch with the South Africans about the warrant. We've only got until Tuesday week before Powers comes up again at Bow Street.'

'The Foreign Office isn't known for moving quickly, sir,' ventured Marriott, and immediately wished he had not.

'You wouldn't think there was a war on,' grumbled Hardcastle. 'I sometimes wonder how we ever managed to acquire an empire. If they carry on at this rate, we'll lose it all one day, you mark my words. Well, Marriott, there's nothing more we can do before Monday. Get that revolver across to Mr Franklin and then go home. My regards to Mrs Marriott.'

'Thank you, sir, and mine to Mrs H.'

'You don't seem too happy, Ernie,' said Alice, when Hardcastle arrived home. 'Your murder not going well?'

'The murder's all wrapped up,' said Hardcastle, 'but that idle fool Ted Brady on Y Division was promoted in last night's *Police Orders*. He's been a DDI for less time than me, and he's never done anything important because nothing important ever happens at Highgate. And now he's been posted to the Yard in some quiet office job where, no doubt, he'll spend all day writing useless instructions for those of us who're really doing the hard work.'

'Never mind, Ernie, you're chance will come.'

'I doubt it,' said Hardcastle. 'I don't say the right things to the right people.'

'That's true, Ernie,' said Alice, with some feeling, 'but you were never one to mince your words.'

On Sunday morning, and still in an irritable mood about Brady's promotion, Hardcastle paid his usual visit to Horace Boxall's shop on the corner of Kennington Road.

'Morning, Mr Hardcastle.' Boxall laid a copy of the *News of the World* on the counter, knowing that Hardcastle always bought that particular paper.

'Morning, Horace. And an ounce of St Bruno and a box of Swan Vestas as well, please.'

Boxall took a packet of Hardcastle's favourite tobacco from a shelf behind him and put it on top of the newspaper together with the matches. 'I see the Huns shelled Paris yesterday,' he said, pointing to the newspaper headlines. 'One of them Krupp Big Bertha guns gave it a real pasting by all accounts. Two hundred-odd Parisians killed, so it says.'

Hardcastle turned the newspaper and glanced briefly at the item. 'Bloody cheek!' he exclaimed. 'Did you see this, Horace?' he said, jabbing a finger at the item that had attracted his attention. 'According to this report the Kaiser said that the battle's won and the English are utterly defeated.' He paid for the paper, tobacco and matches. 'Well, Sir Douglas Haig and General Pershing will soon make him eat his words, and that's a fact.'

'I hope you're right, Mr Hardcastle.'

'You mark what I say, Horace. This time next year we'll be hanging the Kaiser.'

If Hardcastle had been depressed by news of the promotion of DDI Brady of Y Division, worse was to come on Monday morning.

The DDI had just settled in his office when Marriott knocked and entered.

'You don't look too happy, Marriott,' said Hardcastle. 'Someone been promoted over your head as well?'

Having yet to read *Police Orders*, Marriott knew nothing of

DDI Brady's promotion, but sensed that Hardcastle was annoyed about something or someone. Unfortunately, the news he was about to impart would displease his chief even more.

'I'm afraid it's about the revolver we seized from Powers' house, sir.'

'What about it, Marriott?' Hardcastle looked up with a frown on his face.

'It's not the weapon that killed Ronald Parker, sir. Mr Franklin is adamant on the point.'

Hardcastle stared open-mouthed at his sergeant in sheer frustration. He had convinced himself that Powers was the murderer. Everything pointed to it. He had changed his name from de Ritzen and fled to this country to avoid arrest for a murder in Kimberley that followed a dispute over a woman. And now another woman – Daisy Benson – had had an affair with the murder victim and with Powers. The pattern was the same, and surely, Hardcastle had thought, the murderer must be the same.

'What about the search of Powers' house that Wood and Wilmot carried out over the weekend, Marriott?'

'There were no other weapons, sir,' said Marriott, anticipating the DDI's next question. 'The only find of any significance was a substantial quantity of uncut diamonds found secreted in another, smaller safe screwed to the joists in the loft above the kitchen. Initial estimates put the value of the stones at about five thousand pounds. Presumably he took a few of them out from time to time and sold them in Hatton Garden, and he was probably living on the proceeds.'

'No wonder he could afford champagne and caviar,' muttered Hardcastle gloomily.

'What are we going to do about Powers, sir? He's locked up in Brixton prison on a charge that won't stick.'

'Let him stay there,' growled Hardcastle. 'He's going back to South Africa to be hanged anyway. It's only a matter of the paperwork, Marriott, and I was never one to bother too much about that.'

'No, sir.' Marriott knew that Hardcastle found writing reports a chore, although he was never slow to criticize the submissions of his subordinates.

But in the event, and to everyone's surprise, the South African government moved so swiftly that a fugitive offender's warrant for Jan de Ritzen was lodged while he was still on remand in Brixton prison. After a short hearing at Bow Street police court, he was returned to South Africa to stand trial.

'By the way, sir, Mr Collins has just arrived with some information for you.'

'More bad news, I suppose,' grumbled Hardcastle, frustrated at having to reopen a murder investigation that he thought had been brought to a satisfactory conclusion. 'Ask him to come in, Marriott.'

'Morning, Ernie.' Detective Inspector Collins sat down in one of Hardcastle's chairs. 'I suppose you're still complaining about Brady of Y Division being promoted. He must be one of the Commissioner's blue-eyed boys.' Like every detective inspector in the Metropolitan Police, Collins knew where each of them stood in the seniority tables and when they were likely to be promoted, almost to the day.

'Yes, I bloody well am, Charlie. It's a damned disgrace. That man is useless. And I suppose you're going to upset me even more.'

'That's for you to decide, Ernie, but that young DI from Special Branch, Drew, handed me two sets of dabs that the Branch had taken. One set was Mavis Parker's and the other belongs to Lawrence Mortimer that they took when he was nicked for spying. They both correspond with prints on the letter that you found in Parker's piano.'

'Well, I'll be buggered!' exclaimed Hardcastle. 'That means that it was probably Mortimer who murdered Parker.'

'Or Mrs Parker conspired with Mortimer to get rid of her husband,' observed Collins drily. 'Perhaps it's the old eternal triangle after all, Ernie.'

After Collins had left Hardcastle with that suggestion hanging in the air, the DDI spent some time considering the implications of this latest twist in his investigation before sending for his sergeant.

'What do we do now, sir?' asked Marriott, once Hardcastle had told him of DI Collins's findings.

'We go back to Kingston and have a serious talk with Mrs Parker, Marriott, that's what we do.'

As on the previous occasion that they had interviewed Mavis Parker, Hardcastle and Marriott waited near the gates of the

Sopwith Aviation Company for her to emerge. Once she was inside her own home, the two detectives marched up the pathway and Hardcastle knocked loudly on her door.

'Oh, hello, Inspector.' Mrs Parker's greeting was one of resignation, almost as if she had been expecting a visit from Hardcastle sooner or later. 'You'd better come in.'

'It's about the letter from the Ministry of National Service addressed to your late husband, Mrs Parker,' said Hardcastle, once the three of them were seated in Mavis's comfortable parlour. 'The one we found in your piano.'

'I thought it might be.'

'I've had it examined by an expert, Mrs Parker,' Hardcastle began, 'and he discovered your fingerprints on it.' He decided not to mention that Mortimer's prints were also on the letter. At least, not yet. 'Perhaps you'd like to tell me how that came about, given that you told me that you'd not set eyes on it until I found it in your piano.'

It was some time before Mavis replied. 'I'm in a very difficult position, Mr Hardcastle,' she said eventually. 'I've been warned by the authorities not to say anything to anybody about what I've been doing.'

'I know what you've been doing, Mrs Parker,' said Hardcastle, 'and I can only say that your actions deserve the highest commendation. I have spoken to the head of Special Branch and he has told me everything.'

'Well, I'm not sure . . .' Mavis Parker still maintained her reluctance to talk about her activities.

Hardcastle decided to put her mind at rest. 'I've been told officially that you were approached by a man called Lawrence Mortimer and that he was very interested in the new aeroplane that's being produced by Sopwiths. I know also that you quite properly reported this to your manager and he, in turn, informed the police. And you were asked to cooperate with the authorities in conveying false information to Mortimer. The result was that he was arrested for espionage last Thursday.'

'Oh, so you do know what I've been doing, then.'

'About the letter, Mrs Parker,' said Marriott. 'How was it that your fingerprints were on it?'

'Part of what I was doing involved befriending Lawrence and bringing him to the house.'

'As a matter of interest, how did you meet him?'

'At the roller skating rink . . .' Mavis paused. 'I know it sounds dreadful, but Ronnie and I hadn't been getting on too well lately. I suppose it had something to do with the fact that we'd lost our son to diphtheria a year or two ago. We sort of grew apart after that, and my working at Sopwiths didn't help. You see, I'd never had a job before and he was quite annoyed that I'd taken work at an aeroplane factory, but he would've been if I'd taken a job anywhere else for that matter. He said that a woman's place was in the home. And, of course, that meant that we saw less and less of each other as time went by.'

'That's why you took up skating, was it?' asked Hardcastle.

'Yes. A few of the girls used to go there of an evening and that's where I met Lawrence. Of course, at the time I'd no idea why he was so friendly, but, as you just said, he wanted to know about the new aeroplane. He said he was interested in aeroplanes and that I must have an interesting job. He took me out for dinner and for rides in his car and generally made a fuss of me. Well, for a girl working in the paint shop that was quite something, I can tell you. Anyway, I think Ronnie was having an affair, so, I thought to myself, if he can why shouldn't I.'

'And presumably that's why you picked up with Wilfred Rudd,' suggested Marriott.

Mavis blushed and put her hand to her mouth. 'You must think I'm a very unfaithful wife,' she said.

'I suppose it was understandable in the circumstances,' said Marriott. 'You were obviously under a lot of stress, what with this business of Mortimer going on.'

Mavis Parker nodded. 'Thinking back, I wasn't altogether surprised when you told me Wilfred was a deserter. To be honest, I should've worked it out for myself, but I was taken in by all his talk of being an officer and winning medals.' She shook her head. 'Who would've thought he was just a hospital porter?'

'About the letter, Mrs Parker,' said Hardcastle, bringing her back to the matter in hand.

'Oh, yes, the letter. Ronnie had been up for his tribunal in the middle of February, but they didn't tell him the result straightaway. They said they'd write, but he never got the letter. Anyway, one day he just disappeared without a word. Lawrence said that Ronnie had told him that he was going to try to get to Holland so that he wouldn't be called up.'

'I take it that Mr Parker didn't tell you this himself.'

'No, he didn't. I thought it rather strange. I know I said we'd grown apart, but he always told me what he was doing. And I'm sure he would've mentioned getting exemption from the conscription if he'd known.'

'How did your late husband meet Lawrence?' asked Marriott.

'He called here for me on several evenings to go skating. I told Ronnie that he was actually a friend of one of the girl's at the factory, but I don't think he believed me. But by then, I didn't really care what he thought, and I was so worried about what I was doing for the government. I did sometimes wonder if I'd finish up getting murdered.'

'D'you think that Lawrence Mortimer suspected your husband of having found out he was a spy and threatened to tell the authorities?'

'Maybe,' said Mavis. 'Ronnie was certainly curious to know where I went of an evening, because I don't think he believed the roller skating story. I suspect that he might even have followed me on one or two occasions. I mentioned this to the government people – they called themselves my handlers – and they said I wasn't to worry.'

'But you eventually found the letter from the Ministry of National Service.'

'Yes, it was after Ronnie had gone that I was tidying up and I found it in a drawer in the bedroom.'

'And Lawrence Mortimer had been in the bedroom, had he?'

Mavis blushed again. 'Yes, he had, several times,' she said quietly, without elaborating. 'I didn't know what to do, so I hid the letter in the piano. I asked one of the policemen from Special Branch I was dealing with what I should do about it, and he said to forget about it. He said it was no good crying over spilt milk, which I thought was a bit of a cruel thing to say. And I couldn't tell you anything about it because, as I said just now, I'd been told not to talk to anyone about what I was doing, even other policemen such as yourself. I'm sorry, Inspector, but I was only doing what I was told.'

'I quite understand, Mrs Parker,' said Hardcastle. 'You were quite right to follow instructions. It must've been a difficult time for you.'

'It was, and then when you came to the factory and told me that Ronnie had been murdered, I thought about throwing it all in. I spoke to the policeman who was dealing with my case and he said that they were on the point of arresting Lawrence and that I wasn't to do anything for the time being. He said that it would all be cleared up once Lawrence had been arrested.'

'I see,' said Hardcastle, furious that he had, once again, been the victim of what he saw as Special Branch chicanery.

It was almost nine o'clock by the time that Hardcastle and Marriott returned to Cannon Row police station.

'Looks like Lawrence Mortimer is our murderer, sir,' said Marriott.

'Yes, it bloody well does, Marriott.' Hardcastle was still furious that Special Branch had been deceiving him. 'I shall see Superintendent Quinn first thing tomorrow morning.'

'D'you think that Mortimer will admit to the murder, sir?'

'I don't know, Marriott, but if I was given five minutes with him in his cell he'd damned soon cough.'

And of that, Marriott was in no doubt, but he suspected, even so, that the DDI would not have the pleasure of seeing Mortimer arraigned for the murder of Ronald Parker. There would be little point if the man now known as *Hauptmann* Gerhard von Kleiber were to be executed for spying.

EIGHTEEN

Hardcastle was waiting outside Superintendent Quinn's office door at twenty-five past nine on the Tuesday morning following his latest interview with Mavis Parker.

He heard the tap-tap of Quinn's umbrella ferule on the stone-flagged floor well before the top-hatted figure of the Special Branch chief appeared round the corner.

'Come in, Mr Hardcastle,' said Quinn without breaking step. Once in his office, he placed his hat carefully on top of the safe, hung his raincoat on the hatstand and placed his umbrella on another of the hooks. 'Now, what is it you want to see me about?'

He sat down behind his desk and gazed thoughtfully at the DDI standing before him. He did not invite him to sit down.

'The murder of Ronald Parker, sir,' said Hardcastle bluntly, wishing that he could light his pipe.

'And I suppose you've come to tell me that *Hauptmann* Gerhard von Kleiber otherwise known as Lawrence Mortimer was the murderer. Well, Mr Hardcastle, he was.'

'You know this to be the case, sir?' Hardcastle's face expressed a mixture of astonishment and annoyance.

'It was obvious,' said Quinn, 'but we could not jeopardize a delicate operation for the sake of having him arrested for murder. There were far more important things at stake.'

'Has von Kleiber admitted to the murder, sir?' asked Hardcastle.

'Of course he has.' Quinn spoke as though that must have been the obvious conclusion at which to arrive. 'But he'll not be tried for it except in the unlikely event that he is found not guilty of offences under the Defence of the Realm Act. But I don't see that happening. He'll be indicted with the murder, of course, but the Attorney-General has intimated that he will either offer no evidence or ask for it to be adjourned *sine die*.' Quinn paused. 'You do know what is meant by *sine die*, do you?'

'Yes, sir, adjourned indefinitely,' said Hardcastle, furious that Quinn should think he was not familiar with the meaning of the Latin tag that was known to most policemen.

'Very well. You may attend the trial if you wish. I shall have Drew inform you when we have a date. Good day to you, Mr Hardcastle.

It was apparent that the authorities intended to waste no time in arraigning *Hauptmann* Gerhard von Kleiber, alias Lawrence Mortimer, for spying. His trial was scheduled to take place two weeks to the day after his arrest, but the venue came as a shock to Hardcastle.

'Good morning, sir,' said Detective Inspector Aubrey Drew, as he entered the DDI's office.

'Good morning, Mr Drew. Take a seat and tell me what I can do for you.'

Drew was mildly amused that since becoming an inspector, Hardcastle always invited him to sit down. 'Mr Quinn's compliments, sir, and he asked me to advise you that the trial of *Hauptmann* Gerhard von Kleiber is to take place on Thursday the fourth of April. I understand that Mr Quinn told you that you and Sergeant Marriott may attend if you wish.'

'It'll be in the Old Bailey's Number One Court, I presume.' Hardcastle knew that important trials always took place in that particular courtroom, and he had given evidence there many times in the past.

Drew raised his eyebrows in surprise that Hardcastle seemed unaware of the procedure for trying German spies.

'No, sir, not the Old Bailey. Von Kleiber will be tried by general court martial.'

'Court martial?' Hardcastle stared at Drew in astonishment. 'What's wrong with the Old Bailey?'

'The Defence of the Realm Act states that spies, other than British nationals, will be tried by court martial and such courts have been granted the power to impose the death penalty.'

'Good gracious!' exclaimed Hardcastle. 'And where is this court martial to take place?'

'At the Tower of London, sir, commencing at 10 o'clock.'

The court martial was held in camera in one of the Tower's cold and cavernous chambers, and was presided over by Major General the Lord Cheylesmore. He was flanked by a brigadier-general and two army officers of field rank, all of whom were in uniform complete with medals and swords. Also forming part of the court was the judge-advocate attired in wig and gown. On the blanket-covered table were two or three carafes of water and glasses, the New Testament, and copies of the *Manual of Military Law* and *King's Regulations*.

The prosecuting officer was a portly major who had the appearance of someone unaffected by the strictures of food rationing. Another major had been appointed to defend von Kleiber. Each of these majors had been a practising barrister in peacetime.

The one indictment of espionage was put, but no mention was made of the count of murdering Ronald Parker. As Quinn had predicted, that charge had been disposed of at the police court.

Although experienced in criminal cases, and having attended a court martial in the past, Hardcastle nevertheless found the trial of von Kleiber a bewildering affair.

Mavis Parker was the first witness for the Crown. Led through her evidence by the prosecuting officer, she spoke confidently and convincingly of her part in the entrapment of the accused man. It was a side of her that Hardcastle had not seen before. Gone was the timid, almost mouse-like woman of his interviews with her and she was clearly made of sterner stuff than even the DDI had realized.

Mavis Parker was followed by various MI5 officers, including Captain Gilbert Stroud, who gave evidence of the surveillance that had been maintained by MI5. Several cryptographers appeared and produced copies and translations of the coded letters sent by von Kleiber and intercepted by the Post Office. The Special Branch officers who had arrested von Kleiber testified to the finding of the later incriminating documents and photographs that were in his possession when he was detained.

Finally Superintendent Quinn gave an account of his interview with von Kleiber that had immediately followed the latter's arrest. The defence lawyer asked why von Kleiber had not been arrested earlier, given that coded letters had been intercepted. The reply, almost scathing in tone, was that although von Kleiber could have been proved evidentially to have sent the letters, it was preferable to apprehend him with incriminating documents on his person.

The court retired for a mere forty minutes to consider their inevitable verdict, and Lord Cheylesmore pronounced sentence.

'Gerhard von Kleiber, you have been found guilty of espionage against Our Sovereign Lord the King for which there is but one penalty. You will be confined here at the Tower of London where at a time to be fixed by one of His Majesty's Secretaries of State you will be executed by firing squad. And may the Lord have mercy on your soul.'

Von Kleiber remained at attention and impassive during the sentence, but when Lord Cheylesmore ordered that he be taken to the condemned cell, he clicked his heels, bowed and turned smartly. His only utterance throughout his trial had been to plead Not Guilty.

'Well, that's that, Mr Hardcastle,' said Superintendent Quinn, when he encountered the DDI in the street outside the Tower.

'So it would seem, sir,' said Hardcastle, as he and Quinn doffed their hats at a passing military cortège.

'Yes, well now you can get on with your ordinary duties of catching criminals. Good day to you, Mr Hardcastle.' Ignoring Marriott completely, Quinn hailed a cab by raising his umbrella. 'Scotland Yard, cabbie,' he said.

'He might've offered us a lift,' muttered Hardcastle, peering up and down the road in search of another taxi, 'but, there again, I've never known Special Branch to give anything away.' The fact that he had obliquely criticized a senior officer to a junior one – something he would not normally do – was an indication of his annoyance with the entire debacle of the Ronald Parker investigation.

'I'll start on drafting the final report as soon as we get back, sir.'

'Don't be in too much of a hurry, Marriott,' said Hardcastle. 'Despite what Mr Quinn said, I'm far from satisfied that von Kleiber was Parker's murderer. There's more to this whole business than meets the eye. We'll dig a little deeper.'

'But surely the fact that von Kleiber confessed to the murder puts an end to it, sir.' Marriott was beginning to wonder what was really behind the DDI's enigmatic comment.

'Yes, but that's all we have, that he confessed to it,' muttered Hardcastle. 'There's no other evidence to support his admission, no firearm, nothing. It don't hang together, Marriott.' Sighting a cab at last, he instructed the driver to take them to Scotland Yard. Such was his irritation that he omitted to offer Marriott the usual cautionary advice about his reason for not asking to be taken to Cannon Row.

On the following morning, despite Gerhard von Kleiber's confession, Hardcastle reopened his investigation into the murder of Ronald Parker. And he began by once again examining all the statements and reports that had been made since the day that Parker's body was recovered from the Thames by the river police.

'There's got to be something here, Marriott,' said Hardcastle at last, 'but I'm damned if I can find it.' He pushed the pile of paper to one side and let out a sigh of exasperation. 'Get someone to put that lot back where it came from.'

'If you think that von Kleiber wasn't Parker's killer, sir, who do you think was responsible?'

'I haven't the faintest idea, Marriott.' Hardcastle put down his pipe and crossed to the window of his office. Putting his hands in his pockets, he spent some minutes staring down at Westminster Underground station, as if the Upminster-bound train just pulling out would provide the answer. 'We'll talk to Mavis Parker again,' he said, turning back to face his sergeant. 'That'll be a good place to start.'

'When, sir?' Marriott had the feeling that he was destined to lose another evening with his wife and children by a visit to Kingston. And the DDI confirmed it.

'This evening, Marriott.'

'Oh, I didn't expect to see you again, Inspector.' Mavis Parker's face bore a resigned expression when she opened her front door at half past six on the Friday evening. 'You'd better come in.'

Once the three of them were seated in Mavis's parlour, Hardcastle got straight to the point of his visit.

'Did Gerhard von Kleiber, or Lawrence Mortimer as you knew him, ever mention any of his friends, Mrs Parker? Or anyone that he might've known in this country?'

Mavis weighed the question carefully, just as she had done when being examined at the spy's court martial. 'Not that I can recall,' she said eventually. 'He was a very quiet sort of man, rarely talking about anyone. He never mentioned a family or his childhood or anything like that.'

'I suppose not,' said Hardcastle, 'but I'd've thought that the Germans would've given him some sort of story he could tell, just in case anyone asked questions about his background.'

'I suppose so,' said Mavis, 'but I never thought to ask. To be perfectly honest, Inspector, I was concentrating on not giving the game away. It wasn't easy for me.'

'So I imagine,' murmured Hardcastle, 'and I have to say that it was a very brave thing that you did. However, when he was arrested, Mortimer confessed to having killed your husband.'

'So I was told by Mr Quinn on the day of the court martial. Don't you believe it, then?'

'No, Mrs Parker.' Hardcastle paused. 'This is a delicate question, but did Mortimer ever stay here with you overnight?'

'Yes, he did, on one or two occasions, but only after my

husband disappeared. But I told you that before.' Despite being required to establish a close friendship with von Kleiber, she still blushed at the admission. 'It was necessary for the deception, you understand.'

'I'm not criticizing, Mrs Parker, and I quite understand why you did what you had to do. What interests me is whether he left anything here, clothing or a suitcase, or anything like that.'

'He did, as a matter of fact. There's an old raincoat in the cupboard under the stairs. He stayed here the night before he was arrested. It was pouring with rain when he arrived, but the next morning . . .' Mavis paused and blushed again. 'But the next morning when he left, the sun was shining and it had the makings of being a lovely day. I suppose he just forgot all about it, but then he couldn't come back for it because that was the day he was arrested.'

'Did you mention it to the police officers who were dealing with your case?'

'No. I didn't remember that he'd left it here until a day or two after his court martial, but by then it didn't seem important.'

'And the officers didn't ask if Mortimer had left any property here?'

'No, they never asked about anything like that.'

'Could I have a look at it, Mrs Parker?'

'Of course, I'll fetch it,' Mavis said, and rose from her seat.

'Sloppy, that's what I call it, Marriott,' said Hardcastle, when Mavis had left the room. 'Fancy not searching a suspect's drum after they'd nicked him. I've never heard the like of it.'

'But he didn't live here, sir.'

'Don't make no difference, Marriott. It's somewhere he was known to have frequented, and it should have been searched. Even Catto would've known to do that, and he ain't the brightest star in the firmament.'

'This is it, Inspector,' said Mavis, returning to the room holding a fawn mackintosh.

Hardcastle took hold of the garment and examined it closely. 'Would you believe that, Marriott?' he said, turning the collar. 'He only bought it at Harrods. Nothing but the best, eh? I wish I could afford a Harrods' mackintosh, but then I'm not a spy.' He felt in the pockets, both inside and outside, but found nothing.

'We'll take this with us, if you don't mind, Mrs Parker. I dare say that Special Branch will be interested to have a sight of it.'

'Of course, Inspector. I was wondering what to do with it, and I certainly don't want it hanging about here. I've enough of a problem disposing of all Ronnie's clothing.'

It was almost nine o'clock by the time that Hardcastle and Marriott returned to Cannon Row police station.

'It's a bit late to send von Kleiber's mackintosh across to Special Branch now, sir,' said Marriott, glancing at his watch. 'And presumably you'll want to give it Mr Quinn personally.'

'I've no intention of sending it to SB, Marriott. If they weren't sharp enough to go looking for it, that's their funeral. They can have it when I've finished with it. Now then, have you got that Boy Scout knife with you, the one with the gadget for getting stones out of horses' hooves?'

'Yes, sir.' Marriott smiled and handed over his pocket knife.

'Right, now help me clear this stuff off my desk.' Hardcastle placed his ashtray and tobacco jar on the window sill, and waited while Marriott moved the remaining clutter to the top of a filing cabinet.

Once the desk was clear, Hardcastle spread out von Kleiber's mackintosh and began opening the seams with Marriott's knife.

'Ah, this one's been undone and then sewn up again, Marriott,' said Hardcastle, finally opening the seam at the bottom of the garment's skirt. 'And not very well, either.' Extracting a small piece of paper from where it had been secreted in the fold, he studied it briefly before looking up. 'D'you speak German, Marriott?'

'No, sir.'

'Know of anyone who does?'

'I think Mr Drew does, sir.'

'Very likely, but he's a Special Branch officer, and the less that lot knows about this here bit of evidence the better.'

'Can you make anything of it, sir?' asked Marriott, gesturing at the slip of paper.

'There's an address on it, Marriott, and that's in English. Well, it would be, seeing as it's in London,' observed Hardcastle. 'It's says number five Peveril Street, Battersea, and the name Watkins. That's all I can make out, but I suppose it'll have to do.'

'What d'you make of that, sir?'

'I think it's likely to be someone von Kleiber was told to contact if he ever got into any sort of trouble.' Hardcastle handed Marriott the piece of paper. 'And if he turns out to be another spy we'll hand him over to those clever fellows at Special Branch,' he said triumphantly. 'But first thing in the morning, we'll get up to Bow Street for a search warrant, and then we'll pay this bugger a visit, whoever he is.'

Not for the first time, Marriott had serious misgivings about Hardcastle's proposed course of action, but he was in no position to argue.

NINETEEN

Deeming it to be a matter of some secrecy, Hardcastle sought out one of that day's sitting magistrates in his chambers, rather than making his application in open court. He emerged successfully some minutes later, clutching the warrant.

'Right, Marriott, off we go to Battersea,' he said, hailing a taxi.

Peveril Street was a turning off Battersea Bridge Road, and number five proved to be a barber's shop.

'Some things never change, Marriott,' commented Hardcastle. He had known of several hairdressers who had been arrested for spying since 1914.

There were three chairs in the shop, each of which was occupied. Another five men were waiting on chairs along one side of the salon.

'Could be some time, sir. We're always busy of a Saturday morning.' The speaker, a man of about fifty, was shaving a customer in the chair nearest the door, and peered at Hardcastle through gold-rimmed spectacles. He wore a short white coat, had a stooped posture and a small moustache. What little hair he possessed had been allowed to grow long on one side and was swept over his head in an attempt to disguise his baldness.

'Are you the owner?' asked Hardcastle.

'I am indeed, sir.' The man paused, the cut-throat razor he was using held clear of his client's face.

The DDI moved closer to the man so that he was able to speak to him without being overheard. 'I'm Divisional Detective Inspector Hardcastle of the Whitehall Division,' he said quietly, 'and I want a word with you in private.'

The barber dithered and glanced at the neighbouring hairdresser, who had just finished cutting his client's hair and was shaking the gown the man had been wearing.

'Take over shaving this customer, Jack. I've got to have a word with this gentleman.'

The owner led the way into a small back room. 'Now, sir, how can I help you?' Almost craven in manner, he was 'washing' his hands, and gave the impression of being greatly disturbed by the arrival of the police.

'You can start by giving me your name,' said Hardcastle.

'Watkins, sir. Henry Watkins.'

'How well do you know Lawrence Mortimer, Mr Watkins?' said Hardcastle, delighted that the barber's name was the same as that on the slip of paper he had found in the spy's mackintosh.

'I don't know anyone called Mortimer,' said Watkins. 'Is he a customer?'

'I doubt it,' said Hardcastle, thinking it unlikely that a customer would have hidden his hairdresser's name in the lining of a coat. 'Now then, Mr Watkins, I have a warrant to search these premises. Do you live here?'

'Yes, I do. I've got rooms over the shop. But why on earth do you want to search the place?'

'Lead the way, then,' said Hardcastle, leaving Watkins's question unanswered.

The two detectives followed Watkins up a narrow flight of stairs. Arriving at a small landing at the top, they were confronted by three doors.

Hardcastle pushed open the nearest door, which proved to be a sitting room, and turned to survey the barber. 'You can save me a lot of time, Mr Watkins, by telling me where you keep your revolver.'

Once again, Marriott was taken aback by Hardcastle's question, but he knew from experience how often such a direct approach had been instrumental in securing a confession.

'Revolver, sir? I don't have no revolver.'

Hardcastle sighed and held out his hands in an exaggerated attitude of disbelief. 'He doesn't have a revolver, Marriott,' he said sarcastically.

'I doubt that, sir,' said Marriott, playing along with Hardcastle's theatrics.

'So do I, Marriott, so do I.' The DDI faced Watkins again. 'In that case, I'll tell you what I'm going to do, Watkins. I'm going to close this shop, throw out all your customers, and bring in the seven or eight policemen I've got waiting outside to tear this place apart. The floorboards will get taken up, the mattresses ripped open, and the Lord knows what else. It'll make the Sidney Street siege look like a picnic in the park.'

'But you don't understand, sir,' exclaimed Watkins.

'Show me where the revolver is, Watkins, and show it to me now.'

It would not have needed Hardcastle's fictional team of policemen to have found it. Watkins crossed to a worn sofa and lifted one of the cushions to reveal a revolver. But as he was about to pick it up, Marriott seized him from behind and thrust him against the wall, pushing his arm up his back in a disabling hammerlock and bar.

'Oh no you don't my lad.'

'All right, all right,' yelled Watkins, 'I was only going to give it to you.'

Hardcastle crossed to the sofa, picked up the revolver and checked that it was unloaded. There were five loose rounds alongside where the revolver had rested.

'And what are you doing with this in your possession, Watkins?' asked Hardcastle, once Marriott had released the barber from his crippling hold.

'I've been told not to say anything.' Suddenly Watkins adopted an entirely different stance. Gone was the obsequious hairdresser, to be replaced by a man with a confident expression on his face.

'We'll see about that,' said Hardcastle. 'I'm arresting you for the unlawful possession of a firearm, and I'm taking you to Cannon Row police station for further questioning. And that's only going to be the start.'

Ordering Marriott to go first, Hardcastle hustled his prisoner down the stairs and through the shop. 'You're going to be one barber short for the foreseeable future, Jack,' he said to the barber still shaving the man in Watkins's chair. Out in the street, he bundled Watkins into a taxi. 'Scotland Yard, cabbie.' He turned to his prisoner. 'Tell 'em Cannon Row, Watkins, and half the time you'll finish up at Cannon Street in the City,' he said jovially.

Sitting opposite the DDI, Marriott sighed inaudibly and raised his eyes to the roof of the cab.

'We'll let him stew for a while, Marriott,' said Hardcastle, once Watkins had been placed in a cell at Cannon Row police station, 'and get that revolver over to Mr Franklin *tout de suite*. Ask him if he can give me an answer as soon as possible. Then I'll meet you in the downstairs bar of the Red Lion. I reckon we've earned ourselves a wet after all that hard work.'

'You're looking very pleased with yourself this fine morning, Mr Hardcastle,' said the landlord of the Red Lion, as he placed a pint of best bitter on the bar.

'Make that two if you would, Albert. My skipper will be down shortly. Ah, here he is now,' he said, as Marriott appeared in the doorway at the foot of the staircase. 'Yes, I've had what you might call a satisfactory morning's work.'

'Morning, Mr Marriott,' said Albert as he put a second pint on the bar.

'Morning, Albert.' Marriott turned to Hardcastle. 'Mr Franklin said he should be able to give you a result by two o'clock, sir.'

'Excellent,' said Hardcastle, as he drained his pint. 'In that case, we've time for another round.'

But Percy Franklin was quicker than he had forecast, and he knew where he would find Hardcastle at around lunchtime.

'I'll have a pint, Albert,' said Franklin as he joined the two A Division detectives. He glanced sideways at Hardcastle. 'It's a match, Ernie,' he said.

'Got 'im!' exclaimed Hardcastle triumphantly. 'You're absolutely sure, Percy?'

'I'll happily go up to the Old Bailey and swear it on a stack of Bibles, Ernie,' said Franklin.

'Oh, you'll be doing that all right, Percy,' said Hardcastle.

*   *   *

Hardcastle and Marriott sat down on one side of the table in the interview room, opposite the hairdresser.

'Why did you murder Ronald Parker, Watkins?' asked the DDI. He made the accusation secure in the knowledge that he had adequate proof to support his allegation.

'I didn't murder anyone,' said Watkins, but he was soon to discover that that lame response was pointless.

Hardcastle smote the top of the table with the flat of his hand, causing not only Watkins to jump, but Marriott also.

'Don't fence with me, Watkins. We took possession of a revolver at your premises and a ballistics expert will testify that it was the weapon used to kill Parker.'

'I never had a choice,' said Watkins.

'You'd didn't have a choice?' repeated Hardcastle in disbelief. 'I think you'd better explain that.'

'This man came to the shop—'

'What was his name?' asked Marriott.

'Lawrence Mortimer.'

'But you told me that you'd never heard of Lawrence Mortimer.' Hardcastle was not surprised at the man's original denial; it was what he had always come to expect when first he confronted a suspect. 'When was this?'

Watkins gave the question some thought. 'It must've been about the beginning of March, I suppose. I know it was a Sunday evening, quite a while after I'd shut up shop. Anyway, Mortimer said that he'd been sent by a mutual friend.'

'Did he tell you the name of this so-called mutual friend?' asked Hardcastle.

'No, he never said. Anyhow, he went on to say that this friend had told him that I could help him out of any trouble he was in. Well, that didn't sound like one of my friends. I mean, they'd've told me if they'd known Mortimer.'

'And did you believe Mortimer?'

'Well, I had to, because I suddenly remembered that some weeks ago, before Christmas it was, a man came to the shop and gave me a hundred pounds. He said it was an advance payment to help out a Mr Mortimer if he ever needed it.'

'Did this man give a name?'

'No, he didn't.'

'What did he look like?'

Watkins gave a vague description that could have fitted a hundred men.

'Had you ever seen him before?'

'No, never set eyes on him.'

'Didn't you enquire why this strange man should have taken it into his head to give you a hundred pounds?' Hardcastle was having trouble believing this fanciful tale of unknown men appearing out of the blue.

'Yes, I did. I asked him what sort of trouble he was talking about and he said that it was a matter of national security. He went on to say that he worked for the government and that I wasn't to tell anyone about our arrangement, not even the police. Well, it seemed an easy sort of job, and a hundred quid is a hundred quid.'

'So tell me what happened when you say that Mortimer turned up at your shop on this Sunday evening at the beginning of March.'

'He said he'd got a bloke in his car and I was to give him a hand to get him upstairs to my rooms.'

'I presume you did help him, Watkins,' said Marriott.

'Yes, but I got a surprise because the man in the car was only half conscious.' Watkins switched his gaze to Marriott. 'I think he'd been drugged. Anyway, we got him upstairs – it was all quiet in the street, fortunately – but then Mortimer said I was to dispose of him.'

'Did he say how? Or, for that matter why he wanted him disposed of?' Hardcastle dismissed the story of the half-drugged man. Dr Spilsbury had not found any trace of noxious substances in Parker's system. It was more likely that he had been knocked unconscious.

'He said that the man was a German spy and that the government wanted him got rid of. He said that the authorities couldn't arrest him because it would alert other spies to the fact that they'd been rumbled, and that he just had to disappear. And he said that I wasn't to breathe a word to anyone about it because it was secret government business.'

'What did you understand by "getting rid of him", Watkins?'

'I didn't know, so I asked him. He told me I was to kill the man and dump his body in the river.'

'What did you say to that?'

'Well, I was terrified, and then I refused, of course. But then Mortimer said that if I didn't do what I was told, I would be arrested myself for . . .' Watkins paused. 'Yes, he said that I'd be arrested for conspiring with a German spy and that I'd be hanged. Those were his exact words.'

And Mortimer was absolutely right, thought Hardcastle.

'What happened then?'

'Mortimer gave me a revolver, the one you've got there,' said Watkins, pointing to the weapon on the table, 'and an old sack. He told me I was to shoot the man, tie him up in the sack and dump him.' Watkins was sweating now probably because he realized that, in the cold light of day, the story was too incredible.

'I don't believe a word of this.' Hardcastle leaned back in his chair, took out his pipe and began to fill it.

'It's the truth, I swear it,' said Watkins desperately. 'What was I to do, Inspector? It was a case of kill this man or be hanged.'

'Well, my friend, you've scored a double, because you'll be hanged anyway, one early morning at Wormwood Scrubs prison, most likely.'

'But what was I to do?' demanded the anguished Watkins again. He was white-faced now and sweating profusely, and his hands, clasped together on the table, were clenched tight.

'You could've called a policeman *before* you killed this man and told him the story,' said Marriott mildly. 'He might just have believed it, but whether he did or not, he'd certainly have looked into it. And if it was as secret as Mortimer said it was, the police would've known how to deal with it.'

'But Mortimer said I wasn't to breathe a word to anyone including the police,' said Watkins, 'otherwise the government's plan would be ruined and they'd never catch the spies.'

'So, on the basis of this flimsy story, you killed Ronald Parker anyway,' commented Hardcastle brutally. 'Despite it being an outrageous request.'

'Was that his name?' asked Watkins innocently, despite Hardcastle having mentioned Parker's name before. 'Mortimer never told me who he was, other than to say he was a spy. But yes, I did for him. I shot him in the back of the head.'

'And how did you get his body to the river?'

'I borrowed a box-tricycle from the grocer down the road. I told him I'd got some stuff to shift round to my sister's place. I done the body up in the sack Mortimer had given me, dragged it down the stairs and out through the back door into the yard. Then I got it into the tricycle and made for the river. No one saw me, on account of all the street lights being out because of the blackout. When I got to the river, I tipped him in the drink just by the bridge. I took the tricycle back to the grocer the next morning.'

'Bloody amazing, Marriott,' exclaimed Hardcastle. 'Our Mr Watkins, a Battersea barber, murders Parker, sticks him in a box tricycle and calmly pedals his way down to the river in the dead of night and chucks him in.' Turning to his prisoner again, he said, 'Henry Watkins, I am charging you with the murder of Ronald Parker on or about the third of March this year.' He glanced at Marriott. 'Take him out to the charge room and tell the station officer I'll be there directly to prefer the charge.'

'But it was government work,' protested Watkins, as Marriott steered him towards the door. 'That's what Mortimer told me.'

'You're dead right about that, Watkins, it most certainly was government work,' said Hardcastle. 'Unfortunately for you, it was the German government you were doing this for, not ours. Lawrence Mortimer was a German spy and has since been tried and convicted. His real name is Gerhard von Kleiber and he'll shortly be executed at the Tower of London.'

'Oh my God, it can't be true.' Watkins paled significantly, and for a moment it looked as though he would collapse, but for the supporting arm of Marriott.

'Well, Marriott, what d'you make of that?' asked Hardcastle, when he and his sergeant were back in the DDI's office.

'Like you said, sir, it's bloody amazing,' said Marriott. 'But do you believe him?'

'Well, he certainly admitted killing Parker, and Mr Franklin confirmed that the revolver we've got was the one that Watkins used to commit the murder. But if his story's to be believed, he could've genuinely thought he was working for the government, our government. I don't think he had the slightest idea that Mortimer was a spy and that he, Watkins, was therefore indirectly working for the Germans. But murder's murder.'

'I think you're probably right, sir. I don't doubt that Mortimer scared the living daylights out of him with his threat of execution. And I'm not sure our people would've believed him even if he *had* called in at Battersea nick.'

Hardcastle laughed. 'No, perhaps not, Marriott, but they might've prevented the murder. It makes no difference though, he'll swing anyway.' He stood up. 'Bow Street court Monday morning, then. In the meantime, Marriott, take the weekend off, and my regards to Mrs Marriott.'

'Thank you, sir.' Marriott glanced at the clock on Hardcastle's wall; it was five past six. 'And mine to Mrs H.'

'Henry Watkins, charge of murder, Your Worship,' cried the gaoler in Number One Court at Bow Street, as the prisoner entered the dock.

'You seem to making a habit of charging people with murder, Inspector.' Sir Robert Dummett, the Chief Metropolitan Magistrate, cast a benevolent smile in Hardcastle's direction.

'Indeed, Your Worship.'

'Are you ready to proceed?'

'Not at this stage, Your Worship. I respectfully ask for a remand in custody.'

'Very well.' Dummett looked at the prisoner. 'You will be remanded until Tuesday the sixteenth of April,' he said, scribbling a note in his ledger. 'Next.'

Outside the court, Hardcastle hailed a taxi and asked to be taken to Scotland Yard.

'And I mean Scotland Yard this time, Marriott,' he said. 'I'm going to see Superintendent Quinn.'

'Well, Mr Hardcastle, what is it now?' Quinn looked up with an expression of irritation at being confronted, yet again, by A Division's DDI.

'I thought I should inform you that I arrested a Battersea barber named Henry Watkins on Saturday last, sir.'

'And of what possible interest to Special Branch do you imagine that to be?' Quinn laid down his pen and leaned back in his chair, an enquiring and slightly sarcastic look on his face.

'I arrested him for the murder of Ronald Parker, sir.'

'You did *what*?' Quinn was clearly outraged at this announcement. 'But von Kleiber has confessed to that murder, and the Attorney offered no evidence at the police court.'

'Watkins confessed to it, sir, and I seized the firearm that was in his possession. Detective Inspector Franklin is adamant that it was the weapon used to murder Parker, and will testify to that end.'

'What made you decide to arrest this man, Mr Hardcastle?'

Hardcastle explained about his visit to Mavis Parker and his seizure of the raincoat that von Kleiber had left at her house. But when he mentioned the slip of paper he had found that gave Watkins's address, the superintendent interrupted him.

'This is all most irregular, Mr Hardcastle. That raincoat should have been handed over to me at once.'

'I was rather surprised that your officers hadn't found it, sir,' said Hardcastle, risking a reproof, but at once delighted that he had scored a rare point against Special Branch.

But Quinn immediately realized that his own officers had been at fault and, Hardcastle thought, they would be in line for a severe dressing down. Nevertheless, Quinn was obviously undecided what he should do about the problem which the DDI had placed before him and sat in silence for some moments. 'It would seem that von Kleiber, knowing that he would be executed for espionage, confessed to the murder in order to protect this man Watkins,' he said eventually. 'Doubtless so that Watkins could be used on another occasion by another agent, should he be required.'

'That was my thinking, sir,' said Hardcastle, to whom the thought had not occurred until Quinn had suggested it.

'What stage have you reached in dealing with this man Watkins?'

'He appeared at Bow Street police court this morning charged with murder, sir, and was remanded in custody until the sixteenth of this month.'

'I trust no mention was made of von Kleiber at this hearing.'

'No, sir. It was simply an appearance to secure an eight day remand.'

Quinn glanced at the calendar on his desk. 'Well, that gives us a week to decide what to do. I shall consult Mr Thomson about the matter.' Basil Thomson was the assistant commissioner for crime, but in recent years had been taking a far greater interest in Special Branch operations than in ordinary crime. 'I'll let you know his decision, Mr Hardcastle. In the meantime, you're to take no further action.'

'Very good, sir,' said Hardcastle, who could not think of any action he might have taken.

Hardcastle did not have long to wait for the assistant commissioner's decision. The next morning, Detective Inspector Drew appeared in the DDI's office.

'Mr Quinn's compliments, sir, and although he realizes how busy you are, he'd be grateful if you could spare him a moment at your convenience, preferably today.'

'Very well, Mr Drew, I'll see him directly.' Hardcastle was surprised at the conciliatory form of Quinn's summons, but did not comment on it. Putting on his hat and seizing his umbrella, he made his way across the courtyard separating Cannon Row police station from New Scotland Yard, and to Quinn's office.

'Ah, Mr Hardcastle, please take a seat.' Quinn seemed to be in quite a jovial mood. It was certainly the first time that the DDI had been invited to sit down. 'I've spoken to Mr Thomson and he, in turn, has discussed the matter with the Attorney-General. You are to go ahead with the prosecution of Watkins, but the trial will be held in camera. The Attorney has decided that von Kleiber's confession will be allowed to stand, and for that reason, scant regard will be paid to this extraordinary story that Watkins told you. He'll doubtless be convicted as if it were an ordinary sort of murder.'

'But do you think that his story will be accepted by the jury, sir?' asked Hardcastle.

'No question of it, Mr Hardcastle. In fact, I'm quite sure that the Attorney will have no trouble in dismissing Watkins's story as a fiction he dreamed up to justify the murder of Parker.'

'But what sort of motive will I be able to present to the jury, sir?'

'The Attorney will take care of that, Mr Hardcastle.' Quinn waved a hand of dismissal, as though it were of no importance. 'It's obvious now though, that Ronald Parker had been given cause to suspect that von Kleiber was a spy, probably as a result of his wife's friendship with the man, coupled with her employment. In the circumstances, I imagine that von Kleiber was fearful that he would be exposed. With hindsight, it might've been better if we'd taken Ronald Parker into our confidence and told him that MI5 and this Branch had already got the matter well in hand.'

TWENTY

I t was six o'clock in the morning of Tuesday the twenty-third of April 1918, St George's Day. It so happened that it was the day when the Royal Navy was to mount its daring attack on Zeebrugge with the intention of sinking three old cruisers to block the harbour. But there was no symbolism in the selection of that date, for few people knew of it until afterwards; it was merely a coincidence.

The eight men of the Scots Guards who were to comprise the firing squad marched out of Waterloo Barracks in the Tower of London. Their sergeant halted them near the execution block where Anne Boleyn had met her end nearly four hundred years previously.

Within minutes, *Hauptmann* Gerhard von Kleiber, accompanied by an army chaplain with an open Bible in his hands, was escorted from the guardroom in the barracks and secured skilfully and quickly to the execution post by the sergeant.

The Scots Guards officer, a youthful lieutenant, stepped across to von Kleiber and proffered a blindfold. The spy declined it with a brusque shake of the head and faced his executioners with his eyes open.

The chaplain finished intoning a few words and moved out of the line of fire.

As the volley of shots rang out and von Kleiber's lifeless body slumped in its bonds, the Tower of London's ravens rose panic-stricken from their resting places, cawing loudly in the dawn air.

The medical officer stepped forward and, satisfying himself that von Kleiber was dead, nodded briefly to the officer commanding the firing squad. The officer nodded in return, grateful that he would not be required to administer the *coup de grâce* with his revolver. Taking a pace forward, he saluted the corpse.

'Your leave to speak, sir, if you please, sir?' asked his sergeant, snapping to attention. 'What did you salute yon man for, sir? He was naught but a dirty spy.'

'That's where you're wrong, Sergeant,' said the lieutenant. 'A spy he may have been, but *Hauptmann* von Kleiber was also a soldier and a brave man. It was a compliment from one soldier to another.'

'Sir,' said the sergeant. 'Your leave to march off, sir, if you please, sir?'

Under cover of darkness that same evening, the start of a clandestine ceremony took place. At ten o'clock a plain van entered the Tower of London. Moments later a simple, wooden coffin bearing the mortal remains of *Hauptmann* Gerhard von Kleiber was loaded into the van by four men.

The van drove the seven miles to the East London cemetery in Plaistow. Once inside, it continued until it reached a far corner where it stopped. The gates of the cemetery were closed and two policemen stood guard.

The four men placed the coffin on stretchers over a grave that had been dug earlier in the day.

In the light of several hurricane lamps an army chaplain, the same chaplain who had sought to offer von Kleiber solace in his last minutes on earth, conducted the funeral service. Finally, the four men lowered the coffin into the grave and shovelled earth into it until there was just a slight mound to mark von Kleiber's last resting place.

Returning to the van, one of the men brought out a cross bearing a number and nothing else, and hammered it into the ground at the head of the grave. The number on the cross corresponded to the number on the coffin, and was the only clue to the identity of its occupant. It was an identity known only to MI5.

Hardcastle was surprised to see Superintendent Quinn and Assistant Commissioner Thomson seated in the well of Number One Court at the Old Bailey on the day that Watkins's trial opened. As Quinn had predicted, the trial was held in camera, and the only members of the public in court were the twelve men of property comprising the jury.

'Lock the doors,' cried the clerk of the court, and a policeman moved to comply with the order.

The Attorney-General, Sir Frederick Smith, better known to

members of the bar and beyond as 'F.E.', led for the Crown, and Sir Richard Leary KC was faced with the near impossible task of defending the prisoner.

Henry Watkins pleaded Not Guilty and the only four prosecution witnesses – Hardcastle, Marriott, Doctor Bernard Spilsbury and Detective Inspector Franklin – gave their damning testimony.

Spilsbury gave evidence of the cause of death, and Franklin explained how he had deduced that the revolver seized by Hardcastle was the weapon used to commit the murder.

Hardcastle told the court of the statements made by Watkins when he was arrested, and Marriott followed him into the witness box to corroborate what his chief had said.

After each witness had given his evidence in chief, Sir Richard Leary rose to ask a few questions, but he was unable to shake the evidence. Hardcastle got the impression that Leary knew that there was little he could do to aid the prisoner.

Watkins was the only witness for the defence and repeated the story he had told Hardcastle. He seemed quite sincere in his belief that he had committed the murder on behalf of the British government. And despite what Quinn had suggested, the Attorney-General's relentless cross-examination was unable to persuade Watkins otherwise.

In the circumstances, there could be but one verdict.

The judge donned the black cap and pronounced sentence of death. The judge's chaplain intoned the single word, 'Amen', and the trial was over.

There was, however, a surprising corollary to the trial. Even though neither the police, nor the jury at Watkins's trial, had believed the Battersea barber's story, clearly the Home Secretary, Sir George Cave, had some misgivings about it. When the docket requiring him to confirm Watkins's execution arrived on his desk, he deliberated on the matter for over a week before writing his decision.

'I am in some doubt about Watkins's motive,' he wrote. 'It seems to me that he was genuinely labouring under the impression that he committed the murder on behalf of His Majesty's Government, and given that this country is at war, one assumes he imagined it to be an act of patriotism. Having been threatened* *with execution if he spoke to anyone about the task he had been set, he was, I believe, loath to approach even the police. In view of this apparent conflict, the sentence of death is commuted to one of life imprisonment.'*

A year later, Henry Watkins died of natural causes in Dartmoor prison.

A month after Gerhard von Kleiber's execution, Superintendent Hudson, the head of the Whitehall Division, entered Hardcastle's office.

'Good morning, sir,' said the DDI, rising to his feet and putting his pipe in the ashtray.

'There's an interesting item on the Court Circular page of the *Daily Telegraph* this morning, Ernie,' said Hudson. He opened the paper and read aloud. 'His Majesty the King has been graciously pleased to appoint Mrs Mavis Parker a Member of the Order of the British Empire for services to the State.'